"What's going on?"

"I don't know, hurried to the stairwell door, turned the handle, and pushed, but the door didn't open. The feeling of being watched intensified as if the person had moved from behind a closed door. He glanced over his shoulder, but beyond Ted, there was nothing but red shadows.

"The door won't open." He threw his weight against it, but it didn't budge. "I think it's locked."

"There aren't any offices here; that would make sense. I guess it's back to the elevator."

"All right. Hopefully we won't be stuck here too—"

"Jesus."

"What?" Jon turned from the door and froze. Tony, deformed and crippled, shambled toward them. At least Jon thought it was Tony. The man's eyes were sunken and faintly glowing; it looked like every bone in his body was broken. "Tony? Is that you?"

The other man didn't speak, just stared at Ted as if he hadn't heard Jon.

"He's dead," Ted stated.

"What? No, he's not. He can't be." Jon shook his head. "Tony, what happened to you?" His friend couldn't be dead, though he looked … shattered. Things like this didn't happen in real life, Jon thought. Maybe in bad horror movies, but not in the real world. "Tony!"

"Jon, I don't think he hears you."

Tony threw himself at Bacon, knocking him to the ground, and then fell on him, wrapping pale hands around the man's throat. Ted screamed as smoke rose from where Tony's hands strangled him, filling the reception area with the stench of burning flesh.

For information address Crossroad Press at 141 Brayden Dr., Hertford, NC 27944
A Macabre Ink Production - Macabre Ink is an imprint of Crossroad Press.
www.crossroadpress.com

Crossroad Press Trade Edition

INSTITUTIONAL MEMORY

BY GARY FRANK

TUESDAY

SHARON WALTERS

Humming a Burt Bacharach song she couldn't remember the name of, Sharon Walters rode the elevator to the basement. It was a song she'd heard that morning on the radio while her husband, Harry, dressed for work. She'd made him his cup of coffee and prepared his turkey and Swiss cheese sandwich with a pickle for lunch. They'd kissed good-bye; he said "I love you," and she repeated the same. She never liked to say "I love you, too." It didn't sound meaningful, more like an uninspired echo.

The elevator rattled its way down through the old office building as Sharon watched out the diamond-shaped window at the floors passing by with the speed of a senior citizen walking his last steps. Sighing, she glanced at her watch to make sure time moved forward and wasn't coming to a halt. In two hours she'd be having lunch with Marcy Browne, one of her co-workers. After that, she'd leave for her weekly acupuncture session. Though she'd been afraid of the needles at first, acupuncture turned out to be a great way to relieve the weekly tension. After having lunch with Marcy, as much as she liked the woman, she needed something to help her relax. Marcy tended to be anxious and self-conscious of everything she did and said, and that could get overwhelming.

The elevator came to rest and the outside door slid open, then the gate, and finally the inside door. Cool, musty air—tainted with the funky stink like something had died and never been found—crept in and enveloped her, made her cringe, and reminded her of how much she hated the basement. Stepping out into the cavernous area, she was greeted by the buzz and flicker of the fluorescent lights that bleached everything white and made the shadows more starkly black than they should have been.

It was rare that she came down here, but she needed empty boxes to pack up files, and there were none left in the Osprey Publishing office. Without further hesitation, she started across the basement to the stacks of boxes against the far wall.

Something skittered above her. She stopped and stared at the four rows of fluorescents. Was something up there? The lights kept her from seeing anything close to the ceiling.

Get the boxes and get out, she told herself.

But she didn't move. Her gaze sought the dark space above the banks of lights where the unsettling noise came from. Darker shadows wriggled beyond the lights; it had to be her imagination. The sound probably came from somewhere else and she imagined that it came from the ceiling. There were rats down here, and it was most likely one of them had made the sound unless there were bats down here as well.

Maybe it was Leo, the building's creepy maintenance man. He had his office near the elevator. He was too big and spoke too small, making him—in her eyes—the perfect serial killer. And here she was by herself.

That motivated her feet to move. Four sizes of boxes leaned against the far wall, and as she approached the stacks, she looked from one to the next so by the time she reached them she could grab the right ones and flee back upstairs to the fifth floor and the safety of Osprey Publishing. The first ones were too small. The last ones, of course, were too big. Second or third? Third. Those should be just fine to—

A quick, sharp electric buzz filled the air.

The stink of ozone dropped down and enveloped her.

She glanced up in time to see the fluorescents illuminate too brightly, flicker several times, and then grow dim as hungry blackness spread through them until all the light was consumed and the basement was left in darkness.

"Oh, my God." Sharon's pulse quickened. She glanced around, praying her eyes adjusted to the dark before the rats found her. Holding her hand up, she couldn't see it in front of her face. "All right. No need to panic. The emergency lights should come on any minute." Once the lights came on she'd hurry to the stairs—they were faster than the elevator—and leave the darkness. Someone else could come and get the boxes.

Her eyes adjusted to the dark enough so she could see her hands, but little else. If only she had a flashlight to see her way out, but she hadn't thought to bring one along.

Emergency lights flickered on, casting the basement in blood red illumination, pushing the shadows back, but not nearly enough. At the corner of her eye something twisted in the shadows, but when she looked it was gone.

Get upstairs, now, she told herself.

With each step Sharon took, a feeling of exhaustion overwhelmed her until she found that taking another step was too much effort. *What's wrong with me? I shouldn't be this tired. I feel so worn out.* Trudging forward, she felt herself about to collapse, but kept moving, afraid that if she stopped, something bad would happen.

In the darkness to her left, a stack of file boxes fell. In the corner, a long, whip-like shadow snake upward before it disappeared. Her mouth fell open and she made a whimpering sound. Was Leo doing this? Why would he play such a nasty trick on her? But it had to be him. What other explanation was there? A sheen of sweat broke out on her forehead. She had to get upstairs.

Don't stop now. She paused and listened for a sound or something that would tell her where Leo—it was Leo, wasn't it?—was.

Silence.

Sharon almost called out, telling Leo to stop screwing around. But another part of her mind told her this wasn't Leo, this wasn't anyone, but some *thing* that her rational mind refused to accept.

The lights went out and there are rats down here. That's all. No monsters, no boogeymen lurking in the shadows.

But no matter how much she tried to persuade her irrational

self that there was a rational explanation, the more the fear gripped her and sent her into a panic attack.

Without another thought, she rushed to the stairs, gripped the banister, put her foot on the first step, felt her sweaty palm slip on the cold metal handrail, and stared up into darkness.

Was someone waiting up there? It couldn't be a thing because there were no such things as monsters—except wicked humans. No matter how she felt or what her imagination whispered to her, it was a person—probably Leo—who watched her, scared her just because they could. Leo was like that, a real bastard when he wanted to be.

She needed to go up the stairs and out into the lobby, and then she'd take the stairs to the fifth floor and the safety of Osprey Publishing. She would've gone back to the elevator, but if there was someone down here stalking her, they could get her before the elevator doors closed. *Just climb, Sharon.*

Her legs refused to move; fear at what could be waiting for her in the darkness at the top of the stairs held her paralyzed. All she could do was glance toward the main basement, hoping she really was imagining things.

Then she heard a soft metallic rasping in the ceiling moving in her direction.

Come on, Sharon, she told herself. *Move. Please.*

A tiny shadow bolted across the floor, and though she convinced herself that it was only a rat, it was all she needed to get her legs moving. She fled up the stairs, certain that the something was just behind, gaining on her, its gaze boring into her back; any second its cold hands would grasp her legs and pull her back down into the basement and—

Stop it! Just get upstairs and everything will be fine.

The door to safety was right ahead of her.

A few more steps and—

From above her the metallic sound echoed—something was slithering through the ceiling's metal framework. She focused on the door and safety and not the nerve-racking sound of metal on metal that came from the ceiling. She shivered and whimpered and against her better judgment glanced above her head.

A metal cable snaked down toward her. It was nearly as wide around as her arm and it wove through the air, scraping against the metal framework. As she stared in terror and fascination, other cables, not as thick as the first one, snaked through the darkness.

"Oh, God." The door was only ten steps away. "Help me." Her voice was weak, barely more than a whisper. She staggered from the exhaustion that turned her limbs to jelly and her mind to wet cotton. Gravity had multiplied, pulling her down until it took every last ounce of her strength to lift her foot to the next step.

The smaller, faster cables coiled around her wrists and pulled her backward and up.

"No." She wanted to sleep, to give in and rest. But her will to live forced her to fight the cables, to keep her balance and get out. In desperation she climbed one more step before more cables caught her around the waist and she was plucked from the stairs. As she kicked at the air, her shoes fell and clattered on the steps.

"Help me!" she screamed. "Please! *Someone!*"

More cables dropped down and wrapped around her arms, pulling her up to the ceiling.

Sharon knew she was going to die. Her life wasn't supposed to end like this. A heart attack or a stroke or plain old age. But not murdered by some *thing.* "Help me!"

From above her came more slithering. When she glanced up, she could just make out three cables descending toward her.

"*Please, someone help me!*" She glanced around, hoping to see someone, even Leo, but she was alone. Her heart was about to explode. She couldn't catch a breath.

Each of the new cables had jagged edges that danced in front of her, coming close to her face.

"*Help me!*" Sharon screamed, twisting in a useless attempt to get free. "Please!"

A round shape on the thickest braid of cable reflected the red light as it descended from the ceiling, shifting and turning as it came closer to Sharon's face. At first it appeared to be a composite of gears, pieces of sheet metal and jagged bits of copper and silver. But when it smiled, Sharon realized she was staring at some kind of skull. The glass eyes, red points of malignant light, stared back. It made a hissing sound followed by a terrible creaking noise as if it was attempting to speak, but all that came out was the foul reek of motor oil.

"Please … please … please help me." Her voice was weak from screaming. Tears streaked her face. For a moment she dangled helplessly with the impossible skull weaving in front of her. She begged God to help her, praying for mercy, for a quick and painless death, and then swearing she'd—

Cold metal sliced into her upper arm and she cried out.

Her breath came in short jagged bursts.

Warm blood dripped down to her hand, between her fingers.

Another cable's quick jab cut her and she gasped in pain and surprise. It was playing with her. She knew it but could do nothing to stop it, nor could she do anything to calm her jackhammering heart. The next moment she was jerked up into the darkness and all she knew was pain.

MARCY BROWNE

Marcy Browne, tired again, stared at her computer screen wondering what happened to Sharon. Her co-worker and friend hadn't returned from the basement after telling Marcy she was going down to get boxes. Though Sharon was only working a half day, she'd agreed to have lunch with her, and Marcy had checked the cubicle next to her several times, but Sharon never returned. Her computer was still on and the last time Marcy went into Sharon's cubicle, she checked the drawer where the other woman kept her pocketbook; it was still there.

If Marcy hadn't been afraid of the basement, she would have gone downstairs herself, but the cavernous room was poorly lit with too many shadows, and the few times she had been down there, she was sure she'd seen rats the size of small dogs. If that wasn't bad enough, creepy Leo Sedowski always seemed to sneak up on her. He never threatened her or made rude comments, but something was wrong there and she didn't want to be alone with him in the basement or anywhere else.

At two in the afternoon, an hour after they were supposed to go to lunch, Marcy went to her boss's office and knocked on his door. "Bernie, have you seen Sharon? She went to the basement to get boxes a couple of hours ago and I haven't seen her since." Again, her eyes were drawn to his left hand where his pinkie and ring finger were missing; reminders of the torture he suffered in a POW camp during the Vietnam War.

Bernie Thompson looked up at her. His face was sharp, chiseled from his time in the military back in the sixties and seventies, and after all these years, he kept himself in good shape. He was well dressed and usually carried himself with an air of confidence, though recently he'd begun to look worn out, not much different from the way she felt. His desk however, was another matter. Papers were strewn everywhere, files on top of binders, loose CDs tossed on top of files, and empty jewel cases lying all over the place. A dying plant sat by the window, desperately in need of watering. He needed a secretary, and Marcy was the closest thing he had, but it wasn't her job to come in and attempt to straighten his office. So the piles grew until they toppled over and he cursed and straightened them, passing some on to Marcy to file while keeping others because some damned report that he would need had to be in one of them.

"I didn't even know she went downstairs," Bernie said.

"Can you call Security to check the basement?"

"Sharon said she was taking a half day today. Maybe she left already."

"Her computer's still on and her pocketbook is still in her drawer."

Lifting the phone, he hesitated. "Have you checked the bathroom?"

Marcy shook her head.

"Check the bathroom. If she's not there, let me know and I'll call." He looked even more tired than usual.

"Sure." Marcy already suspected she wouldn't find Sharon there, though where the other woman was she couldn't imagine. It wasn't like Sharon to disappear like this. Something was wrong.

The bathroom was empty, and when Marcy asked around she found that no one had seen Sharon since she went to the basement, which led her to conjure a number of scenarios.

Did she fall and can't call for help?

Did Leo attack her?

Maybe Sharon has a secret lover and snuck out with him.

Maybe Harry met her and she just forgot to tell me.

She'd known Sharon for a little over a year and never knew her co-worker to be impulsive to this degree. She had her moments, but she'd never just *leave*.

"She's not in the bathroom," Marcy said as she walked into Bernie's office.

He hung up the phone. "I just talked to Leo. He hasn't seen her. I'll call Security and then I'm going to the basement to see if she's hurt and can't get to a phone." He saw the way Marcy looked at him. "I don't like Leo and though I don't think he's lying, I don't trust him. In the meantime, just relax. I'm sure Sharon's fine."

Marcy didn't believe him. Something told her that Sharon was in serious trouble; the feeling had built since she'd checked the bathroom. Now it was blossoming into fear for her friend's life.

Thompson dialed the Security desk and explained that one of his employees was missing and asked if they could check the basement and the rest of the building to make sure she wasn't in trouble and get back to him.

"Do you want to come with me?" Bernie stood.

"Of course. I want to find Sharon." She would go with him to prove she wasn't afraid of Leo or the basement. There wasn't anything down there that could really hurt her. As creepy as Leo was, he was just a guy, and she'd met plenty of creepy guys in her life.

Bernie led her to the elevators and once they were in and the doors closed, Marcy cleared her throat. "You look tired."

"I haven't been sleeping well, and when I leave here at night I feel exhausted."

"So do I. I don't know what it is, but I've been feeling more tired than usual."

"This place really sucks the life out of you."

She thought it over but didn't know what to say that wouldn't sound stupid, so she said, "I really don't like the basement."

"Then why are you coming with me?"

"Sharon's my friend and I'm worried about her. Finding her is more important than being afraid." She liked Bernie and felt comfortable enough to tell him how she felt. Though she wouldn't admit it out loud, she looked at him as the father she always wished she had.

The elevators opened and when Bernie and Marcy stepped out, Marcy's arms broke out in goose bumps. She could taste the staleness in the cold air.

Looking up at the ceiling, Bernie frowned. "This place needs better lighting."

"That's what I keep saying, chief." Leo stood by his office door. "I keep telling management that the lighting down here is terrible." He limped over to them.

Though curious about his ailment, Marcy never asked what happened to him; she really didn't want to spend any more time talking to him than she had to. The closer he got, the more her skin crawled. There was something loathsome about Leo, though she couldn't figure out what it was. He wasn't a bad-looking man, but he had a plain face that never showed any signs of happiness, and he always looked at her like he was raping her with his eyes. He was a bit too tall and thin, sort of like an angry scarecrow that always leered at her. And he never quite looked like he was all there.

Leo sunk his hands in his pockets and nodded at Bernie. "What can I do for you, chief?" He stared at Marcy a bit too long.

"I know I asked you about Sharon," Bernie said, "but I wanted to come down here and take a look around in case she fell or hurt herself."

Leo shrugged, still staring at Marcy; she felt his hard gaze on her body. "As I said, I haven't seen her since she headed back upstairs, but look around if you want to. Maybe she came back down after I went in my office."

Marcy was only too happy to get away from Leo.

"Thanks, Leo."

"Sure, chief. Any time."

Marcy knew Leo watched her walk away and she wished she had worn pants and not a skirt. "I really hate him," she whispered.

"Don't let him bother you. He's not worth it."

They searched the basement in silence, making sure they checked all the smaller storage rooms. When they came to the locked door at the end of the hallway, Leo joined them and said he never found a key for the lock and figured it was just an empty storage room.

"I'll look into getting a locksmith here to get the door open," Leo said with a polite smile.

"Please do," Bernie said as they walked away. Leo followed them and while they kept searching, he returned to his office.

Only twice did Marcy catch Leo staring at her, making her want to run upstairs, but she wouldn't give Leo the satisfaction of knowing he got to her.

What upset her more was not finding any trace of Sharon. At least if they found something they'd have evidence to show the police. Right now, they had nothing but Marcy's anxieties.

She was about to call to Bernie who was on the far side of the basement when she paused outside Leo's office. Was Sharon in there, tied up and helpless? Shivering from a sudden chill, Marcy knew she had to check. Sure, Bernie would do it if she asked, but she was tired of letting the fear win and she didn't want Bernie to know how afraid she really was. She would just take a quick look around; Leo would understand. He might leer at her, but she'd rather have him stare at her and feel secure that she checked his office than be too afraid and never know if she could've saved Sharon.

Forcing herself toward his office, she hesitated at the threshold. It was empty, though she couldn't remember seeing Leo leave. Then again, she was preoccupied with finding Sharon, and she and Bernie had searched the basement, at times with their backs to Leo's office. But wouldn't Leo have said something to let them know he was leaving? What if they had questions for him? She turned back to ask Bernie if he had seen Leo, but she didn't see him.

Her heart kicked in her chest. "Bernie?" Her voice was timid, weak, the fear stealing her breath. She was alone in the basement. She backed up until the cold cement wall pressed against her. "Bernie?" Still her voice was a whisper and even if he had been five feet away he wouldn't have heard her.

The fluorescents flickered and when she looked at them, she had the impression that the shadows were eating the light. *My mind is playing tricks on me. That's all. Just my imagination. Everything's fine.*

"Bernie?" A little louder but still too soft.

A shuffling noise came from inside Leo's office like—

—Metal scraping on concrete—

—someone moving around, looking for something. But the office had been empty a moment ago. Her heart slammed against her ribs. She couldn't move. It was too cold and too hot at the same time.

The shuffling grew louder; it was moving closer to the doorway.

It's just Leo. It has to be. But Leo's not in his office. I looked. No one was in there. Then who's—

"Boo."

Marcy shrieked.

Bernie came running out of one of the storage rooms. "What's wrong?"

Marcy glared at Leo, who had come out of his office.

"I don't know," Leo said. "I came out here and she was standing there looking all freaked out."

Marcy was unable to speak. The fear had dissipated some, but still pressed down on her.

"Are you all right?" Bernie asked, coming over to her. "What happened?"

"I'm fine. I was going to look in Leo's office for Sharon and then you were gone and I ... I felt *something*. I don't know what, but it scared me."

"Scared *you*?" Leo chuckled. "She nearly scared the crap out of me, chief." Shaking his head, he looked at Marcy. "All you had to do was knock."

"I ... You weren't in there." She stared down at the floor, paralyzed by humiliation and a child's taunting chant in her head: *Mousy Marcy.*

"I was on the floor behind the desk. I dropped a clamp."

"Why don't you wait here, Marcy?" Bernie said. "And I'll check Leo's office."

"Please." He stepped aside. "I've nothing to hide."

Bernie passed between Leo and Marcy and stepped into Leo's office.

Leo's tone made her wonder if he did have something to hide but had already hid it too well for them to find.

As if reading her mind, he grinned at her. "I don't know what happened to your friend. I'm real sorry."

Bernie came out. "She's not in there."

"I coulda told you that, chief." Leo nodded. "Like I said, I haven't seen her since she went back upstairs. A man can get to thinking people think he's lying or something."

"Yeah. Something. Come on, Marcy." Bernie made sure Marcy was all right and the two headed back upstairs.

Marcy kept turning around and staring at Leo, who was most certainly watching her. Did he wink at her?

"We'll find her," Bernie said as the elevator door closed.

Marcy wasn't as optimistic, but she said nothing.

Marcy found Sharon's white Acura in the parking lot on the way back up to Osprey, so that ruled out her driving away. In Bernie's office, his phone light blinked, announcing that he had messages.

"Have a seat, Marcy. Let's see who called." Marcy took one of the chairs as Bernie sat behind his desk and listened to the messages. "It's Security. They checked the offices on the empty floors and called the other companies, but they haven't found her."

"Maybe Harry knows what happened to her," Marcy said. "Maybe he came by and picked her up." If Sharon's husband had come by, it would've been a surprise. Though she didn't expect Sharon to tell her everything, if she had needed to leave, she would've told someone. "You could call his cell phone."

Bernie reached for his phone. "I don't want to upset him if he didn't pick her up." He sat back and steepled his fingers. "On the other hand, I don't want to call the police if they're together." He picked up the receiver. "I have an idea." He dialed, let it ring, hung up, and then dialed again. He waited and hung up. "She doesn't answer her cell phone or the home phone." He pulled Sharon's personnel file out and dialed Harry's cell number.

Marcy fidgeted with her fingers, listening to half the conversation as Bernie explained what had happened. She inferred that Sharon hadn't told Harry about any plans. Bernie hadn't called the police, but he would and would Harry call if he heard anything. "Thanks. Bye." Bernie placed his fingers over the hang-up button.

"Why don't you go back to work and if anything comes up, I'll let you know."

Marcy didn't want to go until she knew where Sharon was. But she did have work to do and she couldn't stay in Bernie's office all day. "All right."

It won't take all day, she told herself as she walked back to her cubicle. Sharon will show up and say she walked to the post office or went out for a cup of coffee and forgot to tell us. Yes, she's fine.

Ten minutes later Bernie knocked on the wall of Marcy's cubicle.

"What's wrong?"

Bernie looked pissed. "The police won't do anything. Unless we can prove there was foul play, they won't send anyone to check on a woman who probably just decided to walk out. We have to wait forty-eight hours."

"Forty-eight hours? Bernie, you know that's ridiculous. You know Sharon." Even if he didn't, she did. "She could be ..."

"I know." He shrugged. "But there's nothing I can do right now except wait and hope Sharon shows up."

"And if she doesn't? Then what?" That familiar, helpless anger she'd known years ago tightened like a fist in her chest. How could the police do nothing for forty-eight hours?

"Then we try the police again."

"Call Harry and tell him. I'm sure he'll call them."

"The police officer told me that because there are so many people who disappear, some because they want to, they can't track down every single one of them. You know, a husband or wife gets tired of the marriage and one day just up and splits."

"But you and I both know Sharon isn't like that. She wouldn't simply disappear like this."

"I know." Bernie looked like he wanted to keep talking. "I've got work to do. If I hear anything or if I think of some way we can get the police involved, I'll let you know."

"I guess there's nothing else we can do." Marcy frowned. Her friend was missing, maybe in danger, possibly … She wanted to scream at someone, but there was no one to blame. It was the way things were done and she just had to accept it.

At five, Marcy shut down her computer, told Bernie to call her at home if he heard anything, and headed to the elevator. Paul Remmick caught up with her just as the door was about to close.

"Hey, Marce." He stepped in and smiled.

"Hi, Paul." She pressed the lobby button. Other than Leo, Paul was the only person who could elicit a response of revulsion. He wasn't an ugly man but his overbearing arrogance—along with his constant fake smiles and less than charming façade—made him undesirable at the very least. It was rumored he'd tried scoring with every woman in both Accounts Payable and Accounts Receivable. He'd hit on her a number of times before, nothing serious that she could call harassment, but close enough she couldn't brush it off as irrelevant. She'd been through enough to know that Paul had serious intentions, so she did her best to interact with him as little as possible. Dealing with an arrogant bastard once in a lifetime was enough; she didn't want to have to deal with Paul the way she'd dealt with *him*.

Though he had the entire elevator to stand in, Paul stood next to her, forcing Marcy to move to her the left, hoping he wouldn't notice.

"So, how's your first month as an official Osprey employee been?" His smile, as genuine as he tried to make it, was fake, attempting to put her at ease.

She'd play along and hopefully the elevator trip would be

quick and she'd be on her way home. "Not much different than the last year." She kept her gaze focused on the lighted buttons next to the floor numbers. "I just have job security now." "That's great." The smile never faltered. "Why don't we go out for a celebratory drink?"

Should've seen that one coming. "I'll pass, but thank you for offering." She hoped she sounded polite; she didn't want to offend Paul as she heard he could get nasty and abusive. *Been there, done that, and never want to do it again.*

"You don't like me, do you?"

Even though he hadn't moved or made any threatening gestures, a familiar claustrophobic sensation tightened her chest and made her blink away a subtle vertigo. Was it too late to keep him calm? "It's not that I don't like you, Paul. I'm—I'm tired and I just want to go home. That's all."

"Some other time, then? Maybe tomorrow night?"

He didn't get it. Was he so dumb he couldn't tell when a woman wasn't interested? It wasn't the first time she'd politely turned down his advances. Did he really think he was so special that no woman could resist him?

The elevator passed the second floor. One more floor and then the lobby. It had grown hot and uncomfortable in the tiny car and Marcy wanted to put distance between herself and Paul.

"What is it, Marcy?" His voice had an angry tone to it. "I'm not good enough for you?"

"It's not—"

"You know, there are plenty of women working for Osprey who would be happy to have a drink with me, and a few of them have."

"Then ask them." The words were out of her mouth before she could catch herself. The last thing she wanted was to piss him off. If he was anything like Jess then ... he couldn't be like Jess. No one was. "I'm sorry. I didn't mean—"

"We went out, had a drink, and that was that. Nothing more. I didn't drug them and take them back to my apartment, or whatever it is you think I'm going to do."

"I don't think you're going to do anything. I'm just not interested. That's all. You're not my type."

"Oh. Your type. I get it. And who is your type? Bernie? Tony?"

"No. It's just—"

"You're just like the other women, so high and mighty, too damned good to have a simple drink with me."

"Paul ..." It was 2003 all over again. Jess, wasted on heroin, screaming at her. The walls of the elevator closed in on her as Paul grew taller, more menacing, and his shadow engulfed her. All she could do was cower in the corner and pray the moment would end before he hit her.

"What is it, Marcy? What's wrong with me that you won't have one drink with me? I'm not asking you to marry me, for Christ's sake. One. Damned. Drink."

"You're shouting."

His shadow disappeared; he backed away from her. She waited for him to yell at her or hit her. His silence was worse than a physical punch. At least if he hit her it would release his anger. This was a storm brewing, strengthening, dark clouds gathering for one moment of devastation, and she prayed the elevator reached the lobby before the storm broke.

"Paul." She chanced a look at him.

He was smiling. "That's fine, Marcy. I apologize. I'm sure you have a good reason for not wanting to go out with me. I'm okay with that."

She'd been through this pre-storm calm with Jess and knew what was about to come, so that when the elevator stopped and the doors opened, she stumbled out into the reception area before she realized she had made a mistake: this wasn't the lobby but the first floor, and the only light came from the red *Emergency Exit* signs.

Paul followed her out of the elevator. The doors closed. He came toward her with a friendly, I-would-never-hurt-you smile on his face that meant he planned to do whatever he wanted and there was nothing she could do about it. She cursed herself for not carrying the gun with her, but after Jess, she refused to.

"Now, you were going to tell me what's so wrong with me that you can't stand being near me."

The reception area was almost exactly the same as on the

fifth floor: four closed, frosted glass doors—most likely locked—and worn carpet. These offices were empty and where the tall plants stood on the fifth floor, here there were only circular indentations in the carpet.

Backing away from him, she saw the door that led to the stairwell, but he had caught her looking. "No, Marcy, not this time. We're going to … talk, and then we're going out for a drink. Do you understand?" He moved between her and the door to the stairs.

The only thing she was aware of was the ugly intent on his face. They both knew no one would hear her scream; the nearest office was on the third floor. Her eyes darted around searching for anything she could use to defend herself, but the area had been cleared of everything. Her heart raced and the claustrophobia closed in again, smothering her.

"Paul, please don't do this."

"What do you think I'm going to do?"

Shifting to her right, she tried getting around Paul, but he cut her off, forcing her back until she hit the wall.

"I only want to talk, Marcy." He offered his hands, palms up. "That's all. No need to be afraid."

But she was scared to death he would attack her. The fears she'd buried after Jess came roiling up again until so many thoughts exploded in her mind that she couldn't focus to save herself.

You encouraged him he's going to kill you there's no escape you should've taken the stairs he's going to rape you what's one drink he's going to beat you it's just like Jess why don't you have the gun you'll never make it out alive they're all the same he's going to kill you Mousy Marcy is as good as dead you should've known better this is all your fault you deserve this after what you did why couldn't you do what Jess wanted why can't you do what Paul wants are you going to do the same thing you should be dead by now you had this coming you shouldn't have done what you did why don't you have the gun like you did with Jess and when he came after you, you pulled the trigger and BLAM—

Marcy pressed herself against the wall, praying for God to

save her. Paul was saying something but all she heard was Jess. "You good-for-nothing whore." Paul's voice was Jess's. "You're fucking useless." What was Paul saying? She couldn't hear him over the torrential flood of voices in her head.

"—just talk, that's all, Marcy."

"Please leave me alone." She sucked in air but it was cold like ice. The fear stuttered her words. "*Please.*"

You are so weak. The voice was hers, whispering in her head. *Mousy Marcy is as good as dead.*

Paul stood too close to her. His warm, stale breath assaulted her. Whatever he planned to do, she had to fight him. She wasn't the teenager, caught by a "friend" who wanted "a little taste" of her while Rod Stewart's "Tonight's the Night" played in the background. It wouldn't be like that or like it was with Jess ever again.

"I can be very accommodating, Marcy. I'm a nice guy." His hand was on her shoulder.

Nice guys don't stand so close. She wanted to tell him to get away, that he wasn't such a nice guy, but the words wouldn't come.

"All you have to do is be nice to me. Is that so much to ask, Marcy?" Fingers on her neck, warm and gentle.

No, she thought, *it really isn't a lot to ask. I can be a nice girl.* She shook her head as the first tears spilled down her face.

His fingertips trailed down the neckline of her blouse. "I'm not going to hurt you."

A door creaked open.

Wiping her eyes, suddenly hopeful that someone had found them, she looked toward the stairwell.

Thank God, thank God, thank—

No one was there.

Paul turned to the door. "Hey! Who's there?" He took several steps away from Marcy; he didn't want to be caught in any compromising situations.

Wide-eyed, her heart slamming in her chest, Marcy prayed someone was there.

The door reached its widest point and then, with painful slowness, begin to close.

"What the hell …" Paul took a step toward the door. "Who's there?"

If she ran she might make it to the elevator doors, but the area was too small and Paul could easily catch her before the elevator came. The only other option was to run to the stairs before the door closed, but without knowing why the door opened she wasn't sure whether it was better to deal with Paul or take her chances on the stairs.

He ignored her, focused on the stairwell door. If she could only calm herself enough, the element of surprise was on her side, but her heart hammered away and her legs refused to obey her.

Above her, something slithered in the ceiling, metal on metal. She gazed up at the tiles and wondered what could make that noise. Could a raccoon have gotten in the ductwork or a squirrel or some other type of rodent? What else could it be? The sound reminded her of a snake, but that was ridiculous. There couldn't be a snake in the ceiling. Well, maybe there could be if someone had accidentally lost a pet, but that seemed too outlandish to be possible.

But at the moment it was the most plausible explanation she could think of. Paul was still distracted when the door clicked shut. They both waited for something to happen, but the first floor was silent. That was worse than the noise. Could she really hear her blood pumping furiously through her veins?

Paul turned back to her, staring at her as if she were a stranger. Then she realized he didn't know what to do. The door had unnerved him, and she wondered if he would suggest they stick together to get out of the building.

"You're not going to say anything about this, are you?" He closed the distance between them until he was within arms' reach. "I mean about what I said in the elevator and what happened just now. You won't say anything, will you?"

The question was absurd. She couldn't think straight from the need to survive, to find the fastest way to escape this place, and he wanted to know if she was going to tell anyone about what he did? "We have to get out of here." Though she loathed the idea, she wanted Paul to help her. "I won't say a thing if you help get us out of here." Her voice trembled. Bracing herself against the wall, she willed herself to stop shaking.

He grabbed her arm. "I can't lose this job. I mean—"

The metal rasping returned and Marcy imagined a snake slithering above the tiles. Pulling away from Paul, she said, "We have more important things to worry about than what happened in the elevator, Paul." Why was he acting like this? He'd always come off as confident and fearless and—Jesus Christ, it was all an act, a façade. He was nothing but a scared little boy, as frightened as she was and would do nothing to save them. He was more afraid of someone finding out about him than the unknown danger they were both facing.

The ceiling tiles cracked, sending a shower of crumbled board down on them.

Marcy ducked out of the way as did Paul, but he still blocked her from the stairs.

"Please," Paul mumbled.

Above them something thumped against the framework of the ceiling and more tiles split and fell.

Paul kept backing toward the elevator, shaking his head as if the mere act would stop whatever was going to happen.

Over a dozen thick cables came writhing down, twisting over each other.

"What the …" Paul tripped over his feet, landed hard, and then scrabbled back.

Marcy watched the cables coming at her. *Run, damn you!*

If those cables caught her, she'd be dead. That got her moving toward the stairwell. She would deal with whatever was there; it had to be better than the snakelike cables that were about to catch her. Even as she stumbled toward the stairwell, they descended on her, coiling around her wrists and pulling her off the ground.

She cried out as her body was wrenched around and up so that her feet kicked air. More cables streamed in her direction. She wriggled and kicked out, hoping, praying for help. But as she hung by her wrists, her body turned and she saw Paul swinging wildly at another half-dozen cables. That was when she believed they were both dead. No one would hear them scream and no one would come to help them. Every office on this floor was empty, and unless the elevator malfunctioned again, it would not stop here.

The jagged-edged cables darted in to jab her and then jerked to a halt inches from her body. Each time one was about to stab her, she jerked away, but then wept in relief when it didn't. Tears streamed down her face as she fought to get free.

On the ground, Paul rolled back and forth as the cables hit him over and over. At first he shouted at them to stop, but then he broke down and cried when they struck every part of his body. The jabs didn't seem vicious, but the constant pummeling must've hurt like hell.

Then, abruptly, the cables around Marcy's wrists slithered off and she fell to the floor. They writhed in the air inches from her so that all she could do was stay as flat to the floor as possible. More cables came down from the ceiling toward her with such menace her breath caught and again she froze. Ahead of her was the stairwell door, and without hesitation she crawled as fast as she could toward it. She didn't care if Paul was alive or dead. All that mattered was getting to the stairs and away from the living cables. If she stopped, if she hesitated even for a second, the cables would attack her and this time they wouldn't let her go.

As she crawled, they slid across her back, tapping her with delicate force, not to injure, but as a reminder they were still there and could grab her any time they wanted to.

"Leave me alone!" She swung at the cables but they danced out of her reach, coming back when she started crawling again. How far was the door to the stairs? It couldn't be that far.

"Marcy! Wait!"

For a moment she was torn between helping him—just because he was a fellow human being—and making sure the snaking cables killed him. When one of the metal tentacles slid down her back, she screamed and forgot about Paul. The bastard could fend for himself.

Staying low to the floor, she kept moving in the direction of the stairwell door. Behind her, Paul yelled for her to stop and help him, but all she thought about was making it to the stairs.

Tears raced down her face as she reached the metal door; she would make it out alive.

"Wait!" he shouted behind her.

She was at the stairwell, getting to her feet, pulling the door open. Glancing back at a dozen cables writhing in the air, she gasped. They were trying to catch Paul, who kept dodging them as he ran for the door. This wasn't real; it couldn't be. Electrical cables didn't come alive and attack people like octopus tentacles, and yet she knew she wasn't dreaming. Paul fought his way through the weaving metal nightmare as they coiled around him.

Not real.

Paul was almost at the door. He was real and if she didn't turn and run, he'd catch her. She fled down the stairs, almost falling several times. Regaining her footing when she reached the bottom stair, she yanked the door open and ran across the lobby. Glen was there, but she didn't stop to say good night, just kept running until she was at her car, breathless, aware her pocketbook was somewhere back on the first floor. She must've dropped it when Paul grabbed her. Luckily she kept her keys in her coat pocket. She fumbled for them, unsure whether she was more afraid of Paul or the living cables.

Once in her car, she couldn't stop crying. Turning the key with trembling hands, she brushed the tears away and wiped her eyes so she could see. Without waiting for her heart to stop doing a jackhammer beat, she drove home with shaking hands and white-knuckled fingers. *Just get home in one piece*, she told herself over and over, repeating it like a mantra. But it was difficult with tears in her eyes and the sensation of the cables dancing on her back.

At a red light she stared at the electrical wires overhead as they pulled free from the pole and wriggled toward her car, undulating like charmed cobras. They wove through the air, creating patterns she couldn't look away from. If they touched the car …

Behind her, a horn blared and when she blinked, the light was green and the wires were still attached to the pole. She offered a wave of apology and accelerated. The next twenty minutes of the drive she stared straight ahead at the road, never once gazing up at the overhead wires for fear of seeing them coming for her.

In the parking lot behind her apartment building, Marcy turned off the car. If she had grabbed her pocketbook, she wouldn't be so afraid that Paul could find it, and then he would know where she lived and ...

She was jumping to conclusions. He was in as much of a hurry to get out of the building as she was. He wouldn't stop to get her pocketbook while a dozen cables attacked him. That would be stupid—unless he saw it and it was in easy reach. Then he would've left with it—if he was even still alive—and could easily find her.

Stop thinking like that. It's pointless. Just go inside and relax, have some wine, watch a movie or something, and then go to sleep.

And then what? Go back to that building in the morning? She shivered, thinking about the building full of cables dropping from the ceiling, plucking people out of their chairs and—

That's what happened to Sharon. The cables got her.

No. The cables must've just fallen out of the ceiling. They weren't alive. The weight of them broke the tiles and they fell. We were unlucky enough to be under them. They weren't—they aren't—alive. That's absurd. Electrical cables are not living things. They are inanimate objects. Plain and simple.

And they came out of the ceiling and attacked us.

Marcy gazed out the windshield, suddenly aware of how many wires and cables there were overhead. She didn't want to give in to the fear.

She walked quickly to the apartment building's back door, alert for anything unusual. The area was well lit and when she glanced over her shoulder, she saw nothing out of the ordinary. She laughed nervously and let herself in, closing and locking the door behind her. The hallway was also well lit, but as Marcy headed up to the third floor, she had the distinct feeling of being watched.

At each landing she expected to find Paul waiting for her, so by the time she got to her apartment, she was trembling, thinking Paul was hiding in every doorway about to pounce on her. She threw her apartment door open, went in, and shut it, making sure all three locks were in place. Before she did anything else, she checked for the gun in her nightstand, the one she bought after Jess almost killed her. The Smith & Wesson Ladysmith revolver was loaded.

She was home and safe. But now that she was home, away from the danger of the building—she was pretty sure that whatever happened there couldn't come after her—her mind turned to Paul and how similar he was to Jess.

No, she told herself. This was completely different. She wasn't living with Paul, they weren't engaged, Paul wasn't—as far as she knew—a heroin addict, and he didn't have a key to her place. Even if Paul did find her, she would have her gun ready before he got in. She hoped she would be able to keep a level head if he ever showed up.

Still, she had to be careful. Though Paul was nothing like Jess, he was just as dangerous in his own way.

She dropped onto the bed, still holding the gun in her hands. "This is insane." She caught a glimpse of herself in the mirror. "You look like shit, Marcy." Her hair was messed up, her makeup ruined from her tears. Running her fingers through thin brown hair, she began crying. *Not this again. Please, God, let this all be a dream and tomorrow it'll be like it never happened.* She hoped God was listening, but She probably wasn't. She rarely did.

Checking the locks on her apartment door one more time, she sat down on the couch with the gun in her lap. *Now what?* The clock said it was dinnertime, but she had no appetite. Her stomach was in knots. She got up and went into the bedroom, sat on the edge of the bed, and stared at the revolver in her hands.

Mousy Marcy, Mousy Marcy, Mousy Marcy!

The woman in her head didn't stop laughing until Marcy fell asleep. Then the dream of the metal octopus came ...

... a continuation of her workday. At her desk, she stared at the computer screen and wondered why it was a shimmering field of white dots like television snow. Then the dots resolved themselves into an elongated shape that expanded until it twisted within the confines of the monitor. Bursting out, long metal tentacles slithered from the screen, leaving trails of sparking wetness everywhere they touched.

Marcy backed away, trying to move her chair on the carpet that had grown thick and plush, making it impossible to roll. Her dream-self screamed as the tentacles reached for her, and where they brushed flesh, her skin crawled. They were cold and wet, soft and pliable. Before she could escape the writhing tentacles, they encircled her and pulled her toward the computer. The monitor had turned into a roiling black hole ringed by electric-blue teeth that shimmered and vibrated, awaiting its meal.

As hard as she fought, the tentacles dragged her closer to the monitor. It drooled dark matter over her desk that dripped to the floor in thick drops. The mouth was dizzying to look at as the crackling and shifting teeth made chewing motions, preparing itself for fresh meat. A tongue made of lightning slowly zigzagged from the center of the darkness and probed at Marcy.

The tongue retreated. The tentacles loosened as they brought her to the waiting mouth and lifted her. When she peered into the mouth/monitor there was nothing beyond the teeth but swirling darkness, and she knew that if she was consumed, she'd cease to exist in the real world. She'd be swallowed into that blackness and become nothing. *Like Sharon?*

Her dream-self screamed one last time and then—

She woke up hyperventilating.

Just a dream. Just a dream. Just a dream.

With each repetition of the mantra, her heart slowed and she was able to breathe again.

Just a dream. Just a dream. Just a dream.

Her body was soaked in sweat and she couldn't stop shivering.

How am I going to go to work tomorrow? Shreds of the dream still clung to her: Foul, ozone breath from the huge mouth that spattered thick mucus-like black fluid on the carpet as cold, slick clammy tentacles reached to embrace her. Too real. Way too real.

In one long breath, the fear overwhelmed her and she began crying until deep sobs racked her body. She let the tears come, hoping to drown the terror that threatened to consume her.

Some time later she woke up. The tears had ended and the tightness in her chest had disappeared. She still didn't know how she'd face the office, but for now, she was hungry. She got out of bed, taking the pistol with her into the kitchen. After checking the refrigerator and finding nothing appealing, she called the local pizza place and ordered a pie, half-mushrooms, half-green peppers, and a liter of Pepsi.

By the time dinner arrived somewhere close to nine, she was ravenous and ate three slices without realizing it. The mushroom-laden slices tasted so good and she felt better than she had all day.

When the phone rang, she stared at it and frowned; she didn't want to talk to anyone. The answering machine picked up and Marcy waited. When it clicked, she held her breath, ready to rush over and pick it up if it was someone she really wanted to talk to, but also wary, afraid she'd hear Paul's voice. When the female voice spoke, she felt herself crumple in her seat.

"It's your mother."

Her mother was definitely not someone she wanted to talk to. Marcy knew why she was calling today and tried to remain calm.

"Twenty-five years since I've seen my baby. Twenty years since my husband left me. I don't know why I call you. You don't care. No one does. I try to talk to your sister—when she decides to pick up the phone, which is almost never—but she doesn't listen to me."

There was a long pause and for a moment, Marcy thought the machine had cut her mother off. But then her mother cleared her throat. "I'm fine. Even though I lost two daughters twenty-five years ago, a husband twenty years ago, and my last child … I don't know if she's gone or not." Her voice was emotionless. "Would you have any idea where my missing children are? I had three daughters. Danielle, Marcy, and Rebecca. They were so beautiful."

Marcy's hands curled into white fists. She couldn't breathe. Tears raced down her face.

"Where is she, Marcy? You were supposed to be watching her. Why weren't you watching her?" Her voice never changed. "Why don't you care?" The phone line went dead.

Before she could stop herself, her mind flashed back twenty-five years ago when she was eleven and Danielle was nine. Becky was eighteen and already living away at college.

October, two weeks before Halloween. They were living in Eastham, New Jersey, a quiet town in the middle of Northwest Nowhere. That year she was going to be a clown and Danielle was going to be a cheerleader. Mommy and Daddy had gone to the supermarket.

"We'll be back in a half hour," Mommy had said as they closed and locked the front door. "Behave yourselves."

They had been down in the family room watching Bugs Bunny cartoons. Danielle was thirsty and Marcy went upstairs to get her some Welch's grape juice (only the best grape juice for our family!), and when she came back, a glass in one hand and a plate of chocolate-chip cookies in the other, Danielle was gone. The sliding glass doors were closed. Nothing had been disturbed. She hadn't heard a sound. Not a cry for help, not a scream. Nothing.

Disappeared.

There were no footprints or any sign someone had come in from the back. Marcy went to the doors and looked out. The backyard was empty.

Danielle had vanished into thin air.

When Mommy and Daddy got home, not more than a half hour later, Marcy told the truth as she'd always been taught to. It had gone worse than she imagined. From that day, her mother spiraled down into an irretrievable state of despair. She talked to Becky when she called and she talked to Marcy's father, but never to Marcy herself, as if on that day she had also disappeared.

Five years later, Marcy's father threatened her mother with divorce because she had slipped into a deep depression. Though she could function, she still refused to acknowledge Marcy or that she'd ever had another daughter other than Becky. She'd started on medication but would not speak to Marcy, telling her husband that when they came home that day from the supermarket, both daughters were gone. Soon after, her father carried through with his threat.

Once her father moved out, Marcy moved in with her father's parents until she was old enough to go away to college. It was when she was in her freshman year that the first letter from her mother arrived and since then she'd received letters or phone calls on every anniversary of Danielle's disappearance, reminding her of what day it was and how she'd failed the family. This year was no different.

Twenty-five years. No clues. No leads. Nothing. Danielle might as well have never existed. No, there were still the memories, the photos, and her mother's accusatory phone calls. Marcy had been to therapy to try to work through the guilt her mother placed on her once a year, but the weight of her mother's blame, added to her own feelings of guilt and failure, made it nearly impossible for Marcy to come out of it.

Too many therapists and twenty-five years later, she still felt it was her fault Danielle had disappeared and still wished she could go back in time and switch places. But she knew it was pointless. Danielle was gone and she had to go on living, working through all the guilt and blame and feelings of worthlessness. It wasn't easy, but she had no other choice.

Marcy went into the kitchen and, with trembling hands, poured herself a glass of white zinfandel. As she poured, the bottle almost slipped from her fingers and it took all her concentration to keep from dropping it.

"It wasn't my fault." The words became her mantra for over ten years of therapy. One therapist after another had told her she hadn't been responsible for her sister's disappearance. But even as she nodded in agreement, she silently berated herself for failing her family. That had been when the woman in her head was created. She became Marcy's voice of torment, constantly reminding her she failed her family and she'd never amount to anything.

Mousy Marcy.

Back in the living room, she erased the message from her mother and turned on the television to an old movie she knew she'd fall asleep watching. It was better to fall asleep than to let the memories come like a tidal wave.

WEDNESDAY

BETTIE WINTERS

Bettie stared at the payable screen on her computer and yawned. This double life would be the death of her; A/P drone by day, hot rocker chick at night. She chuckled. Hot rocker chick. Right. Laughing Jezebel was a fun band and though she wanted it to be more than just a bar band doing covers, unless someone started writing songs, that was all they'd ever be. She'd tried songwriting, but her songs were no better than the rambling poems of the mentally ill, meandering pointlessly through forests of words that made no sense. Maybe she should find some children and ask them to write songs for the band. God knew none of the others—Angelina, Veronica, or Karalynn—could write to save their lives, though Veronica came the closest to being a "songwriter"; her stuff was good but needed polishing, and even though she said Bettie had the knack for it, she doubted herself. But then again, Bettie *always* doubted herself.

Bettie shrugged and turned around, about to say "hello" in her best "I'm not dead though I'm coming close" voice—but no one was there. That was odd. It felt like someone had been standing behind her.

She went back to staring at the aqua A/P screen. It wouldn't be so bad if she had someone other than Ozzy to come home to. A kitten was fine company, but a woman needed more—and she really needed more. Though a lot of men came up to her in the bars the band played in, she turned them all down. After the one time with that guy—what the hell was his name? Scott?—she met on Facebook, she decided there was no way she was dating anyone from a bar or the Internet meat market. Scott was nice, but he also looked like a reject from one of those cutesy boy bands. Though she thought he looked good in an "I want to eat you alive" sort of way, it got old real fast. His looks were all he had. No substance. She played in bars too many nights a week, getting drunk more often than she should, but she still had standards.

Coffee. I need coffee. She rose from her chair and slowly made her way to the pantry. *An IV would be best.* At the doorway, she turned around and smiled, but no one was there. *I need more sleep. I'm going nuts.*

Someone had taken the last of the regular coffee and left an empty pot. The decaf was nearly full, but she needed something high octane to get her moving.

"God damn it."

"What?"

Bettie gasped and looked over her shoulder at Sheila, the Accounts Receivable manager. "Oh. Good morning. I didn't think anyone was here."

"I didn't mean to sneak up on you."

As Bettie started a fresh pot, Sheila handed her a filter. "Someone took the last cup, huh?"

"Yeah, and couldn't bother starting a fresh pot." Bettie got the next pot going and leaned against the counter. "You should come out to one of our shows and bring Laura along."

"She doesn't go for loud rock music."

"Not into rock music?"

Sheila smiled and shook her head. "No, Laura can rock with the best of them, but she doesn't like loud music." She turned to the hallway. "Oh." She frowned. "Was there someone behind me just now?"

Oh, shit. It's not just me. "No. Why?"

"I thought there was."

"I had that feeling before, too, like someone was staring at me."

"Yes. Exactly."

The two women stared at each other. Bettie wasn't sure

what to say, but she did not like the feeling of being watched … without there being someone watching her. She never considered herself acutely aware of people's gazes so when she felt someone staring, it gave her a chill.

"So we're both dreaming?" Sheila took two white Styrofoam cups, poured one for herself and one for Bettie.

"Thanks. I haven't gotten enough sleep because of the band's gigs, so I might be dreaming."

"I think it's this place." Sheila glanced around as if she could find the cause of their worries. "You know, they say work drains the life out of you." Pouring the fat-free milk into her cup, she grinned. "I'm not getting enough sleep either, but that's for good reasons."

"Laura not letting you sleep?" Bettie took her coffee, stirred two bags of sugar in, and sipped it.

"If I'm lucky." She smiled and shrugged. "Back to work. I'll see you later. Try to stay awake."

"It's my only goal." Bettie walked back to her cubicle, hoping the coffee would do her some good. When she sat, her plaid miniskirt rode up, exposing the vicious pink cuts on her thighs. She ran her fingertips over the raised skin, remembering the sensation of the cold blade sinking into her flesh and the chills she got from the rush of adrenaline. This was the power of—

The computer screen was black. *What the* … She placed the coffee out of the way and tapped her mouse. Nothing.

Abruptly, television static exploded from a pinpoint in the center of the screen. Five seconds later it went black again.

"Crap." She moved the mouse, hoping to get her aqua screen back, but the monitor didn't respond. "I'm way too tired for this shit." Tapping a few keys, she waited, but nothing happened. "Marcy, are you there?" No response. "You're not there. I wonder if Sheila's having these problems. I wonder if anyone else is." She could go over to Paul Remmick and ask him, but he'd only leer at her, fuck her with his eyes, and then ask her to dinner or lunch. "Tony? Are you there?"

"I'm here."

"Are you having any problems with your monitor?"

"No. What's wrong?"

"I don't know. The monitor's not working right."

"No, I'm fine."

"Thanks." She considered rebooting the computer, figuring that should correct the problem.

Control. Alt. Delete.

Nothing.

"Crap." She picked up the phone to call Bernie, hoping he would know what to do, but there was no dial tone, only what Bettie first thought was static. *Like the damned monitor.* It wasn't static, but someone mumbling like they were using a tracheotomy microphone. She'd only ever heard one once, years ago when she went to visit her mother's brother. He had one.

"Hello?" The mumbling continued unabated – not words, only sounds – as if the speaker was trying to approximate words but couldn't get it right. The calm buzzing voice chilled her. "Hello," she said louder.

When her heart started beating a little faster, she hung up and stared at her phone. *What was that? Was that a person trying to talk?* The more she thought about what she'd heard, the more details were revealed. Behind the voice was a thrumming, thumping sound like a generator or a motor or—

—a heartbeat—

—an engine of some kind.

I'm too tired and in no mood for this crap—even if it was someone playing a prank with a voice modulator. Holding her head in her hand, she was overcome with fatigue. She unconsciously touched the scars on her thigh. *Just when I think I can't get any more tired ... what is wrong with me? I don't want to quit the band but—*

"What the hell is that?"

Bettie looked up at the screen filled with static. "It's static." She turned around and frowned at Paul Remmick. "What does it look like?"

Paul scowled at the screen. "It looks like a person in silhouette."

She turned back, but saw only static twisting and turning over itself.

"Stand back here."

She got up and stood in front of Paul, but not too close. He'd take that as some kind of sign or come-on. When she glanced at the screen and saw the outline, she forgot about Paul completely. "Oh, my God."

The twisting static formed the silhouette of a genderless person who seemed to squirm on the monitor. Bettie knew the effect was caused by the shifting snow, but it was still unsettling and shouldn't have been on her screen in the first place. Taking cautious steps, she moved toward the monitor.

"What are you doing?" Paul asked.

She didn't answer because she didn't know what she was doing. The being—that was the first word that popped into her mind—fascinated her, and as she stared at it, she felt it staring back at her. Or, rather, felt the sensation of being watched, if not from the monitor, then from somewhere nearby. It wasn't Paul; she was sure of that. His gaze was on her as well, but this was uncomfortable, as if whomever or whatever it was dissected her and sought to see deep into her soul.

The phone rang.

Bettie jumped and stumbled back.

Paul was behind her. "Are you okay?" He had one hand on her arm, the other on the small of her back.

Jerking away from his touch, she glared at him. "Fine. I'm fine."

The phone kept ringing, and as Bettie reached for it, she wondered why it hadn't gone to voice mail.

"Osprey Publishing, Bet—"

The eerie buzzing started again.

Bettie waved Paul over. "Listen to this." She handed him the phone and watched as his brow furrowed.

"What the hell is that?" he asked. "It sounds like someone talking through a voice modulator."

Bettie nodded. *He's trying to talk to you.* Her mind was making connections that didn't exist between some weird shit on her monitor and her messed-up phone.

"All right," she said. "That's enough." She went to disconnect the line but Paul stopped her.

"Wait. I think ... I can barely make out words."

"What?"

"Yeah. He's saying ... he's saying ... tell Bettie ... that she ... she should ... she should have ... din ... dinner with Paul. That's it. He said you should have dinner with me."

"Screw you." She grabbed the phone from him.

"What? That's what he said!" Laughing, he shook his head. "No sense of humor. I'm only joking."

"You think that's a joke?" She nodded toward the static on the monitor.

"No. I just thought—"

"You don't think, Paul, that's your problem." She hung the phone up, and as soon as the receiver rested in its cradle the monitor went dark. "Great." She couldn't figure out what had just happened unless someone was screwing with her phone and her computer. "Tony, how's your phone?"

A few seconds went by.

"It's fine. Why? Now your phone's having problems?"

"My phone was acting up and my monitor just went dark."

"Strange."

"Yeah." Bettie realized Paul was still standing in her cubicle. "Did you come over here for something?"

"Phone number?" He grinned.

"No. Not this time, not next time. Why don't you give up?"

"No reason to." He left her staring at empty space.

What a fucking idiot.

Her screen was aqua again.

Wonderful. She dropped in her chair, feeling the exhaustion from last night threatening to overwhelm her. She was tired after most shows, but today she was especially beat. One way or another she had to come up with a better plan, even if it meant cutting down the gigs and coming in late on the days she had to.

Her gaze drifted to the telephone. The voice or whatever it had been frightened her, but there was no reason to be afraid of someone jerking her chain—except something about the sound unnerved her. It seemed like a voice trying to speak to her in a language she couldn't understand. But what was the odd buzzing that sounded like a trach microphone?

She went to pick up the phone but pulled her hand away, afraid the voice would still be there mumbling or muttering or … whatever it had been doing. That was it: the voice sounded as if the speaker meant to do her harm.

She chided herself. "All right, Bettie, time to forget the phone and get to work." Sliding her chair closer to her desk, she pulled out the keyboard. She knew the best way to forget, and if she wanted to, she could go to the bathroom with the box cutter she kept in her purse. It wouldn't be like home; she'd have to be real careful not to cut too deep or she'd bleed more than she should while at work.

The pain of cutting made her feel alive and powerful; if she cut in the right place she could bleed herself to death. That was awesome power. Life and death, right there in her hand, the cold metal sinking delicately into flesh, drawing blood. At first she was so repulsed by the sight of her skin splitting open that she'd stopped. But the next time, the sensation of the blade breaking skin was so addictive that the sight of her blood wasn't important. The steel, so icy and sharp, cutting into her flesh, took her breath away, made her realize how easy it would be to end her life. That wasn't what the cutting was about, though. Not life and death, but the immediacy of the pain and the addiction of the adrenaline rush that came along with it. She was *alive* when her blood ran in tiny rivulets down her thigh. She felt *something,* and it was a pain she could understand, not like the emptiness that often filled her heart.

"You okay?"

Bettie gasped and tugged her skirt hem down, covering her thighs. "I'm fine." How long had Paul been standing behind her? Could he see the healing pink lines on her skin? "What now?" She didn't turn around because she was afraid her face would give away her pain at that moment. *Get it together, Bettie. Don't let him of all people see how you hurt.*

"I was passing by and you seemed to be in a trance. Wanted to be sure you were doing all right after what just happened."

"I'm fine."

"If you need anything or want to talk, you know where to find me."

"Sure." He'd seen the cuts. She knew it and now he wanted to play therapist and help her. Well, no way was she going to open up to Paul "Mister Every Woman Wants Me" Remmick. No way in hell.

"Have a good day." And he was gone as quickly as he'd appeared.

Bastard. Her heart beat fast and she took a deep breath to calm herself. The last thing she needed was him checking up on her every fifteen minutes to make sure she was okay. She'd be fine without him harassing her. Her last nerve frayed a bit more, and she knew it was all a result of lack of sleep. And loneliness. As much as she loved her bandmates, they were no substitute for a lover, and she hadn't had one of those in too long. The last one had left after he had seen the cuts. He said the lines freaked him out and he couldn't handle such a high-maintenance woman. Gone. Good-bye.

Being alone for so long had weighed heavily on her mind, and there were nights she thought to make the *right* cuts and finish her life. But some insane grain of hope buried deep in her soul kept her from making more than surface cuts, and every morning she woke up, she asked the Universe to make it a better day. Rarely did the Universe listen to her request, but some days were better than others. This one was not starting out as one of those better days.

As she sorted through the piles of invoices on her desk, she prayed the day would get better, but then she swore she heard the buzzing of that voice, felt eyes on her, and the first slivers of cold dread. Wasn't this how all bad horror movies started?

MARCY

Standing outside the Howard Phillips Building, Marcy couldn't convince herself to go in for fear of running into Paul or getting trapped in the elevator with those cables. If she waited around, she could walk in with someone else, but if they took the elevator, she didn't know if she could join them. There was always Security; she could ask to have someone escort her upstairs in case Paul found her.

Mousy Marcy. The woman in her head laughed. *Just walk in the building and get in the elevator or take the stairs. Don't be so pathetic.*

I'm not being pathetic. I'm scared.

Someone passed her and she turned away.

So what are you waiting for? There was your chance to go in.

I can't. The tears ran down her face as she started walking back to her car.

You can't go home, Marcy. You have a job to do.

"I can't. Not today." She picked up her pace.

Are you going to run home and hide for the rest of your life? Are you going to keep running away from everything?

"No, just today." She tried shutting the voice out, but it was too loud.

What about Sharon? She needs you and you're home hiding under the covers? Is that any way to be a friend?

Wiping her eyes, Marcy sighed. The woman in her head was right. She'd failed Danielle twenty-five years ago; she wouldn't let Sharon down. Against her fear, she turned to the office building and headed back. She'd take the stairs up to Osprey and everything would be fine.

Bernie hadn't called, which meant he hadn't heard anything. He might have talked to Harry, but Sharon must still be missing. Only twenty-four hours had gone by, leaving them another day before the police would even come to the office building. She wasn't sure she had the strength to go twenty-four more hours without knowing what happened to Sharon. It was Danielle all over again, and she felt the pull of the years trying to drag her back. Instead of Marcy going upstairs for juice, Sharon had gone downstairs for boxes.

It was your fault. You should've been with Sharon, but you let your friend go down by herself and—

"Stop it." She paused and frowned at the goose shit on the sidewalk. There was so much, it was like navigating a minefield. *Stop trying to make everything about Danielle. That was twenty-five years ago, and it wasn't your fault no matter what your mother says.*

The voice was silent.

As she walked back, Marcy glanced up at the five-story office building and had the sensation that it was some hunkering beast, waiting to devour her and the others. She shook it off and went in, swiping her ID card to get through the second set of glass doors and into the lobby. Glen smiled and said a polite "hello." He was an older, friendly man who had been there longer than Marcy and didn't seem to mind spending most of the day sitting at his desk saying hello to people and making sure everyone had an ID badge. It wasn't the most difficult job, and some days Marcy wished she could trade places with him.

"How are you today?" Glen smiled.

"Fine."

"No offense, Ms. Browne, but you don't look fine."

"I—I didn't sleep well last night. That's all."

As if reading her mind, he said, "Still no word about Ms. Walters. I'm sorry. I'm sure she'll show up."

Marcy nodded and before Glen could see the next round of tears in her eyes, she hurried to the stairwell. By the third floor, exhaustion forced her to stop and lean against the concrete wall. Between expecting Paul to find her and the nightmares of metal tentacles dropping from the ceiling, she'd barely slept.

Five minutes later, when she entered her cubicle and saw her pocketbook on the desk, she almost cried in relief. Everything was in there: wallet, money, credit cards. Who had brought it back? Paul? Leo? Had they gone through it? She shuddered at the thought of either of them rummaging through her stuff.

After concluding that nothing was missing, she dropped her pocketbook in the bottom drawer of her desk, went to Bernie's office, and sagged into one of the chairs. Bernie glanced up from his computer. "No offense, Marcy, but you look terrible. Do you want coffee or anything?"

She shook her head and realized he appeared no better than he did yesterday, maybe a little worse. If not for his change of clothes, she would've thought he spent the night here.

"Are you all right?"

Nodding, she sat up straighter. "Fine. I just didn't sleep well."

"Worried about Sharon?"

"Yes. Any word?"

Bernie sighed and she knew it wasn't a good sign. "No word. Nothing. It's like she vanished off the face of the planet." Marcy stared at the ceiling tiles and shivered. What if those cables got Sharon and she was somewhere between floors? She shook her head and tried her best to keep new tears from coming.

"You're not okay." Bernie followed her gaze. "Want to tell me what's going on?"

She considered telling him what happened with Paul and the cables, but other than Paul making his usual sexist remarks and the brief contact, he really hadn't done anything to warrant Marcy saying anything to Bernie. As far as the cables, Bernie wouldn't believe her. It was better not to say anything and hopefully Paul would just be his normal, idiotic self.

"It's Sharon." Marcy wiped her eyes. "It makes no sense." And by that she meant Sharon's disappearance, Paul's behavior, and the cables that attacked them.

"I'm sure there's a perfectly good explanation as to what happened to Sharon."

She's dead in the ceiling, caught by those metal cables and dragged up there. Marcy frowned, but couldn't look at Bernie. "I should get to work."

"If you want to take the day off, you can. I'll call you if I hear any news about Sharon."

Marcy tried a smile, found it impossible, and gave up. "No, I'll stay. I'll be all right." Without looking back, she left his office, still on the verge of tears. She should've told Bernie everything, but she hesitated too long and now she couldn't go back. If Paul saw her … she couldn't do it. She'd go to her cubicle and get to work.

At her desk she logged in to her computer and stared at the screen.

"Hey. You all right?"

Marcy turned and smiled at Bettie. "Oh." The one constant with Bettie was her wardrobe and her favorite color scheme: black and red. Today was no different. Black top and short plaid skirt. Her hair was dyed black and every now and then Marcy caught violet highlights. Bettie: the Department's Goth Queen.

Right now she wanted to tell Bettie the truth but didn't want to get into all the details. She also had no desire to lie, but it was easier than the truth. "I'm okay."

"Anything you want to talk about?"

Maybe at some point, but not now. "No. But thanks. I miss anything this morning?"

"Have you tried the A/P system yet?"

"No. Why? Did you have problems getting in?" If there was a problem, she'd call the IT guy, who was probably some twenty-year-old who got paid too much money to do too little work.

"No, not getting into the system. I was fine, but then the screen went black and I got this static that wouldn't go away and ..." Bettie hesitated.

"And?"

"And then the screen went black again and finally the system came back up."

"No. I haven't had any problems." Marcy turned back to her computer and checked the four A/P screens; everything was fine. "What was the static like?"

"You know when you're watching television and you hit a channel where there's nothing. That kind of static."

Like her dream. "Oh." Coincidence? She let it go; it probably wasn't the same. When she looked at Bettie she wondered if the other woman held something back. She'd only known her for a month, but Bettie was pretty easy to read and wasn't shy about wearing her emotions like a cloak. "Anything else?"

"Nope. That's it."

If Bettie wasn't going to talk, there was nothing Marcy could do. "All right. If you have any more problems, let me know."

"Sure." Then she was gone.

"Strange." Marcy turned to her computer and started sorting through the mess of invoices on her desk, hoping to immerse herself so she'd forget everything else.

"Uh, Marcy. I need to talk to you."

The sound of Paul's voice made her shiver and clench her teeth, and the memory of his nearness turned her stomach. She had enough to deal with right now without him. "What is it?" It took a great effort to face him, and the smile on his face made her want to strangle him.

"Nothing happened last night. I mean between us. Right?" He frowned and Marcy saw something ugly cross his face. "I wouldn't want to lose this job because you had to go and say something. Right?"

Trembling with rage, she turned to her computer.

"Marcy, you're not going to say anything to Bernie, are you?"

She spun around and glared at him. "Why shouldn't I say something to him? Why shouldn't I tell him exactly what you said and did?" As much as she wanted to scream, she kept her voice as calm as she could.

He stepped into her cubicle and stared down at her. "Because then I'd have to make your life miserable, or worse, and you wouldn't want that." Taking a step back, he smiled politely. "Have a nice day." He was gone before she could say another word.

Tears spilled down her face and she had to turn back to her computer before someone saw her.

At twelve fifteen Marcy decided she had to leave. In Bernie's office, she told him that the situation with Sharon was too overwhelming and she couldn't stay.

Bernie nodded while she spoke, then said, "Well, just relax and take it easy. I hope you feel better."

"Call my cell phone if you hear anything about Sharon. My— um—home phone isn't working right. I'll be in tomorrow."

"That's fine."

Marcy felt bad as she hurried down the stairs. There was her own work to do and with Sharon gone, her work piled up as well. Marcy was so deep in thought she didn't notice the metal pole across the stairs until she almost walked into it. She stared at it, not understanding what she was looking at until she realized someone had bent the banister away from the wall.

The metal was bent at a right angle, effectively blocking the stairs.

She glanced at the wall and saw where it had been ripped from the concrete.

From behind her came the sound of shrieking metal. She turned and saw the banister pull away from the wall like a thin, white caterpillar straining to break free, and curve toward her. As she fled back up to the landing, the end of the banister brushed against her skirt and she felt the cold metal on her skin. She paused, staring up at the door to the second floor. Fifteen steps. But the railing on the right wall waited for her. If she headed up, would it pull from the wall and attack her?

She placed her foot on the first step and saw the bottom clamp strain as the pole tried to pull the screws from the wall. When she backed down, the movement stopped.

The third floor door opened and two people came into the stairwell. They were deep in conversation and hadn't seen Marcy yet. She had to warn them, but the thought of telling them the banister was going to attack seemed idiotic. When she looked down at the other banister, it was flush against the wall as it should be.

The two people saw her and stopped talking.

Marcy smiled and laughed nervously. "Just heading out to lunch." Without looking at them, she fled down the stairs and out to her car. She had the sensation of déjà vu now, like last night; her heart slammed in her chest and she felt dizzy. Though the day was cool, perspiration broke out on her skin.

At her car she paused and looked back at the building. Security told Bernie they'd searched the place thoroughly, including the first floor. Did they find any broken ceiling tiles? A chill wrapped around her as she stared at the windows of the first floor. What caused those cables to attack them? There was probably a rational explanation, but having lived through the experience, she couldn't think of it.

When she got in her car, she hoped by tomorrow morning everything would be back to normal, including Sharon's reappearance. But for now she needed something to do. She certainly didn't want to spend the whole day locked in her apartment like a scared child. Calling her sister Becky in Eastham was an option. Maybe she'd want to have lunch. It wasn't that far of a trip, and she could be there within an hour if the highways were kind to her.

She started the car and pulled out of the parking lot, never looking back.

The afternoon was warmer than the morning, but there was no mistaking the hint of fall in the air. The breeze was October cool and the humidity was low enough that Marcy rolled the windows down and let the breeze ruffle her short hair.

Making her way across the crowded highways of Bergen County, she wound her way to Route 80 West, then headed north onto Route 287 to Route 23 North. The first traffic light was red, so she slowed and stopped, drumming her fingers on the steering wheel. She felt better, but still needed someone to talk to. Then she thought of Connie Floyd, her therapist. She always knew the right thing to say to make Marcy feel better, and Marcy wouldn't have to worry about Connie being distracted by a thousand other things. Hopefully, she'd have time for Marcy; she usually did, but Marcy anticipated the day Connie would say no.

She would've called Becky, but she tended to be a million miles away lately. That was one thing her mother was right about. The last time she talked to Becky, her sister was so distracted, with something on her mind she refused to talk about, that her every reply to what Marcy said was "What?"

The light turned green and the traffic accelerated.

Though she hated using the cell phone while she drove, Marcy didn't want to pull over. She wanted to get a hold of Connie before she left for lunch to be sure her therapist was even in the office; she didn't want to get her hopes too high.

Keeping her eyes on the road, she rummaged through her purse, occasionally glancing over to see if her phone had surfaced. She dug deeper, frowning, trying to watch the road and find the damned phone. Frustrated, she glared at her purse and finally pulled her phone free. She allowed herself a smile of satisfaction that abruptly disappeared when she realized her car was about to veer off Route 23 straight into a tree.

"Shit!" She jerked the wheel, nearly sending her car into the center lane, which was occupied by an SUV blasting its horn. She turned the wheel back the other way, praying to keep the car on the road. "Shit." At the first parking lot, she got off the road, her hands shaking, the phone still clutched between thumb and index finger, and holding the steering wheel. Laughing from the adrenaline rush, she put the car in park and sat there, breathing fast, her heart thumping madly. "Okay, I won't do that again. Promise."

When she felt calm enough to call Connie, she dialed and waited for her therapist to answer. After the pleasantries, Marcy said, "I was wondering if we could meet or at the very least talk on the phone."

"Actually, you're in luck. My one o'clock canceled. Why don't you come by the office and we'll talk?"

"If that's all right." Suddenly Marcy wanted to hang up the phone, feeling incredibly guilty for taking up what was probably Connie's lunchtime. "You know, maybe I'll just schedule an appointment for next week and—"

"No. If you need to talk, you should come by. It's fine."

"All right. I'm on 23 North. I'll turn around. It should take me a half hour."

"I'll see you then."

She slipped the phone back in her purse, found a U-turn jug handle (who thought of these asinine things?) and headed south. Her head was full of the thoughts she wanted to get out to Connie. Sharon's disappearance had brought up so many feelings about Danielle and what had happened twenty-five years ago.

LEO SEDOWSKI

Three o'clock. Break time. Leo had just replaced a couple of fluorescent bulbs on the fifth floor at Dasher Financials. There were a few lookers working there, and some of them knew it. You could tell by the clothes they wore. They wanted every guy to yearn for them, but don't ever, ever think of talking to them or standing too close. God-for-fucking-bid. Like you were diseased or something. They'd shun you, and they wouldn't do it in a subtle way, either. Oh, no. Look at you like you were shit and smelled like it, too. Damned whores.

But it was break time and Leo let a smile creep across his face. Time to go by himself to his private little heaven where no one else could go. Not even those high-and-mighty bitches.

Leo wasn't always this angry, but he'd just come from Dasher and gotten the "look" from a couple of women and it pissed him off big-time.

"I shoulda said something," he said out loud as he got up from his chair. *I shoulda told those bitches they're nothing. They're no better than whores. But I held my tongue because if I hadn't they woulda went screaming to their bosses that I'm harassing them. Bunch of freakin' morons.* He glanced at the pair of red pumps he'd found on the stairs. He knew they belonged to Sharon, but he hadn't said anything to Bernie. No one liked him, and even though he had nothing to do with the woman's disappearance, everyone would blame him and it wasn't worth the effort to defend himself. He'd find a place to drop the shoes and that would be that.

Grabbing the shoes and the key he kept in his locked desk drawer—the one on the bottom right all the way in the back—he left his office, making sure the door was secured behind him. *Not supposed to take midafternoon breaks just in case there's some kinda emergency, but I don't give a flying fuck what those bastards want. Let them have their emergency. I don't give a shit.*

To his right was an unlocked door leading to a hallway that went for twenty feet, made a quick right, and dead-ended with two doors on either side, three of which led to storage rooms. They hadn't been used in over two years, when the building was full of tenants and they kept all manner of crap down here. But because there were only five companies left and they stored their crap nearby, the basement was mostly empty except for the absolute nonessentials no one really needed. Like boxes. The only thing he recalled seeing in any of those rooms was a bunch of pieces of metal ductwork.

At the far end of the hallway was a door on the left. To open this metal door, he withdrew his key and slipped it in the lock. He had lied to Bernie, and as he slipped the proper key in, he allowed himself a smile. Bernie wasn't a bad guy, but Leo couldn't have anyone snooping around so close to *his* room. He turned the key and pushed the door open. It swung into darkness and Leo smiled, knowing what waited for him.

Inside, he flipped the light switch next to the door, which turned on four floor lamps, one standing in each corner of the room. He'd found them at a garage sale while he was looking for lighting for his room; they were exactly what he sought as if some divine hand had led him to them.

Stepping into the room, he relaxed but found himself annoyed that he'd let those people—the women more than the men—get to him. So he wasn't an executive and he didn't have a Ph.D. or a master's degree. He'd barely managed to get his GED, but he knew he was smarter than most of the people he met.

The people in the upstairs offices were just human cattle moving from one pen to another, waiting to be led to the slaughter. What did they long for? Two-week vacations. A luxury family estate in what used to be a forest, so expensive that whoever lived there had to work all hours to be able to afford the mortgage. The high-end SUVs no one could really afford unless they went into such debt they could never pay the damned thing off. Always possessions. That's all they wanted, thinking it would make them happy. Were they? He'd seen the looks on their faces. Miserable. Like death row inmates.

But here in his room, Leo didn't care about them; they couldn't touch him down here. He was in his glory and though the room wasn't finished, he took great pride in what he'd already done and relished the time he would have to spend to finish the walls the way he wanted them.

He dropped Sharon's pumps, closed his eyes, and took a deep breath. The room was lightly misted with Obsession, and he could picture the woman wearing it. Dark, nearly black hair, trailing down her back. Huge coal eyes he could drown in. A sweet, generous mouth with lips that weren't pouty, but full and so kissable. A perfect, tan body full of curves and warmth.

He knew where she was and he went to her. On the far wall, almost in the center, she waited for him with her frozen smile, gentle and friendly. He had found her in a Sears catalog in the women's underwear section, modeling a bra and panties, so vulnerable and yet ... Her skin glowed in the dim lighting and he ran his fingers over the picture, imagining she could feel him touching her arms, her throat, her chest. In her daily life, she paused and gasped, closing her eyes as invisible fingers caressed her and her desire blossomed and she desperately wanted to know who this man was who stoked her fire, who could touch her but yet remain invisible.

Was she working at a desk somewhere? In another photo shoot for another company's lingerie? Her anonymity aroused him and her private life turned him on. If he could only be with her in real life, he could make her feel so good. His fingers trailed down her torso, tracing over her stomach, pausing at the waistband of her panties.

He allowed himself a smile as he ran his index finger across the white cotton panties. He saw her wherever she was, gasping and smiling as his fingers made her tingle, made her wet. Too fast, he thought, and backed away from her. *Soon, my dear, soon.* Turning from his woman in heat, he surveyed the rest of the room, his eyes taking in each wall from top to bottom.

The photos came from wherever he found them. Department store catalogs, mail-order catalogs, magazine ads, and, of course, his pride and joy, the photographs he'd taken himself.

Some of them were of neighborhood girls, from high school down to seventh grade. Anything younger was just not right. The photos themselves weren't as arousing because most of them were only snaps of the girls walking to school or home from school. Those photos Leo used to dream up all manner of scenarios—from simple fondling to more elaborate sexual torture fantasies.

Then there were other pictures that had been much harder to get, but much more rewarding than simple photographs of the girls walking around the neighborhood. He smiled at the tantalizing photo of Ashley and remembered waiting and waiting for that one moment when she stood in her bedroom in the house across the street from his apartment building, at her mirror, unaware he had a camera trained on her. She took her bra off and tentatively touched herself. *Click, click.* Had she known someone watched her as she put on a show, or was she really that naïve? For a seventeen-year-old, she was stacked and apparently curious how her body felt under her fingers.

By the time she disappeared, most likely onto her bed, he had ten shots and was in his own bed, imagining Ashley with him, feeling herself up as he spent himself inside her.

There were other photos of other girls in their bedrooms, in their backyards, mostly in their undergarments or bikinis. Then there were a few photos he had scored of drunk or wasted girls who were willing to show all for a few bucks and a "promise" that he'd show the photos to his editor and they would definitely call for a photo shoot. Those girls were only too happy to give their phone numbers to him, believing his bullshit.

Now he strolled around his room, touching a photo every now and then, pleased he had this shrine to the female body and sad he didn't have any of them for himself. He had heard enough news about pedophiles and pervs and he had no desire to get caught. So he kept his shrine and his fantasies hidden and whenever he needed to, he'd come down and jerk off, dreaming of his neighborhood sweethearts.

When he came to the photograph of Felicia, he paused and stared at the shot. She was one of the most gorgeous seventeen-year-olds he knew and she lived with her mother in the same apartment building right across the hall from him. Her father had left in a drunken tirade several months ago at three in the morning. Good riddance. The guy was an idiot, a drunk, and a wife beater. He was sure the guy had molested his daughter a couple of times, as well. This particularly stunning photo was taken down at the shore where he'd followed her the past summer. She and a few of her friends—all four of them knockouts—spent the weekend down at one of the girls' parents' houses right on the boardwalk in Point Pleasant. He'd gotten a hotel room as close as he could and spent the weekend discreetly snapping photos of the four of them.

But it was Felicia who'd made his heart race and his dick hard, and her pictures—four or five of them—graced the walls of his room. All of them were real, relaxed poses; she had no idea he had been there loving her with the camera. Since then, whenever he saw her, he offered a kind smile while remembering her in that skimpy bikini top and thong and dreamed about what he'd do to her if she ever came on to him.

At first she didn't smile, but when she realized he was an apartment neighbor, she smiled back. He wondered what she'd do for a fifty-dollar bill. He'd never ask; let the fantasy stay intact. If he talked to her and tried anything, she'd probably tell her mother or call the cops and then he'd really be screwed. No, better to let his mind fill with fantasies of her sucking him off, letting him fuck every orifice on her body, asking him to join a fuckfest with her three friends.

He was about to take his clothes off when he became aware of someone staring at him. He looked around the room to be sure he was alone. In the corner by the door was a thing that had no real shape and reminded him of a pile of dirty clothes, except this was a solid mass that shimmered with electrical charges. The reek of ozone filled the room, and it didn't take a genius to know the thing in the corner caused it. The hair on his arms stood on end from the electrical charge filling the room.

"What the hell is that?" He thought to investigate it closer, but without knowing what it was or what it could do, he held his position and realized that until the thing went away, he was trapped. "Aw, shit." His subconscious suggested fleeing the room and he felt that flight instinct trying to push him to the door, but he held his ground; nothing was going to force him out of his sacred place.

The mass squirmed and a tentacle-like growth crept from the top of the thing. The pseudopodium crept along the wall, leaving a trail of smoke as it burned the photographs.

"Hey!" Leo shouted. "You're fucking with my girls!" He looked around for something to use as a weapon, but other than the lamps, there was nothing in the room.

The tentacle grew longer, close to ten feet, flailing against the wall, turning the paper photos black. He thought he should be more afraid, but as his pictures curled and blackened, he was more angry than scared. Sure his heart was racing and his palms were slick, but he was too pissed to let the fear get in his way.

"Aw, man." Leo shook his head, wanting to use one of the

lamps on the thing, but afraid that if it was an electrical creature, he'd be electrocuted.

Another tentacle grew from the thing's side and slithered toward the door. Then it made a thick buzzing sound. Leo thought he heard words within the buzzing, but he couldn't decipher anything.

"Sounds like whatthefuckshisname—Tommy. He had a hole in his throat from too much smoking and used that thing to talk through. Holy shit, it sounds like that." As he watched, the writhing tentacles receded, and the tips grew five smaller appendages that Leo thought looked too much like fingers. Was it trying to imitate a human? The mass elongated up the wall.

It's trying to be human.

An icy chill ran down Leo's spine. He'd seen *Invasion of the Body Snatchers.* What if this was some kind of alien invader, here to take over the world, and he was its first victim? He backed against the far wall, moving next to one of the lamps, ready to yank it from the wall and use it to defend himself.

The thing grew to four feet tall, then there was a loud snap and it was gone, leaving behind the fading smell of ozone and an afterimage on Leo's eyes. It was the form of a four-foot-tall man. He stared where the thing had been and decided he needed to get out of the room that had suddenly turned cold and dank.

Grabbing the key, he slammed the door shut, locked it, and ran back to his office. The image of the small man unsettled him more than he wanted to admit. Had he dreamed it? Other than the ozone and the charred photos, there was nothing to show that the thing had actually been there. But Leo wasn't given to seeing things.

In the main basement he locked the door, still smelling the ozone and realized the hair on his arms stood on end as if he'd been in the presence of a powerful electrical charge. He brushed his hands over his arms, flattening the hairs. What the hell had happened, and what the fuck was that thing? He wanted to be pissed it had interrupted his fantasy, but he was too unsettled— he'd never admit to being scared—by the thing's appearance and sudden disappearance to be angry. Maybe that would come later.

In his office, he closed and locked the door, then brought out the flask of scotch single malt. Good stuff. Smooth and warm going down. It helped him relax. Leaning back, he closed his eyes, feeling the scotch trickling through his system, aware, as he took another gulp, that he was being watched.

JON SIMON

"She did it again, didn't she?" Tony made sure the balls were tight, then slipped the rack off. "I don't know why you put up with her. Your wife's got a messed-up perspective on reality."

Jon placed the cue ball down to the right of the worn spot. "She doesn't get it that the cash from the last book is enough to get us by." Lining up his shot, he let some of his frustration flow through him down the cue and let rip what he thought would be a stunning break, but accomplished very little. "She wants new furniture, new clothes, new everything, so I have to work while she hangs out with Craig and draws."

Tony shook his head and bent to check the angles Jon had left him to decide his best shot. "I don't get it."

Jon watched his friend's deliberate motions, remembering the sequence of events from several hours ago. He had been working on his second novel, furiously typing, in the groove, and then—

He turned and stared at Alyssa. "What?" How long had she been standing in the doorway?

She frowned as if she tasted something bad in her mouth. "Your job starts tomorrow, right?"

Jon felt himself tense. "Yes." After all this time he was going back to work, albeit a temp job, but it was still Corporate America and he resented having to go. The first book had sold well enough to keep him out of work this long and, if it weren't for Alyssa, probably another six months to a year.

"Good. You know we need the money."

"No. We don't." He scanned the bookshelves of novels, reference guides, and how-to books as if somehow he'd find an answer to this conversation that never went away.

She sighed and shook her head like a frustrated mother. "We've been through this before, Jon. There are a lot of things around the apartment that we need, and my job won't pay for all of it. Besides, I need to have more time for my illustrating so I'm planning to cut my hours back. That means you have to pick up the slack and get a job. You can work on your novel at night like the rest of the world."

"Ally, we've got enough money for you to get what you want and for me to stay home and—"

"And what? Look, Jon, the money from your first book has to last. That's all there is to it."

"Ally—"

"I'm heading over to Craig's. Make sure—"

"You're going over there now?" He looked at the old, folk-style wall clock: 3:15. "Isn't he at work?" Still staring at the clock, he wondered when it had been purchased. He didn't remember her mentioning she bought the clock, and God knew he wouldn't get something as ... bland as that.

"He telecommutes so he's home most of the time. We need to get those illustrations finished, so when I called, he said he could get his work done this morning and we'd have time this afternoon and tonight to work."

"This afternoon and tonight?"

"There's a lot to do." She sounded hurt, as if she thought he was accusing her of something, which he was without coming out and saying it. She spent too much time with Craig.

"What are these illustrations for?"

"A limited-edition book called *The Box*. It's a short story by some author Craig knows. From what Craig said, *The Box* is an amazing story. He talked with the author and then contacted the publisher about doing illustrations for a limited edition. They were into it and told him to start working on sketches. It's a very powerful story." She made a face as if talking to an idiot. Then she checked her watch. "I've got to go."

"What time do you think you'll be home?" He already knew the answer: *some time late*, but he wanted to hear her say it. He wouldn't argue, though he knew he shouldn't let her simply walk away.

"We'll be working late."

Her answer annoyed him. Simple, to the point, and no extra information. Usually he'd just shake his head and let her go, but this time he felt more angry than usual. "What's late? How many illustrations can you possibly have to finish? You've been working on these for—I don't know—how long?"

For a moment she stood there as if stunned by his questions, as if never expecting he might ask such things. "The Box isn't the only book Craig has contracts for. He's got a number of other projects that he needs my help on."

Jon heard the petulance in her voice and it pissed him off. How dare she get angry at him for asking why she spent so much time with Craig? After five years of marriage, he had a right to know if his wife was cheating on him, but he didn't want to look like the paranoid husband with no confidence in himself and no trust in his wife. And that's why he said, "All right."

He knew she'd always been a "best of both worlds" kind of woman. If she could get what she wanted from two men, she would. Trust, faith, and marriage be damned. But he had to trust she'd be honest even though he knew she'd never be.

"Don't stay up too late," she called from the front door. "You don't want to be exhausted on the first day of your new job."

"Sure." Anger rose to his throat, but he swallowed it back down. "Don't stay out too late yourself."

But the door closed and she was gone. Not even a kiss good-bye.

"Not even a good-bye kiss." Tony frowned before he sank the seven ball in the corner pocket; he had the solids. "You know why this is happening, Jon? Because you're a chickenshit. There's no reason Alyssa should be spending so much time with Craig. But you think it's all about trust and she knows that. So she's using you, playing on your sense of trust while she's with Craig."

Jon took a fast swig of his Smirnoff Ice and contemplated Tony's words; he was right, of course, but Jon didn't want to admit it.

"If that's not bad enough, there's the whole job issue that she's convinced you is a good idea. You're willingly walking into prison." Tony missed the five, hitting it wide to the left of the side pocket. "I know you well enough, Jon. After all this time, why are you doing it?"

"Because it's not prison," Jon said. "It's just a job. You work there. If you think it's such a prison, why do you stay there?"

Tony laughed, moving out of Jon's way. "I'm not the one with the published book trying to make a living as a writer. You are. To me, it is just a job. But you've got bigger dreams."

Jon took the shot he had hoped Tony would leave him and missed. The thirteen bounced off the edge of the pocket and tapped the six. "I'm just trying to think … practically and rationally."

"You're thinking rationally?" Tony fired the cue ball into the five, sinking it in the far corner. Next he lined up the three and dumped it in the side. "How about the guy who gives up his dream to do what his overbearing wife wants when he knows full well he doesn't have to? He could be home working on his novel and making something good of himself." He bounced the cue ball off the far rail to take the two, but it glanced off the side of the ball instead. "But no, he chooses to listen to some egocentric queen who thinks her dreams are more important than his. Good choice."

"Alyssa's not that bad." But Jon knew what Tony would say.

"She's worse. She makes you believe you're doing the right thing when you're not. You're living her life, not your own."

"That's not true." He took another sip of the Smirnoff Ice and played the fourteen and twelve into the side and near corner pockets. "So why didn't you stop me when I got married? You were my best man. You've could've said something."

"Nice shots." Tony took a drink from his Budweiser. "Because when you got married, Alyssa wasn't like this. Let me ask you something. Do you have to work? Don't you have enough money for at least another year?"

"Maybe it won't be that bad." He missed the ten and frowned.

Tony laughed. "You crack me up, Jonathan! You have a

chance to keep your dream going, but instead you're heading to an office job so you can sit for eight hours, be isolated from humankind, and work for someone else. All because Alyssa refuses to listen to you when you tell her that you've got enough money to stay home." He shook his head. "On your way home tomorrow night, why don't you stop at the men's store and pick up a pair of balls, and then tell Alyssa you're gonna stay home and finish the book?"

"That's hilarious. You know we're trying to save to buy a house, right?"

"Thank you, Alyssa. Men's store. Pair of testicles. It'll do you a world of good."

"She ..."

"She what? Wants stuff? Wants to decorate the place the way she wants it decorated, no matter what you want? So she finds expensive shit, buys it, and guess who has to pay for it? Hm? Wanna take a guess?"

"I get it."

"So what are you going to do about it?"

Jon stared at the pool table. "It's your shot."

"Thanks, but that doesn't answer the question." Tony walked around the table, then came back. "You left me with shit here."

"Too bad." The Smirnoff Ice finished, Jon contemplated another one, but he did have to start a new job tomorrow and the last thing he needed was a headache on his first day.

Leaning over, Tony examined several different angles, frowning at all of them. "Hand me the bridge, will you?" Taking the bridge cue from Jon, he set up a shot that would send the one ball bouncing off the six and—if God was on his side—into the corner pocket. "So what's up with Craig? Do you think she's fooling around with him?" The one crashed into the six and stopped dead.

"I don't know."

"Look, Jon, we've been friends a long time. I've never told you what to do. But if Alyssa's having an affair with Craig, it's all the more reason to split."

Jon had never thought of leaving Alyssa, no matter what she

asked of him. Once they were married, he considered it was for good, taking the vows seriously. Sure his eyes had strayed a number of times, but he wasn't responsible for his thoughts, just his actions.

"You would leave her, right?"

"I never thought about it."

"You wouldn't. Would you?"

Jon passed Tony and took a shot at the eleven. Somehow, it pushed the four out of the way and went in the corner pocket.

"All right. Forget it. At least Osprey's a good place to work. I won't bias you with my attitudes about my fellow co-workers, but the work is pretty easy and the people are mostly good people."

"Mostly?"

"We have a few problem people and a couple of strange ones. Nothing to worry about."

"Good to know because—"

"Fuck you, too!" someone shouted nearby.

"Jackass!" came the reply.

Jon turned around and saw the two men swinging at each other. They were far enough away that he and Tony didn't have to avoid them, but they were close enough that they had to move soon.

"Time to go," Tony said.

They dropped the pool cues, grabbed their coats, paid, and left the bar. Tony had driven so they went to his Avalon.

On the way home, they were quiet, letting WDHA, Tony's favorite station, fill the car. At Jon's apartment, Tony pulled to the curb.

"That was fun. We'll have to do that more often, except without the violence."

"And the interrogation."

Tony grinned. "Just trying to help a friend see the light."

Jon opened the car door and got out. "See you tomorrow."

"Get some sleep, Jon. Don't want to be tired on your first day."

"Thanks, Alyssa. Tell your lovely wife, Maggie, I said hi."

Jon closed the door and checked his watch. 10:43. He wanted to

stay up and work on the book, but he begrudgingly admitted
Tony—and Alyssa—were right. He needed sleep. Tomorrow
morning he'd be a corporate employee, a fact he dreaded as
much as an inmate facing a life sentence.

MARCY

Marcy left her therapist's office feeling worse than when she
arrived. On top of the anxiety that refused to diminish, she
felt guilty for lying to Connie and telling her she was taking
her antianxiety medication. She'd stopped several months ago
because she had hated feeling like the world was nothing but
one beige emotion. Not that she liked the crazy ups and downs,
but at least she felt *something*.

Connie had listened with her usual attentiveness: alert and
interested but mildly distracted and at moments distant. Several
times Marcy had told her she knew how insane the whole thing
sounded but what she was saying had really happened.

Of course Connie had no explanation for the cables attacking,
other than to suggest it was connected to Marcy's anxieties, a
way for her mind to process the events with Paul and how she
got away from him.

Marcy had been there, damn it; she knew what happened
and if she had the guts to talk to Paul, she could confirm her
story, but there was no way she was going anywhere near him.
She couldn't even be in the office today. What would happen
tomorrow? How many days could she call in sick before having
to face Bernie and tell him what was going on?

She couldn't tell Bernie the truth; he would think she was
insane. Maybe she already was and just hadn't admitted it yet.
Denial was a very powerful force. But the cables had attacked
them. The question was, who was capable of doing such a thing?
The first person she thought of was Leo, as he hated practically
everyone who worked there. But this seemed like something
beyond even him. Then she wondered, what if whatever
controlled those cables wasn't human at all?

That was silly. Everything had an explanation, no matter
how outlandish, no matter how far-fetched it might be. It was

Leo. That's all there was to it. Plain and simple. Leo.

But what if?

There was no "what if"; there was reality and an explanation. Just because she didn't know what the explanation was didn't mean there wasn't a rational reason for what happened.

"I sound like every therapist I've ever seen," she said out loud. "Great. Now I'm talking to myself."

Shoving the thoughts from her mind, she drove for a while, stopping at the mall to mindlessly walk around. She'd hoped to let the window dressings distract her, but after a while she hadn't gotten any clarity, and so she went back to her apartment.

Turning all the lights on when she got in, she triple-locked the door and retrieved the pistol from the bedroom. Then she went into the kitchen to get a glass of wine. With pistol in one hand and wineglass in the other, she sat on the couch wondering what to do.

She contemplated dinner, but she had no appetite; her nerves had wreaked havoc on her stomach.

"Okay, Marcy," she said out loud. "You are alone in your apartment. The door is triple-locked. Paul has no idea where you are and there's nothing supernatural—"

A door slammed nearby.

"Shit." She listened but didn't hear any voices or footsteps. It sounded like it came from only a few doors away, which meant whoever slammed the door would be passing by her apartment unless they slammed it on the way in. Marcy couldn't remember if she'd heard footsteps prior to the slamming door, but she was now acutely aware of every noise and voice in the apartment building.

This was no good. She'd never be able to fall asleep later. Glancing at the bottle of wine, she wondered if finishing the whole thing would help her sleep. But Paul could break in any moment and—

The phone rang.

Marcy knocked the pistol to the floor. It hit the rug with a dull thud, like she imagined a body would sound, and she thanked God the safety was still on. Grabbing the phone, heart hammering, she said, "Hello."

Silence. But not silence. A sound like a breeze through trees. Could she hear someone breathing?

"Hello?"

Whomever it was hung up and the breeze was replaced by complete silence. She hung up the receiver, hand shaking, angry at herself for reacting to every little noise, every wrong number.

Was that her first glass or her second? She couldn't remember. Everything felt wrong. She closed her eyes for a moment and took a deep breath, hoping to calm her fraying nerves. Placing the pistol on the arm of the couch, she poured herself another glass of wine, sipping it too quickly so that it spilled over the rim and down her blouse.

"Damn." She looked at the pink liquid soaking into the cotton. "Better do something before it's ruined."

In her bedroom she changed into a T-shirt and sweatpants, then took the blouse into the bathroom where she soaked it, trying to make sure the stain didn't set. Back in the living room, the gun lay next to the wineglass and she realized what a bad combination the two were. The last thing she wanted to do was accidentally shoot someone while she was drunk. Given the woman in her head could start in on her at any moment, that someone might very well be her.

She turned on the TV and surfed through the channels, looking for something to keep her mind occupied and away from the nightmarish thoughts trying to encroach on her consciousness.

At one point she thought the remote had slipped from her fingers and hit the floor, but when she looked, it was still in her hand. She shook herself awake, blinked a few times, and stared at someone on CNN talking about the ongoing events in the Middle East.

Then her eyes were closing. Once. Twice. She sat up straighter to keep herself awake and stared at the TV. CNN had been replaced by a screen of wriggling static snow. At some point she must've changed the channel but landed on a station that had gone off the air or never existed. She had no idea what time it was and thought to go to sleep, but something about the television snow held her fascinated.

Like worms twisting and turning over each other, always in constant motion, always—

A shape resolved itself out of the shifting worms, a silhouette becoming real, taking on solid form.

Marcy watched, captivated by the figure solidifying on her TV screen. Who could it be? What channel was it? The remote lay on the floor. She picked it up and pressed the info button but nothing happened. She couldn't even change the station to find an actual program. It was stuck on this person resolving from the static.

Just when she thought the figure would appear, it remained a thick, black splotch, human in shape but without features.

It's staring at me.

It was impossible to tell what direction the figure was looking as there were no eyes, but Marcy still felt its gaze on her.

The phone rang.

She jumped and her heart thudded in her chest. As she picked up the phone, she hoped it was Bernie with news about Sharon.

"He—hello?"

It was the breeze again. No. It sounded more like machinery this time, like some kind of pump making a sound like a heartbeat. Then a creaking noise—not like a door, but like a voice speaking so slowly it didn't form a coherent word, just a sound—made Marcy shudder.

She was about to replace the phone when a voice spoke. There were no words, only the sound of the mechanical voice as it struggled to form words. Was the speaker in pain? The sound was eerie; a machine voice trying to emulate human anguish.

When she glanced at the television, the figure trembled, and there was no mistaking that the voice on the phone belonged to the shifting shape on the screen.

She slammed the phone down. Her heart hammered and her breath came in sharp rasps. Against her better judgment she turned to the television. The figure grew, obscuring the swirling static worms as if it were coming closer. Fumbling for the remote, she hit the off button, but the television stayed on.

The figure moved closer, blotting out the twisting snow until she knew it could step out of the television into the room.

That same buzzing voice came from the television, and she backed away until her arm hit the wineglass and knocked it to the floor. She tried retrieving it, but her body wouldn't move. A wave of exhaustion overcame her. Her eyelids fell closed and as hard as she tried to open them she couldn't. *So tired.* Then she felt herself rolling over and falling, hitting her head on the hardwood floor. For a moment the world spun and she thought she passed out. When she came to, she was lying on the floor. Survivor was on the television. The wineglass was still on the table, and the gun was on the arm of the chair. She'd been dreaming after all.

Before she could get up, however, she felt disoriented, so she stayed on the floor until she fell asleep. This time, there were no dreams.

THURSDAY

JON

"So, are you going to stay at this job longer than the three months you stayed at your last one?" Alyssa glanced at him over the book she read.

Jon stood by the sink with his morning cup of coffee, staring at her like she was a stranger, feeling the sting of her question go right to his heart. "That's my plan." But it wasn't; it was hers. "I just think—"

Alyssa sighed and put her book down. Something on illustrating bio-organics. "We've been over this and you know how I feel. I just don't understand why you can't see my side of this. It's like you don't care."

He stared at her, nodding when appropriate, not really hearing anything more than "get a job so I can spend your money on shit we really don't need but once we have it I can brag to the neighbors that we're living better than they are."

Alyssa was still talking, but Jon had tuned her out and kept nodding. Hadn't Dr. Phil said this was typical male behavior? Married five years and the selective hearing was kicking in just fine, thank you. There was a time when she hadn't been like this, early on in their relationship, when they had fun and went on trips and it had all been so new. They'd dated a couple of years before they got married, and within a week she started … changing, becoming who she was now. Whatever happened to the woman he knew?

Jon checked his watch, then drank down the rest of his lukewarm coffee. "Why don't we talk more when I get home?"

He rinsed the mug and left it in the sink. "I have to get going." Though he dreaded the temp job, he would make a good show of it for Alyssa's sake.

She stood and came over to him. "I really do appreciate you doing this for me." She kissed him on the cheek. "Good luck on your first day."

"Thanks." Before she could say another word, he put on his suit jacket and left the apartment.

Autumn was in full swing. The morning was crisp and carried the slightest hint of coldness that defined the beginning of Winter. Jon noticed it, but was more concerned with his first day at Osprey Publishing. He hadn't temped in a long time, and it had been a couple of years since he'd actually worked in a corporate environment.

The ride to Osprey was less than memorable but for the ever-increasing pressure inside his head from the feeling of … wrongness. He should be home writing, not sitting in traffic going to some Corporate America job.

His timing was impeccable until he hit a snarl of traffic on Route 17. It was the infamous bottleneck at the Essex Street exit. He should've remembered and either left himself more time or taken another route. This part of the highway always stopped because three lanes went down to two, and most people seemed to be mentally challenged when it came to merging.

The highway stopped. Dead. Jon sighed. *Wonderful.*

He thought about everything Tony had said the night before. Why did he stay with Alyssa? Because, when they dated, she wasn't like this. When they married she wasn't like this. It started around the time his uncle had died. Jon had gone home alone to the Bronx for the funeral; Alyssa had to stay and continue working with Craig on those illustrations. Illustrations that never seemed to get done. Another two years passed before Jon started thinking she was having an affair with Craig. But he never said a word because she'd flat out deny his allegations and refuse to even talk about her relationship with Craig.

The traffic cleared and he accelerated, focusing on Osprey Publishing.

I wonder if anyone there can help me get my novel published.

Maybe working there wasn't such a bad thing. Tony said the people were good to work with, which was comforting to know; nothing worse than having hostile co-workers. Maybe it was fate steering him in the right direction. He couldn't know what life had in store for him from one moment to the next, and though working in a corporate environment seemed like a bad idea, it might turn out to be a great thing. With renewed enthusiasm and a smile on his face, he took the Route 4 exit heading east toward his new temp assignment.

ANNETTE DOWLING

Annette got in the elevator and pressed the 5 button to take her up to Dasher Financials. The doors closed and she waited for it to ascend. Another Thursday morning. Nearly the end of another boring week. *God, if only something different would happen to add a little excitement to life.* She leaned against the back wall and sighed.

A tapping noise sounded above her. She glanced up in time to see one of the ceiling tiles crack and break, falling to the elevator floor in front of her.

"What the—"

Something writhed in the darkness of the elevator shaft.

Like snakes, she thought as two cables squirmed into the elevator.

"What in the world?" She moved away from them, but there was little room in the car to avoid the cables as they curled and uncurled, their jagged ends flicking from side to side, dancing, mesmerizing Annette until she was backed into a corner. Two more dropped into the car with small grappling hooks at their ends. The cables moved swiftly; the grappling hooks opened wider and pinned her shoulders against the wall.

She gasped, struggling against the two cables that held her while the other two danced dangerously close to her face.

A third dropped from the ceiling, but this had some kind of bulblike shape at its end. When it turned and the face—made of spinning gears, wriggling wires, and two glass globes for eyes—glared at her with wicked sentience, she screamed. It seemed to study her, staring into her eyes.

Fighting against the cables, Annette found herself growing tired and weak, as if her strength and energy were being drained away. Her hands grasped the cables, but she no longer had the strength to pull them away even though the grappling hooks dug into her shoulders.

"Please, don't kill me." The words fell out of her mouth. *"Please."*

The malignant skull backed away but kept its stare locked to her eyes. There was a moment when Annette felt a sense of relief. Maybe it wasn't going to kill her after all. Maybe it only wanted to study her. But those eyes bore malice. The face was evil even though it didn't have ability to shape gestures.

The dancing cables swung to the left. Her gaze followed them as they moved to the right. She felt dizzy watching them as the sense of relief passed and she found she couldn't breathe.

Weaving through the air, the cables suddenly paused, hovering in midair.

She blinked.

The cables struck.

It happened too fast; in less than a second the cables came at her and the jagged edges ripped into her eyes. When the cables retreated, she felt a pull from her ruined eyes as they stuck to the metal before they slid off and hung from their sockets. She screamed from the sudden intense pain that tore into the sockets where her sight had been.

The cables holding her disappeared and Annette slipped to the floor, screaming in terror and crying in pain. *"Help me!"* She touched her face and felt the ruined eyeballs and the strands of muscle and sinew still attached.

Cold cables wrapped around her wrists and pulled her to her feet. As hard as she fought against them, they were too strong. The impossibility of the situation settled on her like a heavy, thick blanket she was blind and trapped in an elevator with living cables. Less than five minutes ago everything was fine. When she was jerked up and out of the elevator, all she could do was scream.

MARCY

She did not want to be here, not after last night when the cables attacked. Maybe they'd fallen out of the ceiling and he'd been in such a state with Paul that she thought they attacked. That had to be it because cables didn't attack people. Regardless of the cables, she needed the job. How would it look if she called out sick because ... Why? Maybe she should go in and tell Bernie she wasn't feeling well and needed to leave. Closing her eyes, she took a breath and let it out slowly. No. She was a grown woman and could handle things here.

She was acutely aware that the cubicle next to hers was empty. Everyone knew Sharon had disappeared, and the rumors ran wild.

"I hear she's having an affair with some guy who drove her off on some cross-country adventure."

"She took a flight to someone waiting for her in Paris."

"No, she had a winning lottery ticket she never told anyone about."

But no one said anything about murder because it would mean the façade of safety everyone believed in didn't really exist, and at any moment their lives could end by some random act of violence just because they were in the wrong place at the wrong time.

So they created flights of fantasy that Sharon was on some tropical beach with a Harlequin hunk, drinking pretty drinks and spending her lottery winnings like water. It was safer, better, and fit with their need to control their surroundings instead of their environment controlling them. They could pretend Sharon was just fine and maybe something like that would happen to them. Ah, to be on a beach in the French Riviera sipping fruity drinks and getting a massage from Sven. Or Svenlana.

Marcy wanted to believe Sharon was all right, but knew deep in her heart that she wasn't, that she was gone somewhere and no one would ever see her again. She'd have to keep it together; Bernie had called WorkFinders the previous afternoon to get someone to cover Sharon's desk, and the temporary replacement—and she would be temporary; Sharon was coming back—started today. Marcy would be the one to train her unless she could convince Bernie to have Bettie do it. The last thing she wanted was to spend time in Sharon's cubicle, whether her friend was alive or …

No, Sharon was alive. Somewhere.

Sharon's fine, Marcy told herself. Stop making it like she's … she's fine. Something happened and she'll call me and everything will be all right.

Tears filled her eyes again, threatening to spill down her face.

Even though Marcy had worked there for a year and hired permanently only last month, she and Sharon had quickly become friends. It was rare for Marcy to find someone she was so comfortable around that she'd share all her secrets with them without being drunk.

Overwhelmed, she grabbed her purse and hurried to the bathroom, nodding at everyone who said hello to her. Did they know the pain she felt at that moment when she pushed open the bathroom door and nearly ran into one of the stalls? She closed the door and sat on the toilet, letting the tears come. What was wrong with her? Sharon was missing, that was it. Not dead.

She's dead. I know she is. It's only a matter of time before they find the body.

"She's not dead." Her voice sounded hollow, false. "She can't be." But then she remembered the elevator stopping and the cables. Was it possible Sharon was dead somewhere on one of the floors that was abandoned? Had Security searched everywhere? And would the police even show up and search? Forty-eight hours seemed such a long time to have to wait.

Checking her watch, she realized the forty-eight hours were near to expiring. She should tell Bernie to call the police and demand they come and search the building.

Though Marcy was afraid to go, she wanted to check the other floors and make sure Sharon wasn't lying there hurt or unconscious. What if Paul followed her? She couldn't go alone, but she certainly couldn't ask Bernie to go with her because he would tell her Security had checked the building, and that when the police came they'd check the entire building again. How many offices were there on those three floors that were missed?

No, Security was thorough. That was their job. Wasn't it? She'd seen some of them: Rent-a-Cops who couldn't wait to leave because they had better things to do than look for some woman. She had to tell Bernie to call the police. Maybe he already had and just forgot to tell her.

Wiping her eyes, she realized she couldn't stay where she was. She stood and smoothed her skirt down, then opened the door. At the mirror she checked her makeup to see how bad she looked. She looked horrible. Opening her purse, she tried finding tissues, powder, eyeliner, mascara, anything that would put her back together, but for some reason everything was jumbled up. Loose change fell onto the counter. Lipstick seemed to jump from the bottom of her purse into the sink, losing its top. The tissues had come out of their package, blossoming every which way, falling onto the counter, soaking up water drops.

"Shit."

Her eyes misted as she fought to gain control of herself and the chaos that was the inside of her pocketbook. When would the tears end? Would they stop when Paul left her alone? When Sharon came back? Or would she always be on the verge of crying, never knowing if the building was about to attack her?

The bathroom door opened and Bettie walked in, dressed in her usual short black skirt, stockings, shoes, and lace blouse opened a button or two more than it should be.

Marcy wiped her eyes with the damp tissues, hoping she could clean everything up before Bettie noticed what a mess she was.

"Are you … What happened?"

Too late. "It's … I'm fine." She tried gathering the innards of her purse, but somehow they kept slipping away from her. Mascara fell in the sink. Tissues floated to the floor. Eyeliner clattered across the counter.

"No, you're not," Bettie said.

Marcy reached for the eyeliner. "I just can't …" Pulling at the top, she tried being dignified as she leaned closer to the mirror. "I can't." She threw the eyeliner in the sink. "Damn it." "Wait right there." Bettie disappeared out the door.

Ignoring Bettie's request, Marcy gathered all her effects and stuffed them in her pocketbook. She had to get out before Bettie came back and asked her to explain why she was so upset. Bettie was tenacious when it came to helping someone—as if her life depended on it—especially Marcy. It was as if Bettie's mission in life was to save her and make her a better person.

Well, she wasn't going to wait around for the next installment of *The Making Marcy Better Show*. Tossing the wet mascara in her purse, she made sure she had everything, turned to leave, and froze when the bathroom door opened. *Please don't let it be Bettie.*

"All right." Bettie placed her makeup kit on the counter. "I'm going to fix. You're going to talk." She opened her case and pulled out foundation, concealer, eyeliner, mascara, blush, and lipstick. "Now, tell me what's going on."

"Bettie, really, it's nothing." Marcy stared at the barrage of containers, brushes, and tissues Bettie had strewn out on the counter.

"Of course it's nothing. Everyone comes into the bathroom and cries their eyes out because they're bored and have nothing else to do." The other woman handed Marcy a tissue. "Here, get rid of the makeup you've got. We need to start fresh here."

Marcy scowled.

"I can't work with you if you're going to turn your head. Now, let me help you."

"Why?"

"Why what?"

"Why are you helping me?"

"Because you're upset and you need someone to redo your makeup so you don't look like a raccoon."

Marcy laughed even though she didn't want to and it felt good; she couldn't remember the last time she had. Taking the tissue, she glanced at herself in the mirror and wiped the old, ruined makeup away. Though she wasn't a fan of horror movies, she still knew she looked worse than the Bride of Frankenstein. But then again, Elsa Lancaster had been an attractive woman.

"Good," Bettie said. "Now, look at me."

Marcy did as she was told and waited patiently, as Bettie took up concealer and the powder and came toward her.

"Don't move."

"You're going to poke my eye out!"

"No. I've done this before for Karalynn."

"She was probably too drunk to care."

"Hey. Don't dis the band. Those are some fine women."

"Sorry." Marcy froze as Bettie slowly applied the under-eye concealer. She evened out the color and smoothed it further with the powder. Then she put those down and picked up the mascara.

"Okay. You have to stand perfectly still. Like I said, I've done this for Karalynn so I know what I'm doing." While Bettie stroked the mascara on, Marcy felt uncomfortable with her so close. If she wanted to she could move an inch closer and kiss her. Bettie had joked that she swung either way, and Marcy had no problem with that—Sheila was a lesbian, after all—unless Bettie tried something on her.

"There. See? I know what I'm doing."

Marcy felt Bettie's breath on her cheek. "I'm glad you do. Otherwise I'd be blind."

"You're doing very well holding still. One move on your part and this'll stab your eye and I'd have no idea how to explain it to Bernie. So, are you ever going to tell me what's wrong?"

"It's nothing."

"We had a deal. I fix, you talk. I'm fixing but you ain't talking."

"Really, Bettie, it's just my own problems."

"Good." Bettie stepped back. "Okay. I'm done."

"Wait." Marcy looked in the mirror and saw one eyelash done, the other tiny and undone. "You only did one eye. What about the other one?"

"That was a free one. If you want me to finish the other one, you'll talk and stop telling me it's nothing."

"But it is."

"If nothing's wrong, then there's no reason for you to be crying and no reason you can't fix yourself." Bettie placed the mascara on the counter. "I'll leave this with you. Just drop it off when you're done." She brushed past Marcy and went to the bathroom door.

Marcy said, "Wait."

"Yes?" Bettie said coyly.

As reluctant as Marcy was to open up about all that bothered her, she acquiesced. "Okay. You win."

"I'll finish. You talk." She came back and took up the mascara, then stepped close to Marcy. "One more time; don't move."

Bettie's sudden closeness made Marcy want to take a step back, to put up some sort of defense against the woman intruding into her physical space. But then, she had asked Bettie to help.

"So?" Bettie asked.

"You're going to think it's ridiculous and laugh."

"I promise I won't laugh." Bettie stepped back and looked at each of Marcy's eyes. "I impress myself sometimes."

Marcy turned and saw herself in the mirror. Bettie did a better job than she'd ever done by herself. "You do good work." She glanced at Bettie in the mirror. "I'm scared for Sharon." She waited for a reaction, afraid of what Bettie might say.

"Everybody's worried about her. But you knew her better than anybody else. Why would I laugh at that?"

She turned to Bettie, staring into her eyes as if she could see truth there. "I don't know. It's just that …"

"What?"

Marcy frowned. If only she knew the right words to say so she wouldn't sound like she was nuts. With her attempt to find words, the memories came back. Paul, the elevator, and the attacking cables. "Something happened to me the other night." She opened her mouth but then closed it before she said something stupid.

"What happened?"

Marcy was about to tell her everything, from Paul's actions to the cables, but the bathroom door opened and Sara, the oddly quiet woman from Accounts Payable, walked in. Marcy smiled politely, unsure what to say to her.

Sara winced. "You feel it, don't you?" She turned to Bettie. "Someone's staring at you but no one's there."

"Yes," Bettie said. "I—"

"It's ... different ... somehow. Hungrier."

"What are you talking about?" Bettie asked.

"It's going to get worse very soon." Sara shook her head, went into a stall, and closed the door.

Marcy and Bettie exchanged glances and Marcy shrugged.

"What are you talking about, Sara?" Bettie asked. "What's going to get worse?"

The other woman was silent.

"Sara?" Bettie threw her hands up in resignation. "Whatever."

"I'll talk to you later," Marcy said.

"What about what happened?" Bettie held the eye shadow out. "I know it's not your color, but it works."

Marcy sighed loudly, took it, and brushed her eyelids with the smoky blue eye shadow.

"Here." Bettie placed the eyeliner on the counter.

"Thanks." Marcy handed back the eye shadow and carefully applied the eyeliner.

"Much better." She took the canister Marcy offered her and dropped it in her case. "Now—"

"Later." Marcy nodded toward the closed stall door. "Besides, it's nothing really. You know, just my imagination."

"Right, Marcy." She took the makeup case and headed out the bathroom door with Marcy following close behind. "Things just happen that are in your head. They don't really happen to you."

Outside the bathroom, Marcy put her hand on Bettie's shoulder. "That's not what I meant. I meant that I was probably seeing things."

"Are you going to tell me what these things were?"

Shaking her head, Marcy felt on the verge of tears. "No. Not now."

"All right. Fine."

"Don't be mad at me. I just—I don't want to talk about it right now."

"Okay, Marcy. You know where my cube is. When you're

ready, stop by." She started walking away.

"Thanks." Marcy smiled and shrugged.

"Any time."

Marcy went back to her desk and sat down. She didn't feel any better, but at least she knew she looked better. The computer screen was blank; it was past its screen-saver time frame. She shook the mouse and the static of the screen image reappearing sounded like tiny cables scraping on metal. She looked up, wondering how close the metal cables were from breaking through the ceiling and killing her.

BETTIE

Bettie returned to her desk, frustrated at not being able to get through to Marcy. She'd known the other woman a month and as much as she'd talked to her, Marcy refused to let her in. She couldn't understand why she wanted to be bland and ... mousy, a word she knew Marcy used to describe herself. That infuriated Bettie even more. Why would someone keep putting themselves down?

Marcy was pretty, but the way she dressed, the way she carried herself, and her attitude made it impossible to see her beauty. Not that Bettie dressed any better all in black with black eyeliner, nail polish, and dyed hair with violet tints thrown in just for the fun of it, but she had attitude that Marcy was missing. Marcy was so ... bland. Though she was surprised Marcy had held Paul's advances off for as long as she had, she was glad Marcy had shown enough self-esteem to keep him at a distance. She suspected, in some twisted way, that Marcy was torn over Paul. As much as she was repulsed by him, Paul was one of the few men who showed any interest in the woman, and Marcy was someone who longed for love and attention.

Bettie knew all about that. She thought about the box cutter in her purse. Her heart beat faster and a little part of her wished she could sneak away for a few moments. But this wasn't the place to do that. She turned in time to catch Paul standing outside her cubicle.

"How's the computer?"

"What do you want?" She was in no mood for him. Between her own emotional issues and Marcy's, she felt raw and had no desire to deal with his childish behavior.

"Hey, no need to get mad. I just wanted to see if you were having any more computer problems. That's all."

"I'm sure. My computer's fine."

"Well, good."

Bettie counted to five.

"Watcha doin' for lunch today? I'm heading to the deli. Wanna come with me?"

"I'm having lunch with Marcy." *She was?* The words came out so easily.

"Are you? That's sweet. Marcy's such a wonderful girl. After the other night—" "What?" Her mouth hung open.

"I just remembered something." Paul was gone.

She realized she had been holding her breath. Was that what was bothering Marcy? Sharon was one thing; Marcy was definitely upset about Sharon disappearing. But what was this about Paul? That would explain her reluctance to talk.

After the other night—

What was he about to say? He caught himself before he went on, probably afraid she'd say something back to Marcy or go straight to Bernie. Did something actually happen between them? Bettie knew Marcy better than that. Didn't she? Could Marcy's whole personality be an act for attention?

No. She'd been out with Marcy once or twice and who Marcy was at work was who she was all the time. No act. Which could only mean Paul had forced himself on her. That would explain Marcy's mood and state of mind. It would also mean Bettie would have to go kick the shit out of him for being a prick. It was better that she find out the truth first before inflicting unjustified bodily harm on Paul. Although his very existence justified violence perpetrated against his person.

At Marcy's cubicle she knocked on the metal frame of the entry opening. "What?" Marcy turned. "Oh, hi."

"Right." Bettie stepped in and hauled Marcy to her feet.

"What are you doing?" She resisted, trying to pull away

from Bettie, but the other woman had her by the arm and wasn't letting go.

"We're going for a walk." Taking Marcy from her cubicle, she headed for the conference room.

"Let me go."

"I'll let you go when we're in the conference room."

"Why?"

"We need to talk, Marcy."

"About what?"

"I'll tell you when we get there."

The two people they passed on the way gave them strange looks but got out of Bettie's way.

At the conference room doors, Bettie pulled one open and threw Marcy in.

"Sit."

Marcy sat like an obedient pet and that pissed Bettie off even more. She gave up like she had no spine. What wouldn't she do? Would she ever say no or simply let people have their way with her?

Sitting down next to Marcy, Bettie suddenly remembered a six- or seven-year-old girl hating herself because she'd gotten her favorite dress dirty; her mother yelled at her and, instead of washing it, ripped it to shreds and threw it back at her, telling her it would happen again if she continued acting like a stupid boy and not like the girl she was. Her mother wanted a more feminine daughter, not a tomboy.

But it was Marcy in front of her, acting as timid as ever, almost frightened. God, she hated that look. It was the same one she'd seen on Kimmi, her sister's face, when Daddy came home much later than he should have. He wasn't drunk. At least not with alcohol. He was wasted on lust from being at the bar where the girls danced and now he was hungry and Mother wasn't interested. She'd locked herself in the bedroom, leaving the girls to fend for themselves.

"What's wrong with you?" Marcy asked.

Looking at Marcy as if she were a stranger overlaid with images of her sister, Bettie shook her head, unable to find words.

"Are you all right?"

Kimmi's scared face disappeared and Bettie stared at Marcy again, but her anger was gone. Why were they in here? Then she remembered.

"I just saw Paul," Bettie said.

The color drained from Marcy's face and she trembled.

"What happened?" She didn't think she needed to say more. The idea that anything happened between them was too repugnant to imagine.

"Nothing."

Bettie felt her chest tighten with anger. "Bullshit."

Marcy flinched at Bettie's anger but didn't say a word.

"He started saying something about the other night and then left. What was he going to say?" Bettie knew where this was going. If Marcy had gone along willingly with Paul, she wouldn't be so frightened, which could only mean the scumbag forced himself on her. She decided to drop any pretense that she thought it was mutual consent. "What did he do to you?"

"Nothing." Marcy turned away, but not before Bettie saw tears.

"Why do you keep saying that? Why are you protecting him?"

Tears streaked Marcy's face. "I'm protecting myself." Her voice was loud, and for a moment Bettie expected someone to find them. After several moments, Bettie knew no one had heard them.

"Why can't you just leave me alone?"

Bettie nodded as if in agreement. "Is that what you want? You want me to leave you alone so Paul can keep doing whatever it was he did to you?" She expected Marcy to say Paul didn't do anything to her, but the other woman was silent. "I'll walk out and go back to my desk. I've got a lot of work to do. If you want me to go, I will."

"No." Marcy sounded like a little girl who was too shy to ask for what she needed.

"Are you going to tell me what happened?"

Marcy shook her head and tears slipped from her eyes. "I can't tell you."

"Did he hurt you?"

Marcy shook her head.

"Marcy, did he hurt you?"

Marcy covered her face and wept.

"Jesus. I'll kill him."

"No." She looked at Bettie with wet, red eyes. "Don't say anything to him. Please."

Bettie understood what happened. It had happened to her years ago. *I'm going to do something and you're not going to say a word. Understand?* She understood too well. "I won't say a word." *But I can make his life miserable.* She sat with Marcy until she calmed down.

"Thank you," Marcy said. "I'll take care of everything."

I'm sure you will. "Listen, why don't we have lunch today? My treat."

"You don't have to do that."

"I know I don't, but I want to."

"That's really nice of you."

"I'm just like that." Bettie shrugged, suddenly uncomfortable. "I don't like seeing anyone hurt, especially not by a sleaze like Paul." She imagined the worst between Marcy and Paul and thought of different ways of torturing him. But she didn't want to get Marcy in trouble; Paul might be a vengeful bastard. She would do her best to stay away from Paul until she knew all of what was going on.

"Just … please don't say anything to him."

"I won't. Trust me." She put her hand on Marcy's arm as a sign of female solidarity and thought Marcy was going to jump out of her skin. "Relax. You're really nervous."

"I'm just … anxious. That's all."

"I'm sure." She dropped her hands in her lap, wishing Marcy wasn't so afraid of life. Was that what made her bland? She was scared to death of living? Well, she'd see that changed. "So, lunch today?"

"Yeah. I think that would be nice."

God, that word made her cringe. Somehow, she'd have to get Marcy away from *nice* and move her toward *wonderful* or *excellent.* "Lunch it is. Twelve thirty?"

"Sure." Marcy nodded. "I have a favor to ask."

"What's that?"

Marcy stared down at the hands in her lap. "A guy from my old temp agency, WorkFinders, is starting today. Bernie wants me to train him, but can you do it?"

"Do you know the guy?"

"Oh, no. It's not that. He's going to be in Sharon's cubicle, and I just ... I can't ... you know." She started crying.

"It's all right." Bettie wanted to console her with a touch, but was afraid it would make Marcy retreat. "I'll talk to Bernie and make sure he knows I'll be training the new guy."

"Thanks." Marcy sniffed. "He's here because Sharon isn't and it's just too much for me."

"I know. It's okay."

As if saying she understood how Marcy felt were a signal, Marcy started crying again.

All the feelings of helplessness Bettie had as a child listening to her mother cry when her father hit her came back, making her want to reach out to Marcy and yet run out of the room at the same time. *This isn't the same,* she told herself. But wasn't it? A woman Bettie cared for was in pain because of something a man did to her. Same thing. But Bettie knew it wasn't. Marcy wasn't her mother, Paul wasn't her father, and she wasn't helpless. One way or another, she would make Paul suffer.

"It's gonna be all right, Marcy." Bettie smiled. "It will. I promise."

"Don't make promises, Bettie. It's not going to be all right. Sharon's ... God knows where Sharon is. I'm so scared."

Bettie's chest tightened and her insides twisted. She didn't want to get too close, but she still wanted to help Marcy. There was a lot going on with her, more than she was saying, and though Bettie wouldn't pry, she hoped Marcy would come to trust her and open up. Not that Bettie wanted to be her therapist—she was certain Marcy already had one—but if she could be a friend without Marcy smothering her, then she'd do her best to be there for her.

"You know," Marcy said, "maybe it would be better if I had some time alone."

"Sure." She almost said "thank you," but kept her mouth shut. The last thing she wanted to do was hurt Marcy. "I'll see you for lunch."

"Thanks, Bettie."

Bettie nodded and headed out of the conference room. She needed air and to get her own thoughts together. Right outside, she practically collided with Paul.

"Hey," she said.

He snorted and she almost punched him, but restrained herself. "How's Marcy? She's taking this whole thing about Sharon disappearing pretty hard, huh?"

"Yeah. She's got a lot on her mind." Bettie knew the only reason she was excluded from his little harassment games was because she was the only woman with enough guts to say something to Bernie. The other women were too terrified he'd do something to them.

"I bet." Paul nodded his head like a bobble-head doll.

Karalynn, the keyboardist in her band, was an acupuncturist and Bettie wondered how many needles she could use on him before he passed out from blood loss. That made her smile. "Well, back to work."

"Yup." He walked off to the pantry, humming something.

Bettie went back to her desk, smiling, thinking about Angelina, the drummer, tattoo artist, and piercer, and what the two of them could do to Paul. By the time she sat down, she imagined Marcy there as well, helping them pierce his testicles. She had to stifle her laughter so no one would hear her and ask for an explanation. There was no way anyone would understand.

MARCY

By the time she got back to her desk, Marcy couldn't work. Sharon was missing, probably dead, Paul kept giving her angry glares, and she kept looking up waiting for cables to drop through the ceiling and attack her. If that wasn't enough, she was sure she'd have to help the temp at some time and that would mean being in Sharon's cubicle, something she dreaded. People were talking, most saying she'd found some rich guy and took off. No one suggested she was killed, though Marcy knew some of them thought so. It was Leo, they said in hushed voices. The maintenance guy killed her when she went to the basement the other day. Probably raped her first, then murdered her.

Marcy couldn't listen to them even though she believed what had happened to Sharon was far more sinister than Leo killing her. She didn't want to believe Sharon was ... dead. Thank God Bernie could call the police today so they could start their investigation. Forty-eight hours had passed with no word from Sharon. Harry would probably call them as well.

Marcy wanted to go home and wait for the call from Bernie or whoever would tell her what happened. She couldn't bear the idea of hearing about Sharon while she was at work because she'd be devastated and probably make an ass of herself, bawling like a little baby in front of everyone. But she knew Bernie wouldn't let her go home. She went to his office to find out if he'd called the police yet or if Harry had heard anything.

"You're wondering what's going on," Bernie said as Marcy came into his office and sat down. "I've already called the police and ... what's wrong?"

She was unable to hold his gaze. "I asked Bettie if she could train the temp and she said she wouldn't mind."

"I wanted you to train him."

"Him? Oh. I know you asked me, but that means being in Sharon's cubicle and I can't do it. Bettie can train him. She knows what she's doing." Her hands fidgeted in her lap.

"Except you know the work Sharon was doing better than Bettie does."

Marcy wanted to back down and agree to train the temp but the thought of training someone to replace Sharon was too much for her to handle. It made her feel that Sharon hadn't been a vital part of the department, hadn't made a difference and could be replaced as quickly as a pen with no ink.

As hard as she tried not to cry, tears filled her eyes and

she quickly wiped them away. "I can't." Now she wanted to flee Bernie's office, run out of the building, and never come back.

Stop crying, damn you! You look like a baby!

The voice made the tears come faster and harder, and she couldn't keep from sobbing. "I'm sorry, Bernie."

"It's all right." He pulled a box of tissues from his bookcase and handed it to her.

She wished people would stop telling her it was all right because she knew it wasn't and might never be again. On the other hand, this was a perfect chance for her to tell Bernie everything that had happened. It didn't matter if he believed her or not. She would feel better. But the memory of Paul's wicked smile when he told her he'd make her life miserable forced her into silence. She could mention the cables, but then she'd have to explain how she wound up on the first floor.

Marcy blew her nose and wiped her eyes. "I … I should go. I'm sorry. You must think I'm a real baby. I've got work to do." She shook her head and stood on shaky legs. "I'm sorry."

Just get out of his office. You can fall to pieces in the bathroom. Or better yet, in your car. Just not here.

"I called the police, Marcy. So has Harry. They're on their way here."

Marcy dropped into the seat, suddenly dizzy.

"I know how close you and Sharon were, and I know people are saying all kinds of things. But no one knows the truth. The police will be here and they'll investigate and we'll find out what happened to Sharon. It's all right. I know what it's like to lose someone close to you. You don't have to apologize for being human and being upset."

Marcy looked at Bernie through tear-filled eyes. She wiped the tears away and stared at him, unable to form words, as if a dam kept them from reaching her mouth.

"But I think something else is going on. Wanna talk about it?"

She suddenly realized she wasn't breathing. She shook her head, opened her mouth to say "no," and the dam broke wide open, flooding her mouth with words she told herself she'd never say. "Paul came on to me the other night. He told me he'd make my life miserable if I told anyone. He tried … he didn't really try anything, but he ..." She shuddered from the memory "He touched me and then ... he said things ... that he wanted to talk and he said he was nice and wanted me to be nice to him and have dinner and a drink, but then these ... cables fell out of the ceiling and attacked us like snakes and I ran away. I left Paul there and ran for my life because the cables were trying to kill me. I couldn't stop running. I got in my car and drove home." She stared down at the hands that had gripped the steering wheel with white knuckles. "I don't know how I made it home, but I did and I found my gun and waited. I thought Paul was going to find me or"—she glanced at the ceiling—"or worse."

"Marcy. Hold on a second. Paul made sexual advances? He threatened you?"

She nodded, unable to speak, exhausted from the torrent of words that spilled from her mouth. She wanted to run back to her desk and pretend she hadn't told Bernie anything. What would happen now? Would Paul get in trouble and know it was Marcy who told? Would he really try to kill her?

"Why didn't you come to me yesterday and tell me?"

"Because he said he'd make my life miserable if I told anyone." She trembled and started sobbing again. "But I couldn't hold it in anymore." She couldn't look at Bernie. "Please don't do anything. Don't tell Paul I told you." She imagined Paul coming after her, catching her on the stairs or in the elevator, and pulling a knife and ...

"I'll take care of Paul."

"No! You can't. He's going to—"

"He's not going to do anything." Bernie shook his head. "I need you to tell me exactly what happened so I can talk to Paul and straighten this out."

"I don't want to talk about it."

"Marcy, if you won't tell me, then there's nothing I can do."

That would be better, she told herself. If Bernie didn't know what really happened, then he couldn't say anything. Good. She was safe. No matter how many times Bernie promised her Paul wouldn't do anything, she knew that if he ever found out she told Bernie, he would kill her. "No. I'm sorry. I can't." She started to get up.

"All right. You mentioned something else. Cables attacking you?"

Marcy sat back down. "These cables fell out of the ceiling and I was so surprised I guess my mind played tricks on me." Realizing how stupid it sounded, she wanted to get out of Bernie's office as fast as she could.

Bernie sighed and Marcy winced. "Marcy, look, I'm trying to help you here. You came into my office in near hysterics and it's obvious you're upset about more than just Sharon. You don't want to talk about what happened with Paul, and now you're changing your story about these cables. If you won't tell me what's going on, there's very little I can do to help you.

"I really want you to train the guy from the agency when he gets here, but if you want Bettie to train him, I guess that's fine. She can do it. As far as the rest goes, if you won't talk to me, that's all I can do for you." He leaned forward and folded his hands on his desk. "It's up to you. I'm here if you want to talk."

Marcy knew she should tell him everything that happened, but she was afraid of the consequences and disgusted with herself for giving into the fear. She studied her hands in her lap, and then she started talking without knowing what she would say, without caring what Bernie thought, and without concern for her own life. When she left Bernie's office ten minutes later, she felt oddly dizzy but more at peace than she'd felt in a long time.

THE POLICE

The police arrived shortly after nine. They set up in the conference room, and one by one, interviewed each Osprey employee regarding Sharon. Once the questioning was completed, Officer William Ellison knocked on Bernie's door.

"We're done here," Ellison said. He was tired and wanted nothing more than to be out of this run-down office building. He hated missing person cases because it was rare they were ever resolved. The most likely scenario was that Sharon Walters had simply walked away from her life. It happened all the time. Something in the brain snapped, and either they ran off or they came to work with a gun and started shooting.

"Anything?" Bernie asked.

"We've interviewed everyone here. We'll go to ..." He checked his notes. "Dasher Financials, then to the companies on the third floor and interview them as well to see if they know anything about Ms. Walters's whereabouts."

"Thanks for your help. I'm hoping Sharon'll turn up and the whole thing will be a case of miscommunication."

"That would be nice." He looked around Thompson's office. Someone could be missing in here and they'd never find him. "There's a maintenance man in the building. His name is Leo Sedowski. His office is in the basement. Make sure you question him, as well. He may've been the last person to see Sharon."

Ellison wrote the name down. "Thanks. I'll look into it."

"What's next?"

"Going through the answers to our questions to see if there are any inconsistencies, and once that's done, we'll see where we stand. We also have someone questioning the husband."

Thompson nodded. "All right. Thanks again."

"One way or another, we'll be in touch soon." Ellison nodded, then headed out to join his fellow officer at Dasher Financials, hoping Sharon Walters's disappearance would wind up being routine. They still had A&R Collections to visit, then Dimension Graphics, both on the third floor.

Walking to Dasher Financials, he thought he heard something up in the ceiling like metal grating on metal, but he wrote it off as the common sounds of an old building. He opened the door and prepared himself for the next round of interviews.

PAUL

Score! Elaine had agreed to meet him after work for a little extracurricular activity in one of the abandoned offices, so the rest of the day was going to be just fine. He'd been nervous about metal cables coming through the ceiling, but nothing had happened all morning and now he had Elaine to contemplate.

Sure, he'd get some work done—there was always so damned much of it—but he'd spend most of it wondering what she was like. Would she be a screamer or one of those women whom you could barely tell if she had an orgasm? Did she have multiples or just one big one?

After an hour of this thinking he was ready to go into the bathroom and relieve himself, but he couldn't; he was saving his load for Elaine. There was nothing worse than being with a woman for the first time and dribbling out a few drops.

Imagining what her sweet mouth would feel like wrapped around his—he jumped when the phone rang. The caller ID announced the call was from Bernie.

What the hell does he want? Ruining my fantasy. He picked the phone up and tried to sound pleasant. "Hey, Bernie, what's up?"

"Can you come in my office for a minute?"

He swallowed. Something was wrong. "Sure. I'll be right in." He hung up and headed to Bernie's office with too many thoughts zipping through his mind.

Did I do something wrong?

What if some report get fucked up?

Maybe someone caught me on that porn site and told Bernie?

Are there cutbacks?

Am I going to get fired?

Marcy didn't say anything to him, did she? I'll get fired if she did. God, I'll kill that little bitch.

But he knew he couldn't kill her. He didn't have it in him. He hoped his angry demeanor had kept her quiet and would keep her quiet, especially if another opportunity like the other night arose. Of course those cables or whatever they were really ruined his whole plan.

Maybe that's what Bernie wanted to talk about. The cables.

"Yes, sir." He stopped in the doorway and folded his arms. "What can I do for you?"

"Come in. And close the door, please."

Paul did as Bernie asked and sat down. This couldn't be anything good. When he swallowed, he found his throat had gone dry. Staring at his feet, he knew he came across as guilty and forced himself to look at his boss. Bernie sat behind his desk watching him. Though he looked relaxed, Paul knew Bernie was anxious. Heck, with Sharon gone, everyone was a little apprehensive. Maybe Bernie wanted to know if Paul had heard anything about Sharon. Sure. That was it.

Bernie leaned forward. "I heard a story that's gotten me pretty angry, Paul, and I want you to explain what happened."

"Okay." This was definitely not good because the only thing he'd done that would cause a stir was what he did with Marcy the other night. This was turning into a worst-case scenario. If he had to defend himself against Marcy, he'd lose, be brought up on sexual harassment charges, and get fired. But he was sure they were alone, so if this was about Marcy, then it was Marcy who'd said something. And after he threatened her. Now he'd have to do something to get back at—

Relax. It's probably nothing, his inner voice told him.

"What were you and Marcy doing on the first floor two nights ago?"

The worst-case scenario had arrived, but could he think fast enough to make it sound like Marcy had exaggerated? If only he knew what Marcy said, he could defend himself better. But Bernie wanted to hear his version of the story. So he went for it.

"We were in the elevator together when it stopped on the first floor. Marcy got out, not realizing it was the first floor. I got out with her, trying to explain it wasn't the lobby. Something was bothering her real bad, and she started saying things and we got loud.

"I was ready to leave her there, but these cables came out of the ceiling and … and I don't know what. It was the craziest thing I've ever seen." He shrugged. "Marcy ran for the stairs and left me. I finally got free and left the building. I wanted to apologize, but Marcy was long gone."

"That's all?"

"That's it."

Bernie nodded, looked thoughtfully at Paul as if wanting to question him further, but hesitated. Why? What was he waiting for?

"Tell me something, Paul. What do you think these cables were?" Bernie sat back and glanced out his window. "Where did they come from? Did they fall from the ceiling or did they actually attack you?" He turned to face Paul. "What really happened?"

He doesn't believe me. The jerk doesn't believe me, and now he's trying to corner me with those freaking cables. Okay. Fine. I'll play along. "At first I thought they just fell from the ceiling. But then they seemed to come alive and attack."

"And Marcy left you there?"

"Yes."

"Why do you think she did that?"

"She was afraid. There were like eight or nine cables dropping from the ceiling. We both tried to get away."

"So you don't think it was anything that happened between the two of you that made her mad enough to leave you there?"

Swallowing, he said, "No." His voice came out weak, and right then Paul knew Bernie had him.

"How about I tell you what I heard and then you can tell me why I shouldn't bring you up on sexual harassment charges and fire you right now?"

Paul tried finding words to defend himself, but couldn't. Maybe by the time Bernie finished talking some smart words would come out of his mouth and save his ass.

"You somehow got Marcy out of the elevator on the first floor where you knew no one worked anymore, where you thought no one would see you. Then you tried seducing her. When that didn't work, you got angry and maybe you did something real stupid. Then something happened that allowed Marcy to get away from you. Maybe the cables just fell out of the ceiling, and what you tried doing to Marcy made her decide to leave you there. Maybe she even hoped the cables would attack you."

"You don't know what you're talking about." The words were out of Paul's mouth before he realized he'd said them. "Who did you hear this from? Did Marcy tell you?" *Take a breath, buddy, don't make any stupid comments about how desperate you know Marcy is.* "Who saw us?" Paul rummaged through his mind for anyone who would be down on the first floor. The stairwell door did open and close. Maybe someone had seen them. "That maintenance guy? Leo? He told you?"

"I'm not at liberty to say, Paul. Just explain yourself. If I don't know what I'm talking about, then inform me of the truth."

"I told you the truth. Whoever saw us obviously wasn't close enough to hear our conversation."

"It wasn't your voices that gave you away. The person who told me saw your hand on her, Paul. What the hell were you thinking?"

Paul stared at Bernie. He had nothing to say. Someone saw him with Marcy and now he was royally fucked. "That's not what happened. Whoever told you this is out to get me." He knew he didn't sound convincing, but he had nothing else to go on.

"Do you want me to get Marcy in here? Do you think your stories will be the same?"

"She was distraught. She is distraught over Sharon. I was trying to console her."

"With your hand on her?"

"Okay. Maybe I was a little out of line."

"A little out of line?" Bernie voice grew louder. "Since when is touching co-workers just 'out of line'? She could bring you up on charges of sexual harassment if she wanted to; it wouldn't surprise me."

"For what? Trying to console her? You've got to be kidding!"

Glaring at Paul, Bernie shook his head. "Get out of my office. Get your things from your desk and leave."

"You ... you're firing me?" Paul couldn't believe what he was hearing. Bernie wouldn't fire him over something as petty as this, certainly not over Marcy. "You can't fire me." Paul scanned Bernie's desk for something that would inspire a thought to help him. But all he saw were papers and more papers. "I'm sorry. Look. I ... what can I do to fix this? I'll go apologize to Marcy. How's that?" Bernie merely stared at him and that pissed him off. Here he was trying to get back in Bernie's good graces and redeem himself and the least the man could do was offer him some slack.

"Come on, Bernie. It won't happen again. I promise." He

couldn't be fired. "I have a mortgage that's almost paid off and car payments and a new bedroom set to pay off. Bernie, I'll be honest. I can't afford to lose this job. I'm up to here in debt." He drew a line at his neck with his hand and suddenly realized that was also symbolic for shutting up. Or an execution. "I'm sorry." Bernie was still staring at him. Say something, damn it, he thought, waiting and waiting.

Then Bernie glanced at an open folder on his desk and Paul realized it was probably his file. Had there been other complaints? If so, why had Bernie not talked to him sooner? Either way, he was screwed. It didn't matter if it was Marcy, the little bitch, who said something or someone actually saw them and called Bernie; he had no recourse, no defense. The folder between them, if it was his and he saw no reason to think otherwise, had at least four write-ups, possibly from women who complained about his comments. He couldn't help it if they couldn't take a joke. He almost laughed, remembering a few of those jokes.

"You're not sorry, Paul," Bernie finally said. "How many times have we been here, you sitting across from me telling you to knock off the sexual comments? It's harassment. And now you've taken it one step too far. You know, no one's come forward. I just heard your off-color comments and figured if the person you were talking to had issues, they'd come to me. None of them did. You and I have talked about this, because it's inappropriate. But you don't care do you? I suppose I should've fired you after the first conversation, but I—"

"You let me stay here, just waiting for more women to complain, and now you finally got what you want. Someone misread my intentions, giving you a reason to fire me."

"Are you listening to me, Paul? I just said I've been doing everything to keep you here. Now I have no recourse but to let you go, all because you couldn't control yourself." Bernie shook his head. "There's nothing else I can do. Please clean your desk out. Security will escort you to your car."

"Fine." Paul got up and without another word, left Bernie's office. As he walked away, he thought about going past Marcy's cubicle, but he didn't know what he would say and he certainly didn't want to do anything that would be taken as retribution for telling Bernie what had happened. Oh, he knew it was Marcy who told Bernie. That bullshit about someone seeing them was just that. Bullshit.

But he couldn't let it slide. Because of her, he would be unemployed. Worse, this would go on his permanent record and no one would hire him. Then what would he do? Mortgage. Car payments.

"Shit." He paused by one of the empty offices and stared at the desk. *Should have been mine. Damned bitch.* He had a mind to go over there now and tell Marcy what he really thought of her. What could Bernie do? He'd already fired him. He'd be lucky if the bitch didn't get a lawyer and go after him for sexual assault, and for what? A caress? Jesus shit. He headed over to Marcy's cubicle, not sure what he'd say, but positive he'd let her know what he really thought of her.

She wasn't there. *Where the fuck …*

"Okay," Marcy said somewhere else. "Bernie said you can train the temp." Who was she talking to?

"All right."

That was Bettie.

So, there was a temp starting. Paul wondered what she looked like and if he could meet her before he left. Probably not. Best to pack his desk and deal with Marcy later. Bernie would be calling Security and he didn't want to look like a fool if they had to drag him out. Paul headed to the copy room, emptied two boxes of paper, went back to his cubicle, and started packing, knowing he'd get retribution for what Marcy did to him. Then he paused and smiled; he was still meeting Elaine later. He'd have to figure out a way of sneaking back into the building or having her meet him somewhere else. It would be easier to sneak back in. Security wasn't much of anything and if he was careful, he could get past them with no problem.

Nicole and Yvette were walking toward him deep in quiet conversation and he stepped out of their way.

"Does Sara creep you out?" Yvette asked.

"Yeah," Nicole said. "I don't think her elevator stops on every floor, if you know what I mean."

"Hi, girls." Paul tried smiling, but they ignored him when they walked by.

"She keeps looking at the ceiling like she's waiting for something," Nicole said.

"Maybe she's waiting for the sky to fall on her." Yvette laughed and Nicole joined her.

"Bitches," Paul mumbled and walked away.

Back in his cubicle, he picked up the phone and dialed Elaine's extension. When she answered, he knew that nothing mattered. Not the job and certainly not that stupid little bitch, Marcy. She'd get hers, but first he'd get Elaine.

JON

The Howard Phillips Building was an old 1920s-style brick building full of angles and windows. It was a shadow of its former self; no one had come to clean the building's façade in years, leaving it dingy brown from decades of pollution. It squatted silently, reaching five stories. Where once it stood proudly, higher than most buildings in the area, now it looked as if it were trying to hide amongst the taller structures and not be noticed. The unwashed, senile old man in a crowd of youthful, beautiful people.

In the lobby were sharp angles and dark corners that gave the building a sinister feel to it. This was not a warm and comfy place. A sign to the side of the Security desk announced there were four companies left in the building. Dasher Financials and Osprey Publishing on the fifth floor, Dimension Graphics and A&R Collections on the third floor. That was it. No one on the first, second, or fourth floors.

"Help you?" The middle-aged, uniformed guard looked bored.

"Morning, Glen." A woman walked past the desk, waved a security badge, and smiled like she was pretending to care.

"Doris." Glen nodded.

"My name is Jonathan Simon. I'm from WorkFinders." Jon took a sheet of paper from the inside pocket of his suit jacket. "I'm here to see Marcy Browne. She works for Osprey

Publishing. I'm starting today."

Glen the guard nodded. "I know who Marcy is. One moment." He lifted the phone and tapped several keys.

As he waited, Jon looked around the cramped lobby. A couple of tall plants stood at each side of the double door vestibule and a few other potted plants sat next to two couches that looked like they'd seen better days ten years ago and now were on the verge of collapse. A few magazines—*Time* and *BusinessWeek* along with *Forbes*—lay on the table in front of the couches. But it was the sharp-angled walls that gave him the impression the architect wasn't a kind man, didn't care for comfort, and built this place for cold business.

Jon turned back and realized the guard had been staring at him.

"Ms. Browne? This is Glen at Security. There is a gentleman here to see you. Jonathan Simon. Says he's from WorkFinders and he's starting today. All right. You, too. Bye." He hung the phone up. "Take the elevator to the fifth floor and hang a left. It's hard to miss them."

"Thanks."

The elevator seemed terminally slow coming down, and once he stepped inside the old box, it seemed to crawl up toward the fifth floor. He was amused by the diamond-shaped glass window that allowed him to watch the floors go by. On the fourth floor the elevator stopped.

Jon frowned and tapped the 5 button.

The doors opened. No one was there.

Jon looked out into the dark reception area, lit only by red light that painted the office doors, the carpeted floor, and the plaster walls in blood. Though he didn't see anyone, he felt watched, but shrugged it off as a ridiculously overactive imagination.

The sense of being stared at intensified, as if someone stood outside in the hallway. He cautiously moved to the elevator doorway and peered into the darkness, hoping the doors wouldn't close on him. If someone was watching him, they were well hidden because he couldn't see them. Backing into the elevator, he reached to press the 5 button again and heard someone moving around beyond the reception area in one of the offices.

He tried convincing himself he wasn't afraid as his finger quickly jabbed the door close button then the 5 again. But the doors remained open. According to the sign in the lobby, there were no companies on this floor so there shouldn't be anyone here. Yet he felt someone watching.

He looked at his watch: 9:56. The agency had told him to be at Osprey by ten to give them a chance to get the desk ready for him. The office was one flight up and he had four minutes to get there. There had to be a stairwell near the elevator, but to get there he'd have to leave the safety of the elevator and—

Cables slithered in the shaft above him, and for a moment he thought they were slipping, but the car didn't move. Something tapped on the roof.

Maybe I'm better off finding the stairs.

Whatever was above him wanted in.

"What the …"

But then the tapping stopped and the doors finally slid shut.

On the fifth floor, a sign with two arrows pointed in either direction—left to Osprey, right to Dasher Financials—informing him which way to go. Jon paused outside the frosted glass door, straightened his suit, his tie, made sure his shirt was smooth and wrinkle-free, and then entered.

The office was quieter than he expected; there should've been voices or some noise to indicate there were people around, not morgue-like silence. This was where Tony worked? No wonder he refused to say anything about the place.

A woman appeared from around one of the fabric walls. She was about his age, somewhat attractive in a plain way, with a cautious walk as if she was afraid of taking forward steps. She wore a white blouse and a gray skirt that came down past her knees. Conservative, Jon thought. She extended her hand as she drew closer.

"Hi, I'm Marcy Browne."

He took her hand and shook it. "Jonathan Simon." Her hand was cool and her handshake was loose and quick; she didn't care for shaking hands or maybe it was contact with a stranger.

"Let me show you where you'll be working and then I'll introduce you to our boss, Bernie Thompson. Do you have any things?"

"Just my lunch." He held out the small fabric cooler that contained his sandwich, a bag of chips, and a can of Coke. "I usually bring a sandwich the first day so I don't have to worry about refrigerators or microwaves."

"Oh. Sure."

He followed her through the beige fabric maze. She seemed nice enough, but there was something reluctant about her personality, as if she was afraid to be herself.

"Here we are." Marcy stood outside a cubicle decorated with photos of a happy couple in their fifties. Several framed pictures of kids stood near the desk next to ceramic dog figures, which in turn stood next to pictures of a younger happy couple. Children and grandchildren.

"I have to call the agency and let them know I'm here."

"All right. My desk is next door so when you're done just stop over."

"Sure." He smiled as she walked away.

Other than the personal touches, the desk area was like every other desk area he remembered from too many jobs exactly like this one. Beige fabric walls, beige desk, and the usual office desk accoutrements made up the work space. Setting his cooler out of the way, he called WorkFinders to let them know everything was fine. Then he stepped over to Marcy's cubicle. "All done."

She glanced at him and gave a half smile. "Let me introduce you to Bernie."

Back through the right-angled corridor, he followed her and was pretty sure he kept track of each right and left they made.

"It's okay to call him Bernie." Marcy shrugged. "Just don't call him Bernard or Mr. Thompson. He's too relaxed a guy. I think you'll like it here. We're all really nice people." She glanced at him. "Everything okay?"

"Sure. Fine."

"Nervous? I was on my first day here. I started as a temp, too. It seems so long ago." They went back in the direction they had come. "If you have any questions, just jump right in. Okay?"

"Sure." It sounded like she was still nervous.

They walked to the end of the hallway, and then she paused outside an office that looked as if a tornado had ripped file cabinets apart and left their contents strewn everywhere. A big, old wood desk, covered with papers and folders, stood in the middle of the chaos with a couple of chairs in front of it and a worn, red leather chair behind it. A portable stereo sat on top of more papers and folders off to the right of the desk on a short cabinet. To the left were three four-drawer file cabinets, the old metal kind that always got stuck. In the middle of everything, sagging in the red leather chair, was Bernie Thompson, all six foot, two inches of him, dressed in a blue button-down shirt and a blue and gray striped tie. He seemed incongruously neat in the chaos that surrounded him.

"Mr. Simon!" He rose from the leather chair and came around the desk. "A pleasure to meet you!" His grin was wide and pure with no false pretense. His handshake was firm, but not violent. Jon had once shaken hands with a man who nearly pulled his arm from its socket.

"Same here, Mr... Bernie."

"Why don't you have a seat?" Bernie offered one of the chairs in front of the desk. "Thanks, Marcy. I'll send him out to you in a few."

Marcy nodded and whisked herself away.

Bernie closed his office door and sat down. "She's a great woman; practically my secretary." Bernie's eyes were light hazel, but had what must've been a commanding gaze at one point; now they were weaker with age and stress. Bernie leaned back in his chair. "Tony's told me about you, recommended you for the position."

Jon wasn't sure what to say. As this was Alyssa's idea, he didn't want to be here, nor did he want to sound ungrateful. "We've been friends for a long time."

"Tony said you're a writer and had your first book published. That's great."

"Thanks."

"What the hell are you doing here?"

My question exactly. "My wife and I are saving for a house."
"It's always money, isn't it? Anyway. Feel free to dress casual, just no jeans or sneakers." He ran his hand through his thinning salt and pepper hair, cut short, almost to a crew cut. "I wear a tie because it makes me feel important, but I don't ask it of my employees."

Thank God for that. He disliked wearing suits and ties unless he had to for occasions like weddings and funerals, but otherwise he was happy in khakis and a dress shirt.

Bernie explained what Jon would be doing, which amounted to the accounts payable work Jon had done years before. It was only a matter of getting used to another company's system. He was probably a little rusty with how procedures went, but by day's end he figured it would all come back to him.

"Bettie will be showing you what needs to be done. She's one of my best even though she's relatively new. We don't have any formal lunch period, so whenever you want to go, just tell Marcy. Any other questions you have, you can ask Marcy, Bettie, or me."

"Sure. Do you know how long the assignment goes for? The agency didn't say."

"No." The look on Bernie's face told Jon there was more but he wasn't saying. "I'm not sure how long you'll be here. If it's a concern let me know."

"No. Just curious."

"That's fine. Oh, one more thing. Be careful where you go around the building. Take the elevator, not the stairs, and come straight up here."

"Actually, I took the elevator and it stopped on the fourth floor. I was going to take the stairs, but then it started again. There was some kind of tapping on the ceiling like a loose cable or something. Maybe the stairs would be better?"

"You know what, for right now, make sure you're with someone else when you're coming and going."

"What's going on?"

"Nothing to worry about. We … we've had some problems with cracked stairs and such and I don't want anyone getting hurt. Just be careful." Bernie tapped speaker on his phone and punched in four numbers.

"Yes, Bernie?" Marcy asked.

"Why don't you give Jon a quick tour, introduce him around, and then have him sit with Bettie."

"Sure. Can you send him back? I'm right in the middle of a phone call."

"Not a problem." He ended the call. "Like I said, be careful when you're coming and going. It's an old building, and though Maintenance does their best to keep the place together, time is taking its toll."

"Thanks for the warning." He rose and waited for Bernie to come around the desk and open the door.

"Good luck."

"Thanks." Jon left Bernie's office and made his way through the maze of fabric walls. He imagined someone losing his way, unable to find the right path out, and falling, hungry and exhausted, mere feet from the correct corridor that would've led him to freedom.

At an intersection he hesitated, unsure which way to go to get back to Marcy. As he passed several cubicles, he knew he should ask for directions, but he didn't want to look like an idiot, so he kept going, turning in the direction he thought he should be going. One right, one left, and—

"Hi."

Jon stumbled backward to avoid colliding with the woman in black who appeared out of nowhere. Well, not quite nowhere, but certainly from one of the fabric and carpet intersections that made up this insane prison. A goddamned asylum and he was the newest mental patient.

"Are you all right?" she asked.

Jon stared at the pale woman who was herself the theme of black: tight lace top that hugged her curves, miniskirt, stockings, low-heeled shoes, wavy hair to her shoulders, eyeliner, short nails. The only colors on her were her green eyes, red lips, a shade of purple tint in her hair, and a tiny gold ring above her left eye. Each stood out because they were such a shock against her themed appearance.

"You don't look so well," she said.

"I'm all right."

"Are you sure?"

Jon could tell she wasn't really the nurturing type, though she was trying her hardest to come off as sincere. He almost laughed. "Yes."

"I can get you some water."

"No."

She looked over her shoulder, then moved closer. "I have a flask of rum if you're interested. I don't drink while I'm working, but you know, sometimes during lunch you need something to calm you down or pick you up. You know."

Though he didn't, he said, "Sure," because she was uniquely beautiful and he didn't want to see her frown.

"I'm Bettie." She offered her hand, her fingers tipped with black nails.

"Jon. Bernie told me you'll be training me." He gently shook her hand, but she had a more powerful grip than he expected, and just before she pulled her hand away, he gave it a squeeze to let her know he wasn't one of those people whose handshakes were like holding a tuna. Did she smile a bit more at that? He thought she did.

"You're the new temp everyone's talking about."

"Everyone's talking—"

"Just kidding. I'm a temp here, too. Been here for a month. You need to lighten up or you'll go crazy like most of these people have. I'll be showing you everything you ever wanted to know about Osprey Publishing's accounts payable system." She grinned and it was a good thing to see. "Let me take you back to Marcy. She'll know what to do with you."

There was something in her tone that gave Jon the impression that her dialogue was laced with innuendo. He didn't mind; he could give it right back, but until he knew Bettie well enough to come back at her, he'd play it cool. As he followed her back to Marcy's cubicle, he had a hard time not staring at her legs; they were muscular in a feminine way and quite sexy.

"I found him wandering around the cube asylum," Bettie said when they arrived.

Marcy turned from her desk. "Did you really get lost?"

Jon shook his head. "No, I was just—"

"He was coming back when I found him," Bettie cut in. "I wanted to make sure he got back to you and didn't go wandering off." She looked at Jon. "We've had temps come in here and wander for days before anyone found them and gave them food and water."

"Bettie!" Marcy grimaced, all humor gone from her face. "We have not."

Bettie frowned at Marcy. "I'm just teasing him." She turned to go. "You guys should get along fine. You both need to lighten up." Then she was gone.

"Don't worry about Bettie," Marcy said. "She's harmless. So Bernie's told you all about Osprey?"

Jon told her all that Bernie had told him about what his job entailed and that Bettie would be training him.

She scowled and it made her look like an angry librarian. "I would train you, but I can't … I've got too much to do. First, I'll introduce you to everyone so no one calls Security on you."

He preferred Bettie's lively personality to Marcy's blandness; he needed someone to distract him from the smothering feeling that had started in Bernie's office. It had lessened since he'd run into Bettie, but he still felt it in his chest along with a slight headache.

As they walked through the cubicle maze, Jon noticed she never made eye contact, which, along with the way she dressed and carried herself, convinced Jon she was ultra-shy. Her makeup was the only outstanding feature, and Jon wondered if she had done it herself or had someone else help her.

Outside a cubicle with the name Sara Forrester, Marcy paused and whispered, "Something happened to her before she started at Osprey, but no one knows what it is. She hardly talks and rarely smiles." Then she knocked on the metal framework. "Sara?"

The woman who turned to face them was pretty with shoulder-length, dirty blond hair that looked like it could've used a good brushing, but her blue-gray eyes were apprehensive.

"This is Jon Simon. He's starting today to help us until Sharon gets back."

Sara stared at Jon, then narrowed her gaze. "I ... It's nice to meet you." She turned away from them. "Be careful. That's all I'm saying."

"What?" Marcy asked.

"Nothing," Sara replied.

Marcy shrugged and walked away, Jon following. They'd taken five steps when a man approached them carrying a box of personal belongings.

Marcy stopped and said, "Paul, this is—"

"Get out of my way." He didn't stop walking, and the two of them had to back into other people's cubicles to get out of his way.

After he'd passed, Jon and Marcy joined up again. "That was Paul. I don't know what's wrong with him."

"Looks like he's on his way out."

"Oh, God." Marcy blanched. "Bernie must've—"

"Must've what?"

"Nothing." But Marcy stared after Paul with her hand over her mouth as if she was afraid to say the wrong thing.

"So who do I get to meet next?" Jon wanted to know what had happened, but it wasn't his business. Better to help Marcy along and not pry.

Marcy introduced him to the rest of the Accounts Payable department, all the while distracted by her encounter with Paul. They seemed like nice, pleasant people, nothing as remarkable about them as Sara or Bettie.

Finally she stood outside Tony's cubicle. "Tony, I want you to meet someone."

"It better not be Jon Simon." He never turned, but sounded angry.

"I ..."

Tony spun his chair around and had a big grin on his face. "I know this man. We've been friends for years. Glad you made it, Jon."

"Good to see you, too." They shook hands.

"If you need anything and no one else can help you, come to me. Not that I can help, but at least you'll have someone to commiserate with!"

"Thanks."

"I'll see you later."

Tony nodded as he returned to his desk.

Next was the Accounts Receivable group. After meeting seven of the people who worked there, they stopped at a cubicle that was double the size of everyone else's.

Sitting at a cluttered desk on the telephone, surrounded by calendar pictures of tabbies, calicos, Persians, and Russian Blues, sat a woman in her mid-thirties with short hair colored various shades of blond, from gold to light bronze. She glanced up at Jon and Marcy and took her glasses off. Her dark brown eyes were much smaller now.

"Sheila?" Marcy said in a whisper.

"I've gotta go, Laura, I'll talk to you later." Sheila hung up the phone and turned back with a pleasant smile. "Yes, Marcy."

"Sheila, this is Jon and he's starting today. He's a temp and he'll be with us … I don't know how long he'll be with us." Her laugh was nervous and uncertain. "Jon, this is Sheila, the A/R manager. She works for Bernie, though they're almost equal."

"Almost." She stood up and held her hand out. "Nice to meet you, Jon."

He came into her office and shook her extended hand. Her skin was warm and her handshake was firm. She wore an Irish claddagh ring, turned so the heart pointed toward her; she was attached. But no engagement or wedding bands.

"If you need anything that Bernie and Marcy can't help you with, just drop by anytime."

Jon nodded.

"Is Patti around?" Marcy asked.

"She's coming in a bit late today," Sheila said.

"I just wanted to introduce Jon to your assistant."

"When she comes in, I'll give you a ring."

"Thanks. See you later." Outside Sheila's office, Marcy said, "Patti's a sweet woman, a grandmother, but she's been through a lot this year. She lost her mom, her boyfriend, and her brother. He committed suicide."

"Geez." Jon thought people who killed themselves were one of the saddest things in life.

Marcy showed him where the bathroom and lunchroom were. "That's it. End of the tour. Any questions so far? If you've got any, don't be afraid to ask."

Jon shook his head.

"Then I'll leave you with Bettie. She'll get you started on what needs to be done. Don't worry about her; she's all talk."

"Sure." Jon smiled, but Marcy kept her straight face. Bettie was right; she needed to lighten up.

In the Dark: Sharon Walters

How could any place be so dark? Sharon Walters lay on her side, weak from blood loss. Her throat still hurt from where the cables had pulled her up. But at least she was alive. For now. She tried moving but the pain in her legs was too great. Some time ago the cables came and sliced her legs open until she screamed and finally passed out from the pain. When she came to, she was here, lying on cold metal.

Feeling around, she found the ceiling was only a foot and a half above her. The walls were close, no more than three feet across. This wasn't a room but a chute of some kind. Maybe even the air ducts that ran through the building. If she could crawl, she might be able to find a vent and call for help.

She was about to start crawling when she heard the slithering, clattering of the cables and their knife-like edges coming from in front of her. There was nothing to do but wait for them; she was too exhausted to fight, too tired to move quickly. She knew the routine after—how long had she been trapped in here?—the hours she'd lived through. The cables would come close. They'd stop and she'd anticipate their attack. Her panic would build. Her heart would send adrenaline through her veins. The cables would be silent as if it were a game to see how scared she could get before they attacked her. Then the cutting would begin. And so would the screaming.

JON

"None of this stuff is really that difficult." Bettie placed an invoice down in one pile and sorted through the remaining stack. "Once you get the hang of the system, it gets pretty boring."

"I imagine it would."

They sat in Bettie's cubicle as she went over the basic processes of entering invoices into the A/P system. Jon had to keep refocusing on what Bettie said because her closeness kept distracting him. Her dark clothing coupled with her vibrant personality made her an enigma in his eyes. Who was she really? A goth chick—who were almost always somber—or a spirited woman who enjoyed dressing up?

Every now and then, to make her point, she touched his arm and her fingers left little jolts of heat on his skin. He knew it was ridiculous, but nevertheless it had been years since he'd felt another woman's touch, and it troubled him that he was reacting like a teenager.

"Marcy wants me to set you up at Sharon's desk." Bettie stared at him.

"Is she out on maternity leave? Honeymoon?"

Bettie looked pensive as if she wasn't sure how to answer. "She's missing. She has been since Tuesday. No one knows what happened to her. The police were here questioning everybody."

"Oh." This was a first. All his other short-term assignments had been for people out on maternity leave, honeymoons, injuries, and a few other non-permanent reasons, but never because of a completely mysterious disappearance.

"Does anyone know what happened to her?"

Shaking her head, Bettie said, "She went to get boxes from the basement and never came back. I think Leo, the maintenance guy, knows something. His office is in the basement. He had to have seen something. Besides, he's creepy. He always seems to be lurking around, and every time I see him he stares at me."

Jon understood why a man would be apt to stare at Bettie, but it was inappropriate in a work environment. "Did you ever say anything to him?"

"Once or twice. He apologizes and goes on his way, and the next time it's the same thing. I just stay away from him."

"And you think he had something to do with Sharon's disappearance?"

"I know I shouldn't jump to conclusions, but if there's anyone here capable of hurting someone, it's Leo."

"How do you know she didn't just leave?"

"Sharon's purse was still at her desk and her car was in the parking lot. Her husband hadn't picked her up, and no one but Leo saw her in the basement. What would you think?"

Jon's writer-mind contemplated all possibilities. He didn't like to think Sharon had been murdered, but it was a plausible conclusion given the circumstances. "Have the police questioned Leo?"

"As far as I know they've questioned everyone in the building, and Leo was the last one to see her." She rose from her chair. "Let's go visit Marcy and tell her you're ready to start."

They stopped outside Marcy's cubicle. "All right, he's ready to go. What 'cha got for him?"

Marcy turned to face them. "He's ready? Oh. Good." She frowned. "I guess we have to turn her computer on and get him up and running on the system."

Jon waited for her to get up, but she stared at her hands and bit her lip.

"I'll do it," Bettie said, seeing how hesitant Marcy was.

Marcy shook her head, but didn't make any move toward the cubicle. "I just … it's no big deal. I mean … it's fine." Marcy led them into Sharon's cubicle and turned the computer on. Then she forced a smile, said, "All yours," and went back to her office.

Bettie entered Sharon's password and showed Jon how to navigate around the A/P system screens. "Got it?"

"Sure." Jon sat down and adjusted the seat and keyboard until he was comfortable.

"It's simple data entry." Bettie grabbed a handful of invoices from Sharon's in-box and placed the inch-and-a-half-high stack of sheets next to the keyboard. Then she patted Jon on the shoulder. "Just follow the screen and use the tab key to get from field to field. Any questions, let me know."

"Thanks." Jon watched her go, and then settled in to enter the invoices into the system.

The morning disappeared that way.

"Hey, Jon?"

He turned from the computer at the sound of Bettie's voice.

"Marcy and I are heading out for lunch. Why don't you take a break and get something to eat? There's no real cafeteria here other than the lunchroom, so unless you brought a sandwich, you're on your own."

"Sure."

"Maybe tomorrow the three of us can have lunch together." She nodded toward Marcy's cubicle and winked.

"Sounds good to me."

"We'll see you later." She went to Marcy's office. "Come on. We're outta here."

"Jon's all right?" Marcy asked.

"He's fine."

Jon heard them talking all the way to the elevator. Finishing the last invoice, he decided it was a good stopping point. He grabbed his lunch and stopped at Bernie's office to let him know he was taking a break. The door was open so he stuck in his head.

"I'm heading to lunch."

"All right." Bernie looked as if he were ready to collapse. "Sorry, I'm just really tired." He laughed. "You don't realize how draining work can be. You know?"

Jon nodded.

"You have a good lunch." Bernie smiled. "Looks like a nice day outside."

"That's where I'm heading."

"No, you're not."

Jon turned at the sound of Tony's voice.

"Lunch is on me. Junior's coming with us. Let's go."

The three of them walked to the elevator, but it had already caused him a degree of consternation. "Let's take the stairs."

"Exercise program?"

"No. I ... it's nothing." In the stairwell, he didn't see any of the cracks Bernie warned him about, but he did hear strange creaking sounds like an old door being opened. By the time they were outside the building, the late Autumn sun burned off the trepidation that had built from the five-floor descent.

BETTIE

Outside in the cool October afternoon, Bettie broke the silence that had started the moment the elevator doors closed as if Marcy was so distracted she couldn't talk. "I'll drive." She led Marcy to an old red Chevy Cavalier with bumper stickers that read: "Siouxsie and the Banshees" and "The Runaways."

Once they were on their way, Bettie decided this was as good a time as any to start talking. "Feel any better?"

"I talked to Bernie about everything. I felt dizzy afterward but I guess I'm doing all right now."

"Good. I'm glad. You asked me about—"

"Bernie fired Paul, didn't he?"

"Yes, he did. He stopped by my cubicle on his way out."

Marcy glanced at her. "Did he say anything? Did he say he knew it was me?"

Oh, he said something, all right. He'd come by her cubicle with two boxes in his arms. "Good-bye and tell your bitch girlfriend that she's as good as dead."

Before she could say anything else, Security had escorted him away, leaving her fuming, her hands clenched, her mind racing with a variety of violent ways to make him suffer. Fortunately, two security guards heard him make his threat as well.

"Did he say anything?" Marcy asked again.

Bettie shook her head. "No, he just came by and glared at me, mumbled something about women, and Security took him out."

"I'm scared. Paul's not stupid. He probably figured out it was me even though Bernie said he told him someone saw us."

"Don't worry about it, Marcy. He's gone."

"And what if he finds me outside of work?"

They came to a red light and Bettie looked at Marcy. The woman had tears in her eyes.

"What am I going to do?"

"Paul is just a little boy who talks a lot. He doesn't have it in him to hurt anybody. He just mouthed off to make you afraid. But you stood up to him and called his bluff. Don't worry about him."

"I don't know, I just—"

Bettie had to change the conversation or Marcy would be lost. "So, what do you think of Jon? Seems like a nice guy, huh?"

"Seems like a married guy, Bettie."

"I know. I mean as a co-worker."

"No, you don't. I know you better than that."

Bettie knew Marcy watched her. "Do you really think I'd go after a married man?"

"As I said, I know you better than that."

"Thanks a lot." Bettie pulled into the diner's parking lot.

"Besides, you're not his type."

"Really? And what makes you say that?"

"I don't think he goes for the punk chick look."

Turning the car off, Bettie got out. "How do you know? Did you ask?"

They walked across the parking lot to the diner. "Of course not. I just don't expect too many men in Corporate America to be into punk chicks or goth chicks or whatever you are."

Bettie opened the door for Marcy. "I'm hurt. Punk, goth, you don't know who I am."

"Who are you?"

"I'm a little punk and I'm a little goth."

Marcy shook her head as the waitress seated them.

While Bettie scanned the menu, she wondered what kind of woman Jon was interested in and if she was anywhere close. Probably not. Marcy was right, not many guys in corporate jobs went for the wild women. They were more conservative, more interested in Marcy's type than hers. Well, that was if Marcy was a little more outgoing.

The waitress came and took their order—two salads, a lemonade, and an iced tea—then left.

"Have you been tired lately?" Marcy asked. "More tired than usual?"

Bettie thought about it. "No more so than I always am after playing gigs until one in the morning."

"I've been really wiped out the last couple of weeks. I don't know what it is. I just can't find any energy."

"Not sleeping well? This job isn't exactly exciting work. It's easy to see why you'd be tired."

"No, this is different. It's like I can't wake up. And the other night I had this really weird dream. My television was all snowy and there was this person or silhouette and ..."

"What about this dream?" It sounded remarkably like what happened to her computer. "Tell me about it."

"I thought I was awake, but I was dreaming. The television was on, but it was like the channel had gone off the air and it was just static. Then this silhouette appeared. It was the strangest thing. Then the phone rang."

Bettie shivered. She knew what was coming but didn't say anything.

"When I answered the phone, it sounded like someone with a tracheotomy talking into one of those microphones."

"This was a dream?" Bettie hadn't been dreaming when it happened at her desk.

"Yes. A dream. What's wrong?"

"That same thing happened to me at work yesterday morning. My computer screen went black, and then there was the static. The phone rang at the same time a figure appeared on the screen."

"You told me about the computer and I was so tired and distraught over Sharon, I didn't realize what you were saying. What did it look like?"

Bettie only remembered the black silhouette with no features, but knew the figure watched her as it had tried to communicate over the phone. "I couldn't tell. It was only a silhouette. But it watched me. I don't know how I knew, but I was sure it was." She shuddered at the memory.

"Bettie, you're frightening me." She scowled. "That was a dream. I wasn't awake."

The other woman sighed and sipped her water. It tasted terrible. Where was the waitress with her lemonade? "I'm not trying to frighten you, Marcy. I'm telling you what happened to me."

"So I wasn't dreaming? I was awake?" Marcy thought for a moment. "No, I'm sure I woke up at some point and the television was on to some late show or something."

"It doesn't matter if you were sleeping or—"

"Here you go." The waitress placed the lemonade in front of Bettie, the iced tea by Marcy. "Your lunch will be right out."

"Thanks." Bettie sipped the lemonade. *Much better.* "Look, Marcy, it doesn't matter if you were sleeping or not. We both had the same experience."

"That's too weird."

Too weird didn't even begin to describe it. It wasn't like they had bad computer experiences at work that turned out to be a glitch in the system. This was … like someone was trying to communicate with them. But it was stranger because it happened to Marcy at home.

"What do you think it is?" Marcy asked.

"I don't know. I wonder if anyone else has had any weird things happen to them like this." Bettie thought to ask around when they got back. If it was only the two of them, then it was simply a freak coincidence and she'd blow it off. But if they found other people had had the same thing happen to them … then what?

Marcy sat back and sighed. "Do you believe in ghosts?"

"Why? Do you think the building is haunted? Wait. You told me this morning that something happened to you but you never told me what it was."

"The other night when Paul … you know … we were in the elevator. It stopped by itself on the first floor. I got out. I thought it was the lobby but it wasn't. While Paul was … one of the ceiling tiles broke, and these cables—there had to be a dozen of them—attacked us. Some of them knocked Paul over. Some of them came after me and I thought they were going to kill me." She gazed at Bettie. "You don't believe me, do you?" Marcy asked.

The waitress placed their salads in front of each of them.

"Thanks." Bettie waited until the waitress smiled and left, then said, "I believe you." But she knew her voice had no conviction. "I just don't know what to say, that's all. I mean what if I told you I was attacked by the building?"

"I know. I thought Leo was controlling the cables to scare us. You know how he hates everyone who works there."

"He creeps me out. I could imagine him doing something like that." Bettie knew Marcy wasn't given to flights of fantasy like that. If anything, she was very levelheaded and smart. Could she be telling the truth? "Where'd the cables come from?"

"I don't know." Marcy glanced at Bettie. "I heard them in the ceiling and then they—"

"What do you mean you heard them in the ceiling?"

"Like snakes. The ceiling tile broke and they dropped down on us, writhing and slashing the air. It was more than just cables falling from the ceiling. They seemed driven by something. Or someone."

Bettie tried to imagine what that must've been like. It was bad enough Marcy had to deal with Paul's advances, but then to have the ceiling fall on them and her ... what? Cables attacking her? "Other than you and Paul, do you know if anyone else was attacked?"

Marcy nodded.

"Who?"

"Sharon."

"You don't know that."

"It would explain her disappearance."

"Maybe." Bettie ate slowly, chewing her food, wanting to taste something, to maintain contact with the real world, but the lettuce had no flavor. "All right, Marcy. Let's say I believe you and the building is attacking people. Who's haunting it? What do you think we should do? Get a ... a ghost hunter?"

"I feel like I'm going crazy."

"You're not going crazy." If Marcy was on the crazy train, Bettie was in the same car. "A lot's happened in the last two days. You have every right to be upset."

"What about the building, Bettie? I don't want to go back there. I'm scared."

Bettie forced a smile, unsure what to say. She hoped to talk about how she could help Marcy get out of her own way, not haunted office buildings.

But right now, Marcy was too deeply troubled by what was happening at work to focus on herself, and Bettie started to believe something was genuinely wrong with the place. "All right. Here's what we'll do. When we get back we'll find out if anyone else has seen or heard anything strange like what we've experienced. If not, then we really are going nuts. But if anyone else has, then we'll go to Bernie and see what he can do. The police are already investigating Sharon's disappearance, so hopefully they'll find something."

"They won't, Bettie. Don't you get it? Whatever this thing is, it doesn't want to be discovered. It's taking people and there's nothing we can do to stop it."

Bettie suddenly felt like she was in a bad B-horror movie. This was the do-or-die moment, when the pessimistic characters all gave up hope (soon to be consumed/killed by the movie's monster/slasher) and the optimists took up arms and chased said monster/slasher down for one last fight to the (its) death.

But this wasn't a movie. It was real life and the idea that some ghost or monster lurked in the building they worked in, murdering or eating people, was too absurd to believe. "Hold on, Marcy. This isn't a zombie flick we're in or some alien invasion movie. This is real life, and in real life there's a rational explanation for all this. We don't know how many people have actually disappeared, right?"

"Right. But what is the *rational* explanation for people—even one person—disappearing, your computer and my television doing the same freaky thing, and someone with a tracheotomy microphone calling us while our television and computer are freaking out? Go ahead. Tell me."

People nearby were staring at them, their own conversations forgotten.

"I'm sorry," Marcy said.

"I'm going to find out what's going on."

"How?"

"I don't know. Bernie, Leo, Sara. She seems to know something."

"You're going to talk to Sara?" Marcy laughed. "Good luck. I think she's damaged or something. Sheila keeps her around because she's a nice person and doesn't have the heart to fire her."

"If Sara knows anything about what's going on, we can't ignore her."

Marcy shrugged.

Bettie had no idea how she'd go about playing detective, but it was better than waiting for the police. Of course, it was just this sort of thing that put people in the worst danger in every horror film she'd seen and every horror novel she'd read. Except this wasn't a movie. She reminded herself of that as the waitress came over and asked if they needed anything else, dropped the check, and left.

"I want you to stay with me tonight," Bettie said. "We'll leave work together."

"What if I have to go to the bathroom while I'm at work? Are you coming with me?"

Bettie shrugged. "I'm trying to help you. If you're afraid of Paul, then stay at my place for a few days until he calms down."

"As much as I appreciate your offer, I can't stay with you forever, Bettie. I have to go home sooner or later. I can't spend the rest of my life being afraid of Paul, but in the meantime I don't know what to do."

Bettie watched Marcy, and she saw something pass across the woman's face as if she'd just made up her mind. She took a long drink of her iced tea, placed the glass down, and looked at Bettie. "I used to live in Rhode Island a few years back, where I was engaged to a man named Jess. He turned into a brutal bastard. I won't go into all the details. Maybe we'll have that bottle of wine sooner than later. Just accept that he was worse than Paul. I bought a gun and one day it came down to saving my life so I shot him. Killed him. There was a trial and all and I got off. Self-defense. If I hadn't killed him, he would've killed me. I had no choice. It took me a long time to get over that. I've wanted to kill myself quite a few times since then, but I've never had the guts.

"I know this isn't the same thing, but the fear is the same: the fear that at any moment Paul can show up and hurt me." Marcy leaned closer to Bettie. "Not only am I scared of Paul coming after me, but I'm scared that I may have to make a decision I never wanted to make again. If Paul comes to my apartment and I have to choose between saving my life or killing him, I'm shooting to kill." Her gaze turned glassy before she looked at her watch. "We should probably head back."

Bettie felt like she'd been punched in the stomach, and all she could do was stare at Marcy, unsure of what to say. One minute they're talking about monsters; the next, Marcy was admitting she shot someone. *She killed someone. Shot them. Dead. Jesus. I thought I was the wild one.* She had to reassess her opinion of Marcy. She wasn't the weak, timid woman Bettie thought she was, but someone who kept a tight lid on her emotions after surviving a really bad situation. What would happen if Paul showed up at Marcy's apartment? He probably didn't know any of this. Granted he was an ass, but he didn't deserve to die. Well, there had been moments ... but that was different. She really hadn't wished him *dead.*

"I have to face my fears. I have to go back to work and I have to go home. I can't live in fear the rest of my life."

"There has to be something we can do about the building. Maybe look up the history and find out what happened there, if anything. You know, there's usually some horrible, unsolved murder that took place or something and the ghost of the murdered is hanging around trying to get people to notice him so they can solve the murder and the ghost can be free."

"You've been watching way too many ghost hunter shows." Marcy smiled and Bettie was happy to see it.

"Have you told anyone else about the cables?"

"Bernie knows. That's it." Marcy took her wallet from her purse.

"What did he say?"

"He found it hard to believe. What could he say? This isn't like one of your horror movies where an evil force takes over the building and starts killing everyone for kicks."

Bettie laughed at the switch. "You're humoring me." She slid out of the booth, dropped three crumpled singles from her pocket on the table, and took the bill.

"Can I see that?" Marcy asked, following her to the front counter.

"No." Bettie paid. "My treat. You can get lunch next time."

As Bettie walked to the car, she thought about everything Marcy had told her. The most troubling thing was the information concerning the building. She had to work there as well. If cables really had killed Sharon, what was to stop them from killing anyone else? Maybe they already had. With four companies in the building, should she take it upon herself to go to those companies and ask if any of their employees were missing? She wasn't a cop and she didn't want to create hysteria if everything was fine. No matter how much she liked Marcy, she was going on her words alone. Maybe she could talk to Bernie and get his impressions of Marcy's story firsthand.

"I'm sorry," Marcy said behind her.

"For what?"

"I don't know. I'm sure you didn't expect this when you asked me this morning if I wanted to go out to lunch."

"You're right. I didn't expect most of what you said. But if I was concerned about what you were going to say, I probably wouldn't have asked you." She opened Marcy's door, then her own. "You really have to stop apologizing for being alive, Marcy."

"I know. I'm sorry."

Bettie shook her head and smiled. She was pretty sure Marcy's personality changed after the situation with Jess. Men had that effect on some women, to make them believe no matter what they did, they were wrong and should be sorry for it. She got in the car and started the engine. "How long ago was Jess?"

Marcy stared at her hands. "Five years."

"It's time to move on." She knew how hard that was to do, but if Marcy wanted any kind of life, she had to get past Jess and what happened.

"I can't." She sniffed and tears rolled down her face. "I keep thinking if I was just a better person … He wasn't mean to me when we first started dating."

"None of them are." Bettie remembered her own man problems. "People change. Maybe once he knew he had you, he went back to who he really was and—"

"No, it was me. I'm sure I did something wrong."

"You didn't do anything wrong, Marcy." Bettie felt the knot

of anger in her chest. "Marcy, look at me." She took Marcy's hands, ignored the resistance, and said, "You did nothing wrong, but if you keep believing you did, you will never live your life. You will always be a prisoner of the past. Trust me, I've been there."

"I didn't mean to ... shoot him, but he wouldn't stop."

"You did what you had to in order to protect yourself. Stop thinking you could've done something different. If you didn't do what you did, you might be the one dead right now."

Marcy jumped at the word *dead*. "Sometimes I wish I was."

"Stop it." She knew that dark place well enough, but she had changed her life and it was difficult for her to watch another woman trash herself. "You don't mean that."

"I don't know. Maybe I do." She stared straight ahead, out at the parking lot. "What difference does it make? I'm nobody. The only guy who remotely cares about me is an asshole who just wants to ..." She shook her head. "It doesn't matter."

Bettie pulled out, wishing they didn't have to go back to work. "It does matter, Marcy. You matter. Stop putting yourself down. Damn it, woman, I used to do that all the time, and you know where it got me? Nowhere. I had shit for esteem and used guys to make me feel worthy. I finally realized I was the only one who was going to make me feel better. Same deal here. It's up to you."

"I know," Marcy said, but nothing more.

In the office building's parking lot, Bettie shut the car off and turned to Marcy. "I want to help you, Marcy, but you've got to let me in."

Marcy sat staring out the windshield. "Why are you doing this? Maybe I don't want your help."

Bettie heard the angry tone. "Because I want to see you be more than who you are right now."

"Why?" Marcy scowled at her as if not understanding why Bettie would waste her time on her.

Bettie got out of the car, and then leaned back in. "Because whether you want to believe it or not, you matter to me and I want to help." Before Marcy could argue, Bettie closed the door and headed to the building. Entering the Howard Phillips

Building, she paused and looked around, wondering whether there really were cables slithering like snakes up above the ceiling tiles, waiting for the right moment to strike. She hoped not. She still had the afternoon helping Jon, and she would talk to Bernie about what Marcy had told her. One way or another, she'd get to the bottom of this haunted office building story.

JON

The afternoon was more of the same work: take coded invoices and enter them into the accounts payable system. Nothing exciting, intriguing, or thought provoking, but at least he could contemplate what Tony had told him about Osprey's most eccentric employee: Sara Forrester. From what Sara had told Tony, she'd been involved in some sort of "accident" (Tony's air quotes) and as a result was very sensitive to "outside energies." What that meant she never explained, but after that, Tony distanced himself from the "wacko."

"How's it going?" Bettie asked behind him. "Any problems?"

He turned and took in her refreshing personality. She was one of the few women in the corporate environments he'd experienced who showed any signs of life. Of course she was a temp, so that probably explained it: permanent employees seemed to take on an air of lethargy, as if this were their last stop before the grave. "No. It's just data entry. I haven't come across anything I couldn't figure out."

"You'd be surprised how many temps can't figure out data entry. It's good to know you're one of the more intelligent ones we've had."

"Thanks." He waved her into the cubicle and closer. "Is Marcy okay? She seems really upset."

Her perfume, something flowery that reminded him of spring and all things new, when a young man's fancy ...

Stop that.

Her perfume embraced him and he took a deep breath, trying to be as nonchalant as possible. The scent thrilled him.

"Marcy and Sharon were good friends," Bettie whispered. "She's been really upset since Sharon disappeared."

Jon nodded. "I can't imagine what she's going through."
Bettie shrugged. "I know. I've tried talking to her, but she's
not ready to talk about it. I told her I'd be here when she's ready."
"That's very kind of you." One more quality Jon found
endearing.
"Hey, I'd like to think I come here to do more than work.
This is most of my social life."
Jon laughed and wanted to keep talking to her; he was in
no rush to get back to work as long as she stood in his cubicle.
"I better get going. If you need me, just call." Then she
turned, her skirt floating on air, and exited, leaving her scent
and his imagination wandering in the wrong direction. She
was too young and too pretty to be single, and he was too
married, almost forty-one, to be having those thoughts about
someone too young and too pretty. It wasn't worth it. He was
lousy at hiding things from Alyssa, and an affair with Bettie
would be more than he could handle. "Hey, I just remembered
something."
Jon turned to Bettie, standing next to him again and looking
adorably cute.
"What kind of music do you like?"
"I don't know. All kinds. Why?"
"I'm in a band and we're playing Friday night at the Orange
Lantern in Ridgewood. We're sort of a classic rock, alternative,
goth, punk, folk band. If you're free, come by."
Was she coming on to him? No. He was wishfully thinking
she was and that he was younger and single. "I'll let you know."
"Great. You should come. It's gonna be good times."
Jon nodded, afraid to say more, to commit to something he
shouldn't because of his obligation to Alyssa. What obligation?
It was a show not a date. She probably asked everyone from
Osprey to go, so it would be an Osprey party at the Orange
Tavern. He'd just tell Alyssa he was going out with some people
from work and that would be that.
Bettie disappeared, leaving Jon wondering why he shouldn't
go. He didn't have a lot of friends, less since he'd been married.
Not so much because his friends didn't like Alyssa—though
some, like Tony, really did not—but because he spent more

time with her and not as much time with his friends. While he contemplated all this, he realized he should get together with his friends more often. Alyssa had her artist friends. Why shouldn't he hang out with his friends? That much decided, he keyed the rest of the invoices into the computer.

Some time later there was a gentle knock on the cubicle frame.

"How's everything going?" Marcy asked. "Any questions about the work? Did you have any problems?"

Jon turned to face her. "No. It's all pretty easy stuff. It's just getting used to the system here."

"Good. It's five. If you want to leave, you can. I'm staying a bit late to get some work done for Bernie."

Jon shrugged. "I'll help you, if you want." He didn't really want to stay; he wanted to get home to his novel. But Marcy seemed so sad, and he felt bad she had more work to do. Also he thought maybe they could talk and he could find out what was bothering her.

"You don't have to. I'll be fine. Bernie's staying so I won't be alone."

"If I help, you can get out of here quicker."

"Someone staying?" Bettie stepped from behind Marcy. "Come on, gang, you're not gonna stay late, are you?"

"I have to do some work for Bernie." Marcy shrugged. "It won't take that long."

"I'm out of here." Bettie grinned. "The band's got a gig in NYC and I need to get moving. Jon, you coming?"

"I'll be a few minutes." He should leave with her if, for no other reason, than to spend a little more time with her. Life didn't feel as mediocre when she was around. But he felt bad leaving Marcy, and he really shouldn't be thinking of Bettie the way he was. "I'll see you tomorrow," he said reluctantly.

"Night, folks." Bettie was gone.

"You're leaving, right?" Marcy asked. "I don't really have anything to give you so you might as well get going."

"If that's the way you feel about it." He tried a smile, but she grimaced.

"Well." There was something hesitant about her, like she

couldn't make up her mind if she wanted him to go home or not. "Why don't you go? I'll be fine."

"You're sure?"

"No, but go on. Leave the computer on. I'll see you tomorrow." She walked back to her cubicle.

Grabbing his cooler and his suit jacket, he headed out to Bernie's office. "Have a good night, Bernie."

Bernie looked up from his computer. The desk seemed as chaotic as it had that morning, the only changes being where the folders lay. "You have a good night. Jon, we'll see you tomorrow?"

"Sure." Jon wondered how many temps started here and never came back.

Out in the reception area he found Sara staring up at the ceiling. She appeared frail and older than she probably was. She looked almost frightened. "Sara?"

Her eyes turned to him, but her head stayed tilted up. "I hear them."

"Hear who?" Tony had said she was odd.

"Not who. What. There's a living energy in this building. I sense it. They're in every building. The people who work there are like blood moving through the veins of the building. We keep it alive. But this ... being ... It's different. It's sick." Now she turned her head down. "I'm not crazy."

"I don't think you're crazy." The notion that beings made of energy lived in office buildings was more than he could digest. Though he didn't think she was loony or wacko, he accepted that she had a wild imagination.

She stared at him for a moment. "Either you're lying or you're humoring me to be nice. I know you don't believe me."

"How do you know I don't?"

Sara laughed. "No one does." She nodded toward Osprey. "They all think I'm nuts, some kind of lunatic waiting for the sky to fall. They whisper behind my back and talk about me all the time."

Jon thought she sounded more paranoid than insane, though Tony had said people thought she was wacko and confirmed people talked about her. "So what's the truth?"

"Let me understand this because I'm starting to think one of us is actually nuts. You just started today. I'm sure someone's told you to stay away from me—probably Marcy—but here you are anyway talking to me and asking what I think. Do I have that right?"

Jon nodded. "Truth is subjective, to a degree." He related his elevator experience and how he felt, then told her what Bernie had said.

"He believes something is here?"

"I don't know, but he told me to be careful walking around on my own. Which reminds me—shall we leave?"

They took the stairs and once they were outside, Jon breathed easier. At Sara's Corolla, they talked more about the building and what Sara believed was happening. As much as he wanted to ask her about the "accident," he decided he'd let it go. What she was saying was more than enough to overwhelm him so that when he got in his car, he sat for a few moments taking it all in. Energy beings from other dimensions that siphoned human life force for sustenance. Maybe she really was a wacko. He drove home, pondering her story and wondering what mood Alyssa would be in when he arrived home a half hour late.

TONY

"Good night, Bernie."

"Good night, Tony." He glanced up from his computer and Tony thought he looked beat.

"Go home. Get some rest. I'm sure your wife would like to see you."

Bernie smiled. "It seems this crap never ends. On top of all the work I'm worried about Sharon."

"Hear anything?"

"Not a word. Her husband hasn't heard anything either."

"That's really strange." He shook his head. "I hope she's all right."

Bernie just nodded. "I'll see you tomorrow, Tony."

"You got it." He left the office and went to the elevator. He was tired and couldn't wait to get home. His wife had given birth three months ago, and he was looking forward to seeing little Jenny again. Life had changed so much more than he could've imagined. Even though all his friends who'd had children told him it would, he hadn't believed it would be that different. But now that all his energy and all Maggie's attention was focused on Jenny, he understood. And that was fine by him. Both he and Maggie had wanted children, and this was the first of what they hoped would be three. He realized how much money three would cost, but he and Maggie had settled on that number.

The elevator doors opened and just as he was about to step in, he thought he heard a woman scream in ecstasy. He paused and listened but heard nothing more. When the doors started closing, he snuck in and hit the Lobby button. *That was strange. I've gotta get some sleep. This girl's been keeping me awake worse than Maggie when we started dating. God, those were the days.* He chuckled.

The elevator trembled.

"Whoa. What was that?" He looked around the car as if he could find the cause of the shaking.

The sensation ceased.

Earthquake? In Jersey? I must be dreaming.

The elevator shook, this time more violently.

"What the hell?" He hit the stop button, then the Door Open button, but neither had any effect. "Please, God, don't let me die." Tony rarely attended church, though he believed in God, a loving God who looked after all His children and kept them safe.

The elevator ceased shaking and began its descent.

"That wasn't an earthquake. There's something wrong with this elevator." He hit the Stop and Door Open buttons, but again, neither produced any result. "Damn it." He pressed the Emergency button and wondered where the alarm was and who would hear it. If it was Leo, the man would never show up, and even if he did, he probably wouldn't know what to do. Tony hated that man. He was so … creepy.

The elevator dropped one floor and Tony sucked in air, shouting in terror.

When it settled, he held his breath, waiting for it to start shaking or drop another floor. But it did neither. Instead the doors opened partially, exposing a cinder-block wall.

Tony waited patiently for five minutes, but nothing happened.

"Great. The damned thing's stuck between floors." He took his cell phone out and, heaving a sigh, pressed the button that would dial his house.

"Hello?" It was Maggie's sweet voice.

"Honey, it's me. I'm stuck in the elevator at work. I'll be home as soon as I can."

"Okay, Tony. Someone wants to say hello to you."

There was a moment of silence and then Jenny made cooing noises.

"Hey, baby. Hi, Jenny." He smiled, picturing Maggie holding the phone to Jenny's ear. "Hi, sweetie. Daddy'll be home soon and then we'll play games. Do you want to play games tonight?"

Jenny made cooing noises and Tony smiled. Then Maggie was back on the phone. "I'll see you in a little while."

"All right. Love you."

"Love you, too."

He disconnected the line and slipped the cell phone in his belt clip.

The elevator creaked. The floor cracked and split open. Tony braced himself against one of the walls. There was no railing to hold on to, so when the floor opened wider like a grinning mouth with jagged wooden teeth, he forced himself into the corner and held his breath. As if the elevator demanded a sacrifice, the mouth split down the middle forming an X in the floor. Gravity yanked Tony through the cracked floor. As he plunged down the four story drop, he let out one long scream of terror. Then he hit the floor of the shaft; his spine shattered, his legs broke in three places, one arm under him broke in too many places to count, and his head slammed against the floor. As consciousness fled him, he heard a buzz like thousands of flies descending on him. Something cold and metal snaked around his wrists, ankles, and midsection and lifted him, pulling him up. Something cracked in his chest. His breathing was wet and shallow. Below him he thought the elevator doors opened and someone stepped into the shaft and looked up. Did the person say something? He wasn't sure. As he floated higher his world turned black.

PAUL

"Shh." Paul grimaced. Elaine knew how to scream, no doubt about it. But this wasn't the place to let her animal side out. Christ, they were only a handful of yards from Osprey's doors and Paul had no idea if anyone was still there. As he had figured, it was easy to sneak back in. He'd told Elaine he had to leave for the afternoon, but would be back and to meet him in the empty office across from the elevators. It had been some company named BioTribe. He had no idea what they did, though they had hired really pretty women.

The company was gone and the office was empty, though some of the furniture was still there. He and Elaine had started on the couch in the reception area and then moved back into the main office to avoid being seen.

But even though they had moved out of the reception area, sound still carried. All he needed was for his ex-boss to hear Elaine and come investigate. But what the hell? What could he do? He'd already fired him. Paul could do what he wanted, even if that included screwing his ex-co-workers.

"Sorry," Elaine whispered, smiling down at him. Her hair tented his face. "I get really worked up and I forget where I am."

"It's all right. Just ... try to keep it down." He was proud of himself for picking the lock of the abandoned office. He'd tried a number of times over the course of several weeks but had to stop because someone was always passing by. But this morning he arrived early and tried several times before the lock clicked open.

"I'll try," she said demurely, gently rocking on top of him.

He'd wined and dined Elaine a few times over the last couple of months. He really wanted to go down to one of the abandoned floors where he was certain no one would find them, but he'd learned she liked doing it in unique places where there was a chance of being caught. So when he mentioned this office, he knew she'd go for it.

No one would find them in the office anyway, but he let her think what she wanted to as long as he got some. And, God, was he getting some. He never realized Elaine was such a sex kitten. She was quiet and never picked up on Paul's innuendo, preferring to ignore it. Or was she just not playing with him because she was married and didn't want to appear interested? Well, she was doing a good job of being interested right now.

The rug was starting to burn his back, and he wanted to roll over and take command, but Elaine had her legs spread wide to maintain control. Leaning back, she began bucking her hips and he joined in, thrusting up as hard as he could.

Suddenly he paused and a moment later she did as well. "What's wrong?" she asked, slowing but never stopping her rocking motion.

"I thought I heard someone shout or scream."

"Maybe you just thought you did." She laughed and ran her finger down his chest. "I didn't hear anything."

"Oh, well." He held her hips, arched his back, and drove up into her. He quickly forgot everything around him except the damned carpet, but even that faded when he felt himself rushing toward his orgasm. Focusing all his attention on his erection, when he could no longer hold back, he squeezed his eyes shut and thrust up as hard as he could.

But abruptly Elaine stood and warm wetness spattered on his stomach as he came. Cool air wrapped around his shrinking erection as his anger rose. How dare she just stand up? So she was married. If she didn't want his load inside her, she should've said something before, not waited until the last second and stood up. What the hell was that about? And why did he still feel warm droplets hitting his stomach? He was quite finished.

"What's wrong with—" He opened his eyes. His mouth fell open.

Elaine stood over him with her hands at the back of her neck, making an odd choking sound like a cat trying to dislodge a hair ball.

He stopped breathing.

In the dim light, something protruded from her mouth

where her warm blood spilled on his body and though he couldn't make out what it was, he knew it wasn't supposed to be there. He crawled away from her as she continued making choking noises and fumbling behind her neck.

Breathing too fast, he looked around her, trying to understand what was happening when he saw the silver cable going from the back of her head up into the ceiling. It must've come down and pierced the back of her neck, catching her like a fish on a hook. Elaine hadn't gotten up. She was yanked to her feet by whatever it was that came from the ceiling. The tip curled upward and the thing lifted her toward the ceiling.

"Oh, my God," Paul mumbled, watching her rise.

Elaine's fingers grabbed at the part that went into her neck, but there was nothing she could do but moan as more blood spilled from her mouth and ran down her body, streaking her skin with dark red. The cable shook violently and she flailed like a rag doll.

Paul watched helplessly as she rose into the darkness and disappeared into the ceiling. His eyes focused on the dark place where she'd gone and all he could do was kneel there and stare. "Holyshitholyshitholyshitholyshitholyshitholy—"

He wasn't sure how long he looked into the black square in the ceiling, but when he moved, his knees ached badly. Maybe getting fired wasn't such a bad thing. First with Marcy and now Elaine. It was time to get out of here and never come back. As much as he wanted revenge on Marcy, he'd never set foot in this building again.

Paul wiped himself clean with Elaine's dress. Then he found his clothes, scooped them up, and got dressed as quickly as he could. No way he was staying here a moment longer than he had to.

Paul started laughing and crying at the same time. Only the fear of the cables coming down and impaling him made him crawl to the door and flee the office, praying no one saw him, praying no one saw him and Elaine enter the office, and praying that tomorrow his sanity would return. No more chasing women in this building; it was way too dangerous.

He opened the door to BioTribe's reception area and was

halfway across to the office door when the first cables slithered from the ceiling and grabbed him. *This isn't happening,* he thought while he was pulled far up into the ceiling. And then the cutting began.

MARCY

She thought about going home, but there was nothing at the apartment worth going home for. She could try Becky—no, she wasn't ready for that. What else was there? She didn't like the bar scene because of how self-conscious she was, and she hated going to restaurants by herself. Maybe she should stop at a bookstore and find a good book to read. That would distract her from all the weirdness that had suddenly become a part of her life. She might even wander into the café and get something sweet, sit for a while, and read magazines.

Her mind made up, she headed for the local Barnes & Noble and discovered, to her amusement, that some author was at the store talking about her new book, *Love, Sex, and Relationships: How to Have the Best of Everything.* She sat for a while and listened before getting a mocha latte at the café and returning to the lecture.

"Any questions?" The author was a woman who seemed to be in her late forties, but she was still beautiful with a perfect body.

Marcy had a million questions, but she couldn't bring herself to stand and ask them. People would look at her, compare her to the author, find her unattractive, and she'd see the disdain on their faces. Better to keep quiet, buy the book, and discover the answers for herself.

Several people, mostly women, asked questions about love, finding the wrong guy, and how to know who was right and who was wrong. Marcy knew she belonged with these people who kept getting into bad relationships. Since Jess, there hadn't been anyone serious, though there had been a couple of short, loveless relationships. But as she sat half-listening to the author answer the questions, she thought about Jon and how nice he was to offer to stay late with her. As much as she wanted him around, to talk to him, she couldn't bring herself to say yes. But he had wanted to stay. He almost seemed—dare she say it?—interested. But he had a wedding ring on. So why was he being so nice to her?

Of course he's married, Mousy Marcy. No single guy would ever give you a second glance! The woman in her head laughed. *Mousy Marcy. Always an empty bed. Mousy Marcy. Go home and put a bullet in your head.*

Hot tears slipped from her eyes, and she quickly wiped them away, not wanting anyone to see her pain. She had to leave the store before someone looked at her and laughed. Taking the latte with her, she rushed out to her car where, once in the driver's seat, she let the tears come.

"I'm not mousy," she mumbled through her sobs. "I'm not mousy." She wiped her eyes and sniffed. "Bettie thinks I'm special and Jon—"

Not mousy? Oh, no, not you. You're brave, courageous, fearless, outgoing. You're not mousy. What you are is pathetic.

Marcy let out all her rage in one long, primal scream and pounded the steering wheel with fists clenched so tight her nails dug into her palms. But she didn't care about the pain. It was physical pain, though it barely distracted her from the emotional anguish tearing her apart.

"Leave me alone!" She couldn't stop sobbing. *"Please!"*

The woman in her head was silent.

Still crying, she started the car and wiped her eyes. She drove out of the parking lot and headed home, thoughts of the author telling her that if she really wanted happiness, then finding someone to love her was her priority. Sure, people said you had to love yourself first, but she needed someone to show her what was lovable about herself. Once she could see what it was, then she'd love herself as deeply as that other person loved her. Everyone found love in their own way, and no one had the right to tell anyone else how to find true love.

But could she allow herself to love again? Everything she'd felt after Jess had been the love one felt at the beginning of things—before you saw a person's dirty laundry and listened to them talk about how miserable their day had been at work one day after the next.

With Jon it could be different. But he was married. She'd seen the ring on his finger. He was being nice because he felt obligated to, not because he had any feelings for her. The notion that he *might* have feelings for her was absurd. As much as she wanted to hope he might—maybe his marriage was falling apart—the truth was, she wasn't loveable.

Driving home, as hard as she tried to put him out of her mind, her thoughts kept returning to Jon. When she imagined their first kiss, their first caress, and their first lovemaking, she accelerated a little faster and felt like a teenager dreaming about the hunk on the football team. In her fantasy, it wasn't important if he was married or not; he wanted her and that was all that mattered.

When she got home, she triple-locked the door as usual and went straight for the wine. The latte wound up on the counter by the sink, forgotten. Her nerves were fraying from everything that had occurred, and now her heart raced from all the fantasizing she'd done on the ride home. A glass or two of zinfandel before dinner would calm her down enough that she could think straight. She drank the first glass while she reheated the pizza. Downed a second as she ate. By the third, she was finally relaxed and after finishing two slices, decided a bath would be for the best.

Staggering her way to the bathroom, she plugged the drain and turned on the hot water. Adding in lavender bubble bath, she mixed the hot water until a thick layer of bubbles lay across the water's surface. When she knew the water was high enough to cover her up to her neck, she shut the tap off, stripped, and slowly got in, letting her skin adjust to the hot water. As she settled into her bath, she was grateful she'd left the latest novel she was reading on the counter by the tub.

Pouring another glass of wine, she relaxed and sipped, enjoying the taste of the zinfandel on her tongue. She reached up and brought the book down, careful not to get it wet, then turned it right side up and read the cover: *Insatiable*. What a ridiculous title, she thought, but the story was full of lust and love betrayed.

She placed the wineglass on the tub's ledge and opened to where she'd stuck her bookmark: a Stop & Shop receipt. The main characters became she and Jon, and after the first scene of intense sex, she let the book slip from her fingers onto the bathroom floor, closed her eyes, and imagined the same scene playing out, but in her room on her bed with them naked, holding each other as he rolled her on her back and hovered over her. She took his hot, thick erection, gave it a gentle squeeze and several loving strokes, before guiding him into her. He smiled down at her and she closed her dream-eyes, wanting only to feel him enter her, his sexual energy consume her, make her a whole woman.

Then she sank lower in the tub until her chin touched the water and she wished Jon was there with her. It didn't matter if he was married or not. She could find the courage to seduce him, couldn't she? She had to.

Somewhere nearby a phone rang, and it wasn't until the answering machine kicked on that she was able to raise herself out of her fantasy enough to realize she was still in her apartment. She listened for the voice to know who it was. She giggled, thinking maybe it was Jon reading her mind, wanting to come over and—

Her message abruptly cut off; the person had hung up.

She frowned, annoyed at the interruption, but fell back into her fantasy, imagining it was Jon trying to reach her, but was then suddenly too shy to leave a message.

If only she could find the courage to open up to Jon, then she would ... then she'd see what an idiot she was for thinking he could feel anything for her. But the woman author said all you had to do was overcome your fear and believe in yourself enough to know you're worthy of love. She had to do it if she ever hoped to find a relationship and not spend the rest of her life alone. All she had to do was get past the abandonment issues and her fear of intimacy and she'd be fine. No problem.

JON AND ALYSSA

"You're late. Is everything okay?" Alyssa was in the kitchen and never turned away from the stove. "You didn't call so I kept dinner hot. Next time you're going to be late, please call."

Jon stood in the kitchen doorway watching his wife. "Sure. I'm all right." He wasn't, but he had no interest in reiterating his feelings.

"How was your first day at work?"

"Fine. It's like every other office job I've had." Alyssa sighed and turned to face him. "I don't know what to say anymore, Jon. I'm sorry you don't like it, but this is real life and we have bills to pay and you have to work."

He thought she stared at him like he was a child who just refused to understand the way life worked, and he felt his heart thud in his chest as it tightened in anger. *I bet Bettie isn't like this.* Then he smiled like a little boy. "I know. At least the people are pleasant."

"Well, that's good. So, why were you late?" She turned back to the stove and stirred something in a small pot he prayed was not asparagus.

"I ... stayed to help someone."

"That's very nice of you. Trying to make a good impression on your first day?"

"Just trying to be helpful." He headed to the bedroom. "I'm going to change."

"Don't take too long. Dinner's ready."

In the bedroom he looked around as if seeing it differently, as if it were alien and not his own. Though he didn't really have an affinity for decorating, he realized this room was exactly the way Alyssa wanted it, and for the first time, it angered him. The bed, the dressers, and the nightstands were all pieces she'd wanted, and even when he had voiced his opinion, she had still went ahead and bought them. They weren't terrible, but the wood was too dark and gave the bedroom an ominous, gloomy feel. He thought a lighter wood would make the room feel more hospitable and welcoming. But she had the final say.

In the kitchen, Alyssa spooned some kind of chicken stew into two bowls. "Craig called and said he had shown the illustrations to the editor and he wanted some changes made. Craig invited him over, so after dinner I'm going by his apartment. I've never met the editor before, and this way we can brainstorm and come up with some really good images. Just a shame the author can't be there." She handed the bowl to him.

"So you'll be out most of the night." He went into the dining room and sat to eat.

"Yeah. I was going to go over there earlier, but I thought I'd make dinner for us first." She followed and took the chair across from him.

She was doing it again. No matter what Alyssa did, regardless of Jon's feelings, she always made sure he knew that she thought of him first. But most times her actions said otherwise. She might say she always put him first, but most of their life together was him doing what she wanted so she could have what she wanted.

He almost said something about her relationship with Craig, but decided not to; she'd deny it and he'd get angry. Let her go. It would give him a chance to work on the novel undisturbed, and that was fine by him. Truthfully, he was happy to have her out of the apartment.

"I need you to do me a favor tonight."

Jon stared down into his stew, watching unidentifiable vegetables floating around each other like striated green planets. Planet Celery orbiting the Carrot Discworld. For God's sake, he felt like crying. He hoped his disgust didn't show. "What do you need?"

She got up from the table and pulled a sheet of paper—the grocery list—from under the PNC Bank refrigerator magnet. "Can you go over to A&P and pick up a few things?" She placed the list down at his elbow. Her writing covered the entire page in two columns. This would take at least an hour if not longer. His chest tightened further and he wanted to yell at her, ask her what she'd done all day, and why they couldn't go together to make it a faster trip. But he already knew the answer. She had to go over to Craig's apartment and screw him. Maybe Craig was planning an orgy tonight.

"Sure. No problem."

"Thanks. I would've gone today, but work was such a disaster."

"Wasn't today your half day?"

She nodded as she spooned something that might have been a potato cube into her mouth. "Yes. But, uh, we were really busy."

Her tone of voice and her pauses made Jon believe something else was going on, but maybe he was just paranoid because she'd seemed to be losing interest in him the last couple of months. It bothered him only mildly that this was happening to the marriage. He should be trying to save it, make it a better place for both of them, but he didn't care.

"Sorry to hear you were busy."

Then she was done and bringing her bowl to the sink. "Hopefully, I won't be home too late tonight. I haven't been sleeping well lately."

Maybe it's your attitude toward this marriage, he thought. He couldn't even bring himself to call it *their* marriage. Maybe they needed a break from each other. It had only been five years; should this be happening so soon? Didn't the shit really hit the fan closer to seven?

"I'll see you later." She came over and kissed him on the cheek.

He listened as she gathered her stuff and left the apartment. For a while he sat, keeping himself from taking the bowl and its soupy contents and throwing it against the wall in anger. Then he sighed and cleaned up what was left of his dinner. He'd lost his appetite. He spilled the stew down the sink and washed his bowl and spoon, then he put the rest of the stew away; Alyssa had left it on the stove to cool.

Jon grabbed his keys and headed to the supermarket, praying for short lines. But once outside the apartment, he hesitated. It was still early and he felt the need to walk around among other people, to be with strangers all going somewhere. Putting both the supermarket and his writing on hold, he got in the car and headed to New York City.

BETTIE

In less than an hour, Bettie had to change, eat, and get her bass guitar so she could take the bus into Port Authority and walk the three blocks to where Laughing Jezebel played. If she was lucky, Angelina, Karalynn, and Veronica would already be there and they would help each other set up. Nothing worse than someone missing and coming in at the last minute all apologizing and shit because their cat threw up, or the damned van wouldn't start, or the boyfriend took his time when it should've been a quickie.

Bettie had none of these problems, and though she was glad she didn't have a vomiting cat or a damned van, she wouldn't have minded the slow boyfriend. As she reheated the leftover Thai food from three nights ago, she decided that thinking about boyfriends was a waste of time because there was no one lining up at her door asking her out. The only guy she could be interested in was married, which meant it couldn't go anywhere.

Once the Pad Thai with shrimp was hot enough, she sat down at the kitchenette table and grabbed a pen and paper. After she and Marcy had gotten back from lunch she had gone around and asked if anyone had had any sort of weird things happen to them. She hadn't wanted to give any examples because she didn't want them making things up.

She didn't have to. Several people said they had gotten weird phone calls full of static and a voice that reminded them of buzzing bees trying to talk. A couple of people said they saw a silhouette of an unidentifiable person on their computer screens, but it only lasted a few seconds. A few people said that while they were walking around the building, they heard strange noises as if snakes rattled through the walls or around the elevator. In the stairs were metal shrieks or loud thumping. It turned out more people had experienced something strange than hadn't, but no one had said anything because they didn't want to sound ridiculous. So better than half of the A/P and A/R staff had confided strange occurrences, but no one had any ideas what caused them.

Of course there was Sara, who explained all of these occurrences as encounters with an alien energy that lived in the building and drew its food from the people working there. It had turned agitated as of late, unsettled and a bit—for lack of a better word—*schizo*. Oh, there was one in every office building; they were drawn from their own dimension to a particular vibration in each building. But this one ... it was sick or something. Yeah, Bettie thought, sick all right. In the head.

Bettie wrote down names and the corresponding experiences they had. Nothing matched up. It wasn't as if all the women had one experience and the men another or people in a specific area heard noises while people elsewhere did not. It was all random. But the one thing that struck Bettie as important was that none of the incidents were harmful. They were all just ... scary ... as if someone was trying to frighten everyone.

Once she was done writing everything down, she decided tomorrow she'd check out the other companies for missing people or weird events. She had no idea what she would do once she gathered all the information, maybe go to Bernie or the police and try to get them to understand that something ... supernatural? ... was happening. Was it ghosts? Was someone like Leo screwing with them for fun? If it was Leo, he was doing a lot of work for very little effect. Although she'd sooner believe it was Leo than a haunted building.

She'd never given much thought to the supernatural or any of that paranormal mumbo jumbo. Reality was enough of a burden, and she didn't need any ghosts or poltergeists or UFOs intruding on her life, making it worse. Right now, she'd stick with Leo as the source of the weirdness, regardless of what Sara said, and if something else happened to prove otherwise, she'd deal with it then.

Folding her notes, she slipped them in her purse to take with her to work. She finished the Thai food and left the dish in the sink for another day. Right now she had to change in to her "rock chick" clothes and get over to the club. As much as she looked forward to playing with Laughing Jezebel, getting up the next morning would be pure hell. Soon, she knew, something would have to give. Singing to herself, she headed off to the bedroom and stripped out of her work clothes, leaving Bettie Winters, A/P clerk, on the bed. Her gig wardrobe wasn't very different from her regular work wear, but it leaned more toward red and showed more cleavage and added Keds high tops instead of Doc Martens. She wasn't a slut, but she knew what brought the boys in. A/P clerk left in the bedroom, Bettie, hot rocker chick, grabbed her bass guitar case and headed out. Something told her this would be a special night.

BERNIE

Sitting at his desk, Bernie stared at the mess of papers piled and scattered around him. He couldn't remember the last time he'd actually seen the wood surface of the desk, and he really wished he had a secretary to help him go through it all. Marcy helped as best she could, but she had her own work to do and he couldn't ask her to do any more.

Between her and Sharon, he rarely had to wonder if everything was getting done. But now Sharon was gone. Two days she'd been missing with no clue to what had happened. Worse, he had that nagging feeling things were going to get worse real soon.

He sat back and stretched. It was getting close to six o'clock, and as much as he wanted to go home, he was too tired for the hour-plus drive home. Living in Sparta was nice but the commute was less than desirable. If only he lived closer or had a job closer to home. Fifteen years ago this was a comfortable job not far from the apartment in Rutherford, and though it wasn't exactly what he wanted to be doing, it was fine for their financial needs; it even gave him and Linda some spare money so they could save for a house. Once they had started looking—the apartment had gotten too claustrophobic—they found a beautiful old Colonial within their financial means in Sparta. The drive would easily be an hour on a good day, but they couldn't have said no.

Bernie had thought that once they had settled into their new home he'd look for a new job closer to the house, but it had never happened. House repairs and an overload of work had prevented him from taking the time he needed to look for a new job. Eventually he had reasoned that the job was fine and had settled in for the long haul. It wasn't glamorous, but it paid the bills and gave them money for vacations, something he desperately wanted and needed right now.

It was bad enough Sharon had disappeared, but now Marcy was in terrible shape. Then again, with her friend disappearing, Paul sexually harassing her, and that whole thing with the cables … What the hell was that about anyway? He'd checked with Leo to see if he knew anything, but he'd said he didn't. Nope, sorry, chief, not a thing. If it had been up to him, he would've fired Leo and gotten someone a little more psychologically stable. It wasn't as if Leo had ever done anything to him, but there was something about the man that bothered him, and he could never quite figure out what it was. That none of the women liked him was a certainty. They all said he creeped them out.

As if on cue, someone knocked on Bernie's office door.

"We need to talk, chief."

Bernie stared at the papers scattered on his desk like white leaves after an October storm. *I'll never get this place organized.* He glanced up at Leo, who looked unusually pale. Something was wrong. "What is it?"

As if the words opened an invisible door, Leo practically ran in and fell into one of the chairs in front of Bernie's desk. "We've got—there's some kind of—I don't know what's happening around here—I'm … I don't know what to say."

"What are you talking about?" Bernie sat forward, concerned that something had shaken Leo so badly.

"All right." Leo took a deep breath. "I was in the basement when I thought I heard someone scream. It came from the elevator shaft. So I went over and pressed the elevator button. Nothing happened. Then I tried opening the doors by hand. They opened way too easily. But that's not the problem, chief. There was no elevator there. Just the shaft, but I heard a noise coming from above me. Sounded like bees. Thousands of them. Just up there buzzing. So I looked up and someone was in there, floating up into the shaft. I tried to get a—"

"What do you mean, someone was floating in the shaft?" Bernie wondered if Leo had been drinking again. He knew the man drank but hadn't said anything because the building's owners didn't care—they planned to sell the place soon or demolish it, whichever was cheaper—and Leo hadn't let his drinking affect his work. Lame-ass excuse but Bernie had more important things to worry about.

"There was someone—I think maybe it was Tony—floating up the shaft. He was spread-eagled with his arms out like this." Leo demonstrated by holding his arms out and above his head.

Bernie sat back and steepled his fingers. Sharon gone. Paul fired. Marcy too upset to function. Now Leo was going off the deep end. He wasn't sure if he should believe him or not. But why would Leo lie?

"Look, chief, I gotta tell you something and I should've told you before, but I was afraid I'd get blamed for it. But now that I saw what I saw—though I'm not even sure what I saw—I think I need to—"

"Just tell me." Could this get any more absurd?

"I found Sharon's shoes the other day. The day she disappeared. They were in the basement. One was on the stairs, the other was—"

Bernie leaned forward, almost jumping over the desk. "You found her shoes and you didn't say anything? What the hell is wrong with you?"

Leo sat like a little boy who'd just been reprimanded for stealing a cookie. Calmly, he said, "I didn't say anything because I didn't want to be blamed for something I didn't do. Bernie, I've had a lot of problems with the police and I don't need any more."

"So you took the shoes, lied to me, and lied to the police. That makes perfect sense."

"It does. I mean I only found her shoes. I didn't find her body or anything."

Bernie sighed. "You found her shoes, Leo. The police could've started their investigation sooner because then it would have been a crime scene. But because you took the shoes so it looked like there wasn't anything suspicious, the police wouldn't do anything." Bernie gritted his teeth. "What else, Leo? What else aren't you telling me?"

He shook his head. "Nothing. I swear. Just the shoes. That's all I found. Wait. There was something else."

"Leo, so help me, if people have died because of your damned stupidity ..." Bernie's hands were clenched fists, turning whiter by the second.

"No, it was nothing. One of the ceiling tiles was broken on the floor, and some kind of yellowish fluid in the elevator. That's all. I cleaned it up."

"A broken ceiling tile? Do you have any idea what the fluid was?"

Leo shook his head.

"What was it like?"

"I don't know. Slimey and yellow. There wasn't much of it. And there was some red streaks in it as well. I'd never seen anything like it before. It was slippery but it didn't have no smell."

"Red streaks? Like, maybe, blood?"

Leo stared at Bernie as if struck dumb by someone else's genius. "Hadn't thought of that."

Bernie sat back, clasping his hands together. It would do no good to either leap over the table and beat the holy shit out of Leo or continue screaming at him. "Let me see if I've got all this straight. You found Sharon's shoes in the basement but didn't say anything to me or the police because you didn't want to get in trouble. Any mysterious fluid you found you cleaned up and you're in here now because you might've seen Tony floating in the elevator shaft and you thought that was a problem."

Leo nodded.

"And you decided to come in here and tell me this, why? I mean, why the sudden change of heart?"

Leo looked like he was thinking real hard, with his brows knitted and a scowl on his face. He kept his gaze down, then suddenly glanced up at Bernie. "I don't like getting involved in other people's trouble, chief. But when I see people floating up elevator shafts ... well, that's more than a little trouble. Whatever happened to Sharon, I can't do anything about 'cause I didn't see nothing. Same goes for the peculiar fluid. But I know I saw someone in the elevator shaft. Truthfully, chief, you're one of the few people I trust. I mean, I could call the owners, but you know they don't give a damn about this place. So you're it."

"You're not drunk, are you? You know I have to ask."

"Of course you do, and no, I'm not. Big of you to think I'm off my rocker here and seeing things. But I know what I saw."

Bernie stared at Leo, trying to decide if the man was telling the truth. He'd just found out Leo had lied to him, probably more than once. So how could he believe him now? On the other hand, Leo had no good reason to come up here and lay some bullshit on him. But people didn't float up elevator shafts. Maybe the sensible thing was to go check the elevator and see if anyone was floating there. The whole idea was ridiculous. People didn't fl—

Something heavy dragged across the ceiling. Both men stared at the tiles.

"Something damned weird is happening here, chief."

Bernie thought to tell him he was an ass for stating the obvious.

"That's the roof up there," Leo said. "Sounds like it's in the ductwork, though, like someone's dragging themselves through or something."

"What in the world would make you say that?" Bernie stared at Leo as if he'd gone insane.

"I don't know. First thing that came to mind."

The sound of something being dragged across the ceiling continued, but when it reached the opposite wall it ceased. Or maybe whatever it was had continued on and the sound just didn't reach them.

Bernie stared at the ceiling where he last heard the noise. Should he pull the tiles down and have a look up there? Leo could help him. "Give me a hand." He pushed one of the chairs to the wall.

"What are you doing?" Leo moved out of the way.

"I'm going to have a look up there." Making sure the chair was flush against the wall, he climbed onto it.

"I don't know if that's such a good idea, chief. It's probably just ductwork."

"Then that's all I'll see." He reached up and angled one of the ceiling tiles down. "Here. Take this."

Leo took the tile and stood it up next to the desk.

As he reached for the next one, Leo said, "Hey, chief, you

better take a look at this."

"What?" He followed Leo's gaze to his computer screen. His e-mail account was gone, replaced by static snow. "Oh, what the hell is that?"

"Static."

"Thanks, Sherlock." He glanced up. "Help me get these few down, and then I'll take a look at the computer and see what's wrong with it."

Leo shrugged. "Guess it ain't goin' anywhere anyhow." He took the next two tiles and stood them with the first. "What's up there?"

"Just what we figured. Air ducts." He looked closer. "Looks like something was dragged through it, though; it seems to be bulged out a bit."

Hunnn ... grrr ...

"What did you say?" Bernie looked down at Leo, who stared at the computer screen. "What ..."

Within the static was the form of a man.

Leo went closer. "It looks like Tony."

"What? That's ridiculous. It can't be—" Something spattered on his shoulder, and a single fat, red drop rolled down his shirt. "What the hell?" He looked up. Where two duct pieces met, the same red fluid dripped a single drop every few seconds.

"It's Tony, chief," Leo said.

"Hunnngrrr." The sound came out of the computer speakers like bees.

Bernie glanced down at the screen, balanced by his hands on the metal framework of the ceiling. From here it did sort of look like Tony, but that was ridiculous and impossible. The way the static tumbled across the screen just gave the impression of—

Metal coiled around his wrists, his neck, his chest, and he was jerked up into the darkness.

LEO

"Shit." Leo backed away from the computer, afraid that whatever was on the screen was going to get him. "Just like the sound I heard in the elevator shaft. What do you think it is?" He heard Bernie climb off the chair, gasping as he did. The guy was not in good shape.

He waited for a reply, but there was none. When he turned, he said, "Oh, shit." Bernie was gone. Disappeared. Leo ran over to the chair and looked up. Blood dripped onto the chair from a joint in the ductwork. "This is not good." He looked around, hoping something would give him an answer, but it was just Bernie's office and it looked like a tornado had swept through.

On the monitor, the static still roiled and a low buzz came from the speakers. "Hunnngrrr."

"Shit." He glanced up at the ceiling and then at the blood on the chair. He had to call the police. This was out of his league. But he wouldn't do it from here where Tony watched him. Oh, yes, he was sure it was Tony, the same Tony who had floated up into the elevator shaft earlier. And now he was on Bernie's computer, his voice a buzz of mad bees.

"Hunnngrrr."

"I know you're hungry. Shut the fuck up!" Leo fled the office and headed to the hallway. He was alone, and though he couldn't remember ever being scared of anything, right now, as he stood in the fifth floor reception area between the elevator and the stairwell, he felt his heart beat faster and he felt hotter than usual.

"All right, Leo, don't freak." He stood still. "Okay. We get out of the building, then call the police and … Glen's downstairs. He'll know what to do. Well, he probably won't, but at least maybe we can figure something out." Hurrying into the stairwell, he jumped when the door clicked closed behind him. "Why the hell can't Osprey be on the second or third floor? Jesus Christ on fire. Five flights of stairs." He began walking down, taking the stairs two at a time, praying he wouldn't fall, cables wouldn't drop from the ceiling, and he wouldn't run into Tony.

At the third floor landing he heard the door to the second floor open and click shut. Had someone come into the stairwell or gone out? Maybe whoever it was got scared and left the stairwell because they didn't know who was coming and didn't want to take any chances. Maybe they'd had some kind of crazy encounter just like he did and they were scared shitless.

"Shit." There were no companies on the second floor. He wished he had taken something from Bernie's office to defend himself with because if he ran into Tony or any of the others who disappeared, he was sure they wouldn't be friendly. He had no idea what had happened to them or what state they'd be in if he did see them, but he preferred to make it out without running into anyone.

As he listened, he wondered what had happened in Bernie's office. Aliens? Poltergeists? Or that thing he saw in his private room? What the hell had that been? It was like electrical ooze. When it disappeared, he figured it was his twisted imagination seeing things. But now he wondered if it really had been his imagination or if some kind of monster had been in his room probing with that tentacle.

Leo had always considered all that New Age nonsense a crock of shit, spoon-fed to gullible assholes who were so weak they'd believe anything. There was no such thing as ghosts. When you were dead, you were dead. You might go to heaven or hell, but you certainly didn't hang around haunting places. People were so freakin' gullible it astounded him how many fell for that New Age garbage. UFOs, Bigfoot, all that was for children and—

On the second floor landing someone shuffled around.

It's just someone who got themselves lost. That's all. They thought they'd found the lobby and missed. Probably a temp from Dasher or one of the companies left on the third floor. Just a human being. No big deal.

But Leo didn't move. He stood frozen to the spot and kept his eyes locked on the lowest part of the stairs he could see in case whoever it was wasn't friendly and he had to go back up.

Jesus Christ on fire, just walk down the stairs, you fuckin' pussy.

"Right," he whispered. "Just down the stairs." He demanded his feet move and they did, though very slowly as if they knew something his brain didn't. Crouching, he made his way down the stairs, keeping his eyes on the next landing so he wouldn't be surprised.

At the midway point he stopped. Someone was definitely moving around down there. He could hear them breathing like they had asthma or something. Whoever it was sounded like they had a problem walking, as well. A step, shuffle, step . . . stumbling. A gasp and . . . *What the hell was that?* It sounded like they were trying to scream but no sound came out.

This ain't good, Leo. Granted, we don't believe in any of that New Age crap, no aliens or ghosts or poltergeists or whatever. But what about ... zombies?

He'd seen every George Romero zombie flick, as well as numerous other movies with the living dead or the walking undead or whatever you called them. Suddenly everything made sense in a way he wished he'd never thought of. Tony had been turned into a zombie. That explained why he kept repeating hunger over and over. He was hungry for human flesh.

"Jesus Christ on fire," he whimpered. Was Bernie being turned into one of those things even as he crouched there? And what about Sharon? Was she a zombie as well? He leaned farther out over the stairs, hoping to glimpse whoever was on the second floor landing, because he needed to know he was being a stupid idiot thinking there were actual zombies walking around the building.

Tony stood on the landing below him. Leo couldn't see his face, but he recognized him from his clothes. The man staggered forward, almost falling down the stairs. At the last moment, he backed away and fell against the opposite wall.

"He's a fucking zombie! Holy motherfucker!" He prayed his voice didn't carry down to Tony or else he'd wind up as zombie vittles.

No. Tony is not a zombie, you freak. There's just ... there's just something wrong with him. That's all. He did fall down an elevator shaft. Then again, you didn't see him fall, you just saw him floating. So why ain't he dead? He should be dead. D-E-A-D. Not walking around. He's still alive. He's just really hurt and while he's having problems, you're up here afraid to help him 'cause you think he's going to eat you. Dumb jackass.

Leo resolved to help Tony if he needed help, but he didn't move, couldn't move. The scene with the kids being pulled out of the truck from *Night of the Living Dead* came back to him in stark black and white. Zombies ripped those helpless kids open and pulled their intestines out, feasting on the gore and—

The Tony-thing opened the stairwell door and shambled back to the second floor lobby.

There was no hesitation. Taking the steps two and three at a time, Leo fled to the lobby and only when he threw the door open and saw Glen did he laugh—not weep—in relief and thank God he was still alive.

Glen was at his desk looking, for all the world, like nothing was wrong. Of course he couldn't know what had just happened, but Leo wished the other man appeared slightly agitated.

"Leo, how are—"

"Glen, I need you to call the police and get them over here. I was just in Bernie's office and something strange happened and then he disappeared."

"Another one?"

"What do you mean, 'another one'?"

"A few people have gone missing. There's been at least one a day since Tuesday." Glen lifted the receiver and dialed.

Leo wondered who else, other than Sharon, Tony, and Bernie, were gone. Maybe those bitches from the third floor. He didn't wish anyone harm, but a good scare never hurt anyone. Well, except him. He didn't need the pain in his chest from the fright he got when he realized Bernie had disappeared. No, he didn't need that at all.

"I'm heading home, Glen. I'll see you in the morning." Before Glen could answer, Leo walked out. The security guard may've said, "Wait," but he didn't. Once again, he wanted nothing to do with the police. If there were so many people disappearing, surely there were other witnesses the police could question.

Now, he'd catch the bus and be around people. Even if he disliked most of them, at least they were real and not zombies and they didn't just disappear. Nor did any of them talk like bees.

Waiting at the curb, he glanced back at the Howard

Phillips Building. No way was he ever coming back to this place. Tomorrow morning he'd call the owners and tell them they could find someone else for the job because he quit. As much as he wanted to find Bernie and Sharon, he didn't have the equipment or the inclination to fight zombies, and to be absolutely honest *his* life was more important than *theirs*.

Sure, he'd seen all the zombie movies and knew *how* to kill them, he just didn't want to; let the police or the National Guard do it. That's what they got paid for. Emergencies like floods, riots, and zombie infestations.

If he did have any thought to come back, at least in the morning the sun would be out and he'd have all day to look. Now the sun was setting and it threw shadows that reminded Leo of monsters.

When the bus arrived, he got on, dropped his change in the change receptacle, and took a seat. For a few minutes, he watched the office building for signs of movement but there were none. He turned to find an obese woman—she'd be a real feast for zombies—sitting across from him reading a book on alien abduction. He snorted; the gullible were everywhere. If there was a zombie attack, people like her would be the first to go, and he'd thank God for it.

GLEN

After Leo left, Glen waited for the phone to connect. He had asked Leo to wait, but the other man never heard him. He had a dial tone, but then once he dialed, the phone went dead.

"Oh, now what?" He pulled out his cell phone. "Just call them on the cell." He pressed the on button and waited.

A noise by the elevator caught his attention. When he looked, the elevator door opened and Tony was inside but he didn't look right.

"You okay, man?"

Tony dropped to one knee and shook his head.

"Ah, shit." He set the cell phone down and went over to help the man out of the elevator.

Tony stumbled backward out of Glen's reach.

"It's all right. I'll have you out of here in no time and then we'll—"

The elevator door closed.

"What the heck?" Glen turned to the door. "Did you ..." He turned back to Tony.

The other man rose up on what Glen thought were broken legs.

"What happened to you? You don't look—" A noise above him made him glance up in time to see a half-dozen metal cables descend into the car. "Oh, no." The elevator began to ascend as the cables methodically cut Glen apart.

IN THE DARK: ANNETTE

She wept, but no tears came from her ruined eyes. She had tried placing them back in their sockets but they kept slipping out. Now she lay on her side feeling every cut and every slice of skin the cables inflicted on her. Her clothes were useless ribbons that stuck to her from the numerous trails of blood that covered her body.

The cables were controlled by something intelligent. She was sure of it. Whatever it was played with her, terrorizing her until her throat was shredded from screaming, and then disappearing, only to come back hours later and start again.

The cuts, as bloody as she knew they were, weren't deep, which meant the thing wasn't trying to kill her. It was torturing her, carving her body methodically to cause the most pain. The cables came out of nowhere and each time scared her so badly she cried.

How much longer could she endure this nightmare? She would bleed to death sooner than later, which was a mixed blessing. Not that she wanted to die, but she didn't think she could endure the pain or the fear of never knowing when the cables would strike. In the dark, it was impossible to know where she was, though she'd surmised she was up in the air ducts somewhere in the building. It was narrow and hot and made of metal from the sound of it when she knocked.

Annette heard them coming, though she couldn't guess how many. Four, maybe five? They scraped along the metal of the duct, the rasping sound echoing around her so it was impossible to tell which direction they came from. This time she could not fight them as she had tried to do before. The cuts on her hands stung from the last time she tried to protect herself. But while one cable had sliced her hands open, the other cables cut the rest of her flesh. She would die from the next round of attacks. That was her fate and she accepted it. Better to die than to live in this nightmare until the cables decided it was time to kill her. No one would rescue her as she first prayed someone would. But no one knew where she was, and even if they tried to find her, who would look in the air ducts? No one.

As the first cable danced on her skin, brushing up her leg, she lay back. God, I am sorry but I can't fight anymore. I have no fight left in me. I have no hope that someone will save me. If this is my time, please, I beg for mercy to make it quick. The pain ... She cried as cold, jagged metal edges sliced into her skin. Warm blood flowed down her calves, down her thighs, pooled on her stomach, trickled down her arms. And still the cables continued ripping her apart until there was nothing left of her.

JON

Times Square was bathed in electric daylight as billboard-sized video screens played commercials and neon signs dazzled and illuminated the night. Even in the middle of the week at close to nine p.m., the city street bustled with humanity like a river of strangers swept along the sidewalk.

Jon headed uptown from Port Authority with no particular destination. All he wanted was to forget life in New Jersey and all his troubles back home. Just being immersed in the thick crowd moving from one street to the next was enough for him after feeling caged at the job and, worse, caged at home.

Hundreds of voices around him spoke at once—to the person next to them, on their cell phones, or to themselves—some in English, some in languages he couldn't understand. It was easy to imagine that his life in New Jersey was a bad dream and now he was truly awake in this strange and wondrous place. In a way, he was as much a tourist as the German family next to him; he just spoke the same language as most of those who walked with him.

The aroma of fresh, New York pizza drifted out of a pizzeria as he passed, making him slow down and take a deep breath; there was nothing like the smell of pizza in New York City. Inside, people shouted at each other in Italian and a teenage girl laughed before saying something that made the older man behind the counter roll his eyes as he kneaded dough for the next pie. Jon contemplated getting a slice, but he wasn't all that interested in food. Next time, he told himself before moving on.

Jon often wondered if he could live in this utter chaos. The only way he'd ever work in the City was if he lived here. No way would he commute from Jersey every day. As he walked along the street, noticing every beautiful woman, most on their cell phones, he believed he could move here and start completely fresh with no ties or strings. It troubled him he could give up his marriage so easily, but some of these women passing him had to be single and kinder than Alyssa.

Is Alyssa really that unkind? Yeah. At times she's pretty selfish and cruel. His thoughts meandered to the times when she was nasty to him. It was obvious she cared more about her own life and dreams than she did about sharing their lives together.

Walking along Eighth Avenue, he was aware how many people there were at this hour. He could never remember being in the city when there weren't hundreds of people walking somewhere. As he walked passed Forty-second Street, he felt alive. Between the people and the bright lights turning nine o'clock at night into midday, it was hard not to get swept up in the excitement that was New York City.

I bet Bettie likes the City, he thought. He thought of her in black stockings, miniskirt, and lace top with Doc Martens, and the violet—not purple—highlights in her hair walking with him, talking and laughing about anything and everything. Where he should've felt guilt, he felt none, and that bothered him. Granted, he wasn't happy in his marriage, but not everyone was. Could all those people be thinking of having affairs? That's what counselors were for. Except no matter what happened in their marriage, Alyssa refused any kind of counseling, telling Jon it was him, that she was mentally and emotionally healthier than he was because she understood how life worked and he continued to live in some kind of fantasy world.

But she didn't. She'd carefully constructed a life that she could control. He wasn't one of those A personality types and could be easily coerced to doing what she wanted. The whole "I always put you first" attitude, though a lie, was so Jon would feel bad for her and let her do what she wanted. So far, it had worked well.

"Hey, bud, wanna hear some kick-ass rock?" A thick, balding man, dressed in black jeans and a T-shirt, stood in the doorway of a bar with some sort of pass in a plastic holder around his neck. "You look like you know good music. Right?"

"Sure." Jon was taken aback, unsure whether to walk away or find out what was behind door number one.

The man held out a pass in his sausage-like fingers. "Go inside. Have a drink. Enjoy the show." He glanced at his watch. "Band's playing right now. Probably take a short break in like fifteen minutes, then go on again. Here. Check it out."

What was one drink and some good music? He took the pass and walked in, hoping the band was good or he'd be leaving sooner rather than later.

He went through a vestibule, then pushed another door open and was assailed by loud guitars, a thrumming bass, and a hard, steady drumbeat. What caught him off guard, though, was the quality of the female singer's voice. She was smooth with a rough, bluesy quality that would lend itself to pretty much anything she sang. Before he even saw the band, he knew she'd be good-looking.

They were cranking their way through Blondie's "One Way or Another," and as Jon sat down at one of the few empty seats at the bar, he took a look at the band. Four women, all good-looking (what a surprise), stood on the tiny stage playing with intense passion, especially the bass-guitar-playing singer. Not only could she sing, but she was stunning in her plaid miniskirt, Keds high tops, a tight black tank top, and—his jaw dropped.

It was Bettie. She was hot and she sang with such passion—like the world was on fire and the only way she could save it was to sing for her life. Jon realized that he wanted—no—needed to know her better. He told himself that this wasn't anything sexual, so there was no reason to feel any deception or guilt;

he wasn't sleeping with her. He just wanted to sit and talk. All night. And drive down to the Shore and watch the sunrise. And ...

Jon ordered a SoCo & 7 and watched the band. Bettie kept slinking across the tiny stage when she wasn't singing. All four women sang, which complimented the band exceptionally well. A few songs showed off their harmonies like the Eagles' "Seven Bridges Road."

After four songs, the guitarist, an Englishwoman, announced they were taking a short break and would be back. The audience was appreciative and applauded them as they left the stage.

"What are you doing here?" Jon realized Bettie stood in front of him. Somehow she'd snuck up and now she smiled at him. "You don't live in the city, right?"

"No, I don't."

"So what are you doing here? I don't remember telling you we were playing tonight." She turned to the bartender. "Water."

"No, actually, you mentioned tomorrow night at the Orange Lantern. I was just walking around and this guy outside offered me a free pass."

"So you had no idea we were playing?"

Jon shook his head.

"Wow. What a coincidence. How long have you been here? What do you think of the band?"

"I heard four songs and I'm amazed. What are you doing working at Osprey? You guys should be on a national tour or something."

"That's sweet of you. Believe it or not, this doesn't cover most of my bills, so I have to slum it at Osprey. If I could quit and do this full time, I'd give my notice tomorrow."

"I know what you mean."

"You're a musician?" She took the glass of ice water from the bartender. "Thanks, Gerry."

"No. A writer." He sipped his drink, making sure what he felt was just his own emotions and not the alcohol, although if he stayed long enough and kept drinking, it would factor into his reactions to Bettie.

"What do you write?"

The guy who had been sitting at the bar next to Jon left, and Bettie quickly took his seat.

"I'm working on my second novel."

"Wow, that's awesome." She grinned and sipped her water. "I always thought about writing a novel, but it seemed so ... immense ... that I couldn't do it. So I picked up the bass instead. Actually, after I heard The Runaways I wanted to play guitar. They were amazing to me after hearing so many bands that were just guys; to hear these women ... it changed me. But everybody was playing guitar, so I started playing bass so I could join a band. Not many bands are looking for a woman guitarist, but there were plenty looking for bassists. I played around for a while and then I met Karalynn, our keyboardist. I went back to the guitar and we played here and there. Then Veronica—she's our guitarist—heard us at one of our gigs and wanted to join on, and then Angelina, our drummer, found us and here we are. Laughing Jezebel." She paused to take a drink. "And you didn't ask for any of that. Sorry."

Jon shrugged. "It's fine. Nice to know there's more to my co-workers than just going home and watching TV until it's time to go to sleep."

"If only I had that easy kind of life!" She laughed.

"You'd be bored."

"You're right. So, what's your novel about?"

"Infidelity." The word slipped out before he could shut his mouth. Worse, he found himself staring into Bettie's dark eyes. He opened his mouth to say more, but as the book was about a guy who has an affair with a co-worker, very much like he imagined he could have with Bettie, he couldn't speak. *Not responsible for my thoughts. Not responsible for my thoughts.*

"Oh," Bettie said after she seemingly waited for him to say more.

"There's more to it than that." He stared at his glass before taking a fast drink. *I shouldn't have used the word infidelity. I should've thought of something better. What the hell am I thinking, and why am I not saying anything else?* "The book's about life and dreams and sacrifice and grand themes like that." He hoped he'd recovered so that infidelity wasn't stuck between them. He wondered if she had any feelings for him.

"Sounds important and very serious." She shifted her gaze, looking around the bar.

"It's not that serious. The characters are pretty screwed up so there's a lot of sarcasm and irony in it."

"Just like real life, huh? I mean, screwed-up people."

"Yeah. Well, they say write what you know, and I guess I know a lot of messed-up people."

"Don't we all?"

Jon was about to ask her if she'd be interested in reading it, just so he could get her impressions, when Veronica came over to them.

"Hey, what's going on?" She took a slug from a bottle of Heineken. Her accent was distinctly English. She grinned at Jon and threw her arm around Bettie. "Name's Veronica, but please, call me Nica." She bowed slightly.

"Jon, nice to meet you."

"Jon started today at Osprey," Bettie said.

"So you guys are co-workers, then," Nica said. "Very nice. She teachin' ya good?"

"Of course I am," Bettie said. "Right, Jon?"

"Absolutely."

"Cheers to that!" Nica raised her bottle in salute and drank back.

Jon raised his glass and tapped Bettie's water. "Cheers."

"Listen, I hate to break up this lovely Kodak moment," Nica said with a sly grin. "But we're on again."

Bettie frowned at Jon. "Gotta go. Are you sticking around?"

"Just for a little while. I have to get home to write." He wished he could stay all night. It wasn't like Alyssa would be home anytime soon. But he really did want to get some writing done, and then there was the issue of sleep so that he could be functional the next day at work. *One day and already the job is getting in the way of my life,* he thought as Bettie slid off the bar stool.

"Thanks for coming." Bettie leaned over and kissed him on the cheek. "It's great to see you." She smiled and the two women headed through the crowd toward the stage.

"Sure." Watching her go, he still felt Bettie's lips on his cheek. What was that for? Did she kiss every guy who came to see her? Probably not.

Back up on stage, the band was ready. Bettie came to the microphone, glanced at Jon—or so he believed—and smiled. "Siouxsie and the Banshees. 'The Last Beat of My Heart.'"

Angelina kicked the song off with a slow drumbeat. As soon as Bettie sang the first word, Karalynn and Nica came in on keyboards and guitar. The place was silent as Bettie sang through the hypnotic song that wound its way around the bar, settling over the place like a warm summer breeze.

When she came to the chorus, she turned her gaze from the crowd and stared straight at Jon. Their eyes locked and she sang only to him. Words got through to him, asking for his hand, asking that he not turn away, but how could she wish not to be torn apart until the last beat of her heart? He heard the song, knew it was one they probably did all the time, but this night was different because she sang it only to him, opening her heart to him.

She backed away from the mic and looked down at the stage floor. When she stepped back to the mic, she continued the song, gazing at him.

She's not singing to me. That was his first thought as he stared at her. *But she's staring right at me.* There was no mistaking it. Her eyes were locked to his as she sang. But he had already seen her look at his hand, checking for a ring. She knew he was married.

But the softness of her voice, the desperate loneliness in the words, wasn't playing around. She genuinely wanted him to be there, not to turn away from her, but to reach out to her.

His heart raced. He took a fast gulp of his drink and watched her, captivated by her beauty and – the alcohol was definitely talking here – sexual energy that simmered in her. *I should leave*, he thought, but didn't move. Instead, he sat riveted by her performance, imagining that she sand and swayed only for him.

When the song ended, he expected her to smile, but she only

stared at him as if reinforcing her need. Then the band went off into The Runaways' "I Love Playin' with Fire"—Karalynn announcing the song and then singing it—and Jon threw the pass and a twenty on the bar. "Whatever Bettie wants," Jon said when the bartender gave him a strange look. The man nodded and Jon left, stepping out into the cool, autumn night. He felt the energy of the bar fade away, replaced by the energy of the crowded street, leaving him feeling alone. Behind him, Bettie and the band played on and Jon walked away, wondering what Bettie's kiss meant, if anything. And then their song choice. "I Love Playin' with Fire." Granted, the lyrics didn't fit the moment, but the title did. What was she thinking, kissing him on the cheek? They had to work together. She knew he was married, didn't she? Maybe she didn't care.

What am I thinking? He had somehow jumped from Bettie the co-worker to Bettie the … what? Maybe it was the kiss or the look she gave him as she sang "The Last Beat of My Heart" that had him heading down a road that at once thrilled and scared him. He had to back up. He had to do two things: put his feelings in perspective and deal with Alyssa. Whether she was telling the truth or lying, at that moment, he would rather have been with Bettie. But until things were either straightened out with his wife or ended, he had no business considering Bettie as anything but a co-worker.

At the door to the apartment, he thought he heard a man's voice and paused. Was Alyssa brazen enough to bring Craig over to the apartment? Maybe she wanted Jon to meet him to prove once and for all nothing was happening between them. He let himself in. "Hello?"

No answer. Alyssa wasn't home yet, either.

The answering machine beeped its notification that someone had called, left a message, and hung up. Checking his watch, he realized it was close to midnight. Who would be calling unless …

He tapped the Playback button.

A telemarketer.

His mother.

Maggie asking Jon if he knew where Tony was because he hadn't come home and he wasn't answering his cell phone. Unfortunately, it was too late to call her back now.

Then the fourth message began. For several seconds there was the sound of someone breathing, then a man's voice, obviously drunk. "Hey! What the hell's going on, dude? Yeah, it's midnight over here and the wine bottle's empty. Damn. Hold on. Can you get another bottle?"

"Can I have my phone back?" It was Alyssa's voice.

Jon's heart slammed in his chest. Why did this guy have Alyssa's cell phone? Why was there an empty wine bottle?

"Just get another bottle from the fridge, Ally. I'll give you your phone back in a second." Then into the phone, he said, "Women."

"Craig!"

"But Ally's all right. You know?"

So this was the infamous Craig talking.

"What number did you dial?" Alyssa asked.

"I don't know. Sorry, dude. She keeps buggin' me 'bout her cell phone and what number I dialed. Truth is, I don't know what number I dialed."

"Craig! Give me my phone!" Her voice got louder as if she were now right next to him.

"But it's all right. I don't mind her buggin' me 'cause I let her suck my dick and she's so good at it. I don't know what the fuck's wrong with her husband. Man, he's one stupid prick if he keeps ignoring her. Right, babe?" The sound of flesh slapping flesh was sharp.

"Hey! Cut it out and give me my phone." She was drunk, as well.

"Just go get more wine."

"I have to go."

"Don't get dressed. Come here." A kiss. "Now go get another wine bottle."

"Who are you talking to?"

"Nobody. I just hit a button and then it connected. I don't—"

"That was the Redial button, you ass! I've gotta get home and erase this message before Jon hears it! I can't believe you're so damned stupid!"

"I didn't know—" The line went dead.

Jon stared at the answering machine, expecting someone to get on the line and say it was all a joke. The illustrations were done and Alyssa was coming home. But no one said anything. The machine beeped to let him know there were no more messages. But Craig's voice repeated in his head.

I don't mind her buggin' me 'cause I let her suck my dick and she's so good at it. I don't know what the fuck's wrong with her husband. Man's he's one stupid prick if he keeps ignoring her. The slap of his hand on her ass? *Don't get dressed.* A kiss. *Now go get another wine bottle.*

His breath grew ragged and his vision blurred from the tears that filled his eyes and spilled down his face. He couldn't turn away from the answering machine because he kept hoping the phone would ring or something else would explain what he'd just heard.

I let her suck my dick and she's so good at it.

It was a practical joke. Someone who knew him was being an idiot and playing on his insecurities by pretending to be Craig.

I don't know what the fuck's wrong with her husband.

The tears were hot on his face but no hotter than the anger in his heart making his chest hurt. He had been concerned about being faithful to Alyssa while Bettie gave him a tiny, insignificant kiss on his cheek. After all the arguments with himself about whether or not Alyssa was honest and if he should be honest and not act on his feelings, after all the goddamned bullshit excuses he made for her, to imagine she really was working on illustrations and not screwing Craig, this was what he was left with.

Man, he's one stupid prick if he keeps ignoring her.

In his mind's eye he saw her smiling at him, telling him how much she loved him. Fast-rewind back five years. *I do. I do. Better and worse. Richer and poorer. Sickness and in health.* It didn't mean a damned thing. Not one word of it. Not one goddamned word.

Five years of memories. Her illustrations, his short stories.

Her smiles, her caresses, and gently whispered words of love. Romantic candlelit dinners. All the plans they'd made while in bed on lazy summer weekends. Gone. Exploded in one two-minute period. His whole life had changed in those 120 seconds. How easy it was for a heart to self-detonate as the mind processed words. They were, after all, only a string of words.

He remembered the joke about the author who spent a lifetime searching for the right words, and when he finally found them, he wept because he couldn't figure out what order to put them in. Songs drifted through his mind about words and how they could heal, cut, burn, kill, make it all right, or completely crush a heart and soul. They were just words, letters summoned together either by pen or voice to make a statement, to say something, an announcement, a proclamation, a decision.

Did Craig think it was funny? He had no idea what number he dialed? Bullshit. He knew exactly what he was doing, and now Jon wanted to find him and beat the shit out of him, but he knew there was no point in it.

He wiped his eyes.

We're doing illustrations.

Sucks my dick.

All his rage boiled over. The fire in his chest exploded into his mind. He grabbed the answering machine, yanked it from the phone, and hurled it as hard as he could against the wall. It shattered in a less-than-satisfying explosion of plastic parts, which left a dent in the plasterboard.

The hell with it.

He reached for the nearest chair, fell into it, and let the anger and tears assault him, not getting up for fear of smashing everything in the apartment to bits. There weren't any sledgehammers around, and he was grateful for that. Fortunately, he wasn't given to drinking and violence or else there'd be a hell of a lot of empty bottles and just as much destruction.

What if he'd come home later after Alyssa had realized what Craig had done and made it home in time to erase the message? He'd never know, though he'd have his suspicions to nag at him until they were proven true somehow.

Now he had to deal with Alyssa, who was on her way home, hoping to erase the message before … what? Where did she think he was? Even if he had been sleeping, he would've woken up when the phone rang. It was midnight, for God's sake. He suddenly realized he was supposed to have gone to the supermarket, but in his state of mind (a quick kiss from Bettie had turned into a lingering kiss of passion on the lips in his thoughts), he'd completely forgotten about it. But that didn't matter now. He would wait right here and confront her as soon as she walked in.

He glanced at the answering machine lying in pieces by the wall. The action had helped dissipate the surface level of anger, but not the deep-down, harbored-for-months rage he felt at believing Alyssa's lies.

What he really wanted was to tell Alyssa their marriage was done, that she could go back to screwing (or sucking) Craig, and then he'd go back to the bar, get another drink—or five—and listen to Laughing Jezebel. He was sure Alyssa was laughing at him. What a fool he'd been since she first mentioned Craig. Had they been going at it from the beginning, or was it something that had developed over time? Like a tumor.

Jon was ready to fight; his adrenaline was racing. If she had a side of the story, he didn't give a damn. What could she say in her defense that he would believe?

Then the apartment door's lock clicked. Jon wiped his eyes as the door swung open and Alyssa rushed in. She dropped her pocketbook, took two steps toward the phone, froze, and stared at Jon.

"Uh," was all she said, confirming what Craig had said was true. Why else would she have rushed home? If it wasn't true, she would've called right back and told the answering machine Craig had been screwing around and making things up to be an asshole. Why hadn't she called back? Too shocked to think straight? "Hi."

"The answering machine is right there." He pointed to the pile of plastic rubble. "I'm sorry you can't hear the last message I got. It was really something." He wanted her to tell him it wasn't true, that it was a joke because Craig was that kind of jackass.

"Jon—"

"What? Are you going to tell me he was just having some fun?" He stayed in the chair, but his hands grasped the arms tightly. "Are you going to say nothing happened? That what he said was just him being an ass?" His voice got louder but he didn't care; the neighbors be damned. "Say something, Alyssa." He rarely used her full name; it was only in anger that he used it.

"I'm sorry." She stared down at the answering machine as if suddenly mesmerized by it. If she was drunk, she didn't show it. Maybe finding him here sobered her up fast.

Jon needed to say something, but the words were jammed up in his throat, clogged by his rage. When he finally looked at her, still staring at the answering machine, the image of her going down on a man he'd never met filled his head. "I'm moving out. We're done."

He stood and went into the kitchen, found his keys, gripped them until the teeth dug into his flesh.

"Jon, please, I'm sorry. I don't know what happened. I was—"

"You don't know what happened?" He laughed. "According to Craig, you sucked him off. Were you too drunk to remember that? Or did you just figure to play the victim here like you usually do and blame Craig like you blame me for all your problems?"

"What are you talking about?" When he turned to face her, she was finally looking at him. "I don't blame you for anything."

"You don't? Why am I working? It's my fault you don't have everything you want. It's my fault you have to work instead of drawing your goddamned illustrations. I had to get a job so you could buy all the furniture you wanted and pursue what you wanted, and my dreams be damned. We talked about this and agreed I'd have the time off. But all of a sudden you were the most important thing and the hell with me."

"I'm always thinking of you, Jon." Her voice shook.

"You're always thinking of ways to make sure I know you're the martyr, that you work so hard for me, when it's only to gain sympathy so you can do what you want." The words poured out of his mouth.

"That's not—"

"So, what, you decided to suck Craig off as some way to get back at me?"

"No. Why would you—"

"Did you fuck him, too?"

She jumped at *fuck*, but quickly shook her head. There were tears in her eyes.

"Don't, Alyssa. Don't even think to pretend you're the one who's hurt. I get home and find a message from Craig that rips my heart out and you have the audacity to cry?"

"I said I'm sorry."

"You know what, Alyssa, *sorry* works for broken dishes. *Sorry* works for not doing something I asked you to do. *Sorry* even works if you spent too much time somewhere and weren't home when you said you'd be home and I worried about you. Though at this point I don't know why I'd give a shit. But. *Sorry.* Does. Not. Work. For. Fucking. Blow. Jobs."

Alyssa stared at Jon, tears running down her face.

"I'm sorry, too, Alyssa." He came up to her with his heart racing in his chest at five hundred miles an hour. He looked into her eyes for what seemed like hours though he knew only moments had passed. "I'm sorry I didn't see what kind of person you were long ago so I could've gotten out before it came to this. Why couldn't you just tell me you weren't interested in being married anymore? We could've tried to work things out, and if that didn't work, I would've given you the divorce you wanted. But to do this … I don't know what to say." Jon shrugged. "What would you like me to say?"

"I don't know."

This close, he could smell cologne on her. *His* cologne. Whether they'd had sex or not didn't matter. He didn't believe anything she said, especially that she was sorry, because if she truly was sorry, they wouldn't be standing here having this conversation. She never would've done what Craig said she did.

"I have to go. I can't stay here tonight." He moved past her, heading to the front door.

"Where are you going?"

With his hand on the doorknob, he stared at the door. He

had no idea where he was going, but he couldn't stay here with her. Even if she said she'd sleep on the couch, he would still leave. On the other hand, why should he leave? "Nowhere." His hand came away from the door. "I'm not the one leaving." He walked back to the chair and sat down. "You are."

"I—"

The phone rang.

"I wonder who that could be?" Jon went to lift the receiver.

"Don't answer it." Alyssa came toward him, but stopped when he glared at her.

"Why not? It might be important." He lifted the receiver but didn't say anything.

Alyssa looked puzzled. "Aren't you going to—"

"Ally, did you make it in time?" Craig's drunken voice came over the phone.

"No, she didn't." Jon's teeth clenched. "But don't worry, she's just leaving to come back to your place. Turns out it was too late when she got home. I already heard the message. She's all yours."

"Oh, shit. Jon? Man, I'm sorry. I was just screwing around. Nothing happened. I thought I was calling one of my friends and busting on them."

"On her cell phone? Do you always keep your friend's numbers on her phone?" This was absurd. He should tell Craig to go fuck himself and get off the phone. Then he could send Alyssa on her way back to him.

"I thought it was my cell—"

"You know what, Craig, go fuck yourself. Don't try to apologize because it's a load of shit to me." He hung up and turned to Alyssa. "Get out. Go back to Craig's, go to your mother's. I don't care. Just get out of here."

Alyssa opened her mouth to say something.

"You better be saying good-bye because I don't want to hear anything else out of your mouth."

The few tears turned to earnest crying. She said, "Good-bye," and ran out of the apartment.

He closed the apartment door, sat down in the chair next to the phone, and wept until he fell asleep.

BETTIE

Laughing Jezebel had finished their final set at close to one in the morning. She wouldn't get in bed until close to two and had to be up at seven. Except she would be too wound up to fall asleep for at least another hour. Four hours of sleep. She'd be a zombie again, but did she really need to be much more? Probably have to help Jon again. Shit. But at this point, she had no choice.

Helping Angelina pack the drums, she couldn't wait to get home.

"This shit's killing me," Angelina said. She was a tall, muscular woman in her late twenties. "Work's a fuck and I'm not worth shit without sleep." She slid the bass drum into her van.

Handing the snare drum to Angelina, Bettie rolled her eyes. "You work at a tattoo parlor, hon. You pierce people's parts. That's more exciting than sitting at a desk."

"No shit." Angelina laughed. "Which reminds me—hand me that snare over there, will ya?—when are you coming to get a clit ring?"

Bettie rolled her eyes. "I'm not. We've had this discussion. No clit rings. There are some parts of the body that should never be pierced."

Angelina stopped packing the van. All the fun was gone from her face. "And there are parts of the body that shouldn't be cut, either." She shook her head. "You talking to anyone?"

Bettie shook her head. She just wanted to get home. The last thing she wanted to do was get into a "head" conversation with anyone, especially Angelina.

"Why aren't you?"

"Can we just load this crap and get out of here?"

"Do you like having scars on your thighs?" Angelina took a cymbal stand and threw it alongside the drum stands. "Wouldn't you like to wear real short skirts and have men stare at your legs for your legs and not the cuts?"

Bettie wondered how to get out of the conversation gracefully without hurting Angelina's feelings. Though she appreciated the woman trying to help her, it was way too late to get into this discussion. She hefted the case and brought it to Angelina. "I'd love to be able to wear short skirts, Angie, and I know what I'm doing isn't smart, but can we have this conversation some other time, maybe a few hours earlier in the day?"

"Sure." Angelina took the case. "Hey, baby, I'm just trying to help a fellow soul. So long as we have that conversation before you start cutting anywhere else. You know, like your wrists or your throat. It's all I'm asking."

"Sure. I don't plan on ending my life just yet."

"That's good." Karalynn had her mini-keys under her arm. "'Cause there's still too much equipment to load and we can't afford to lose you."

"Thanks," Bettie said. "I appreciate the love. Can I ask you guys something?"

Both Angelina and Karalynn stopped what they were doing. At that moment Nica came out with her guitar case. "We having a moment of silence or something?" Her English accent made her sound like she was always singing her words. "Should I go back inside or kneel in prayer?"

"Bettie was about to ask us something profound," Karalynn said.

Nica set her case down. "Let's hear it, babe."

"I met a guy at work today and—"

"Ah, one of those questions." Nica grinned. "I'd say if you let him once, he'll always think he can. Make him wait."

Bettie smirked and shook her head. "Not quite the answer I wanted, but I'll keep that in mind anyway."

Nica laughed. "Good girl, listening to Nica. She always knows what she's talking about."

"Go on," Angelina said.

"I met this guy at work. He seems nice, a bit shy, but really nice. Except he's got a ring on." She waggled her left hand ring finger.

"That's a bitch," Angelina said.

"You're not talking about the guy at the show, are you?" Karalynn asked. "The one you were talking to?"

"That's him."

"And he came to the show to see you?" Nica asked. "How sweet!"

"No, he was wandering around the city and stopped in. He had no idea I was here."

"But he stayed," Karalynn said. "That's something."

"He's married, though." Nica shook her head. "I don't know, hon. Sounds like more trouble than he's worth."

"Is he happy in his marriage?" Karalynn asked.

Angelina laughed. "Who the hell is happy in their marriage?" Hefting the last of her drum kit into the van, she grunted, shouted, "Fuck me!" and shoved the case in. She turned back to the rest of the band. "I was married for three wasted years, and by the middle of it, all I wanted was some guy to come along so I could fuck somebody else and listen to him make promises I knew he couldn't keep just so I could get out of the damned marriage. And it worked." She looked straight at Bettie. "If you think this guy'll be good for you, I say the hell with the wife. Go for it. And I'll tell you why, Bettie. If he goes for you, then he doesn't give a shit about his marriage. If he's tight with his wife, then he'll say no." She shrugged. "It's fucking late. I'm outta here." She gave the other women a quick kiss on the cheek, Bettie last. "Keep me up to date on this, will you? I've got shit going on, so I'm going to have to live vicariously through you."

Bettie said, "I'll let you know what happens."

After Angelina got in the van and left, Bettie weighed the worth of her words. The truth was that she'd put herself in situations to test herself, never intending anything to happen. The last thing she needed was some jerk breaking her heart because he was trying to see if he could be tempted. But Jon didn't seem like a jerk at all. Quite the opposite. More like a lost soul looking for someone or something.

"Well, is he happy?" Karalynn asked.

"He only started today. I just met him."

Nica came up beside her. "Did he mention his wife at all tonight?"

"No. He's a writer and he said he had a lot on his mind and needed to go for a walk."

"He lives in New York City?" Karalynn asked.

"No, he drove here and started walking around."

"Wait a minute." Nica held her hand up like she was stopping traffic. "Let me get this straight. You meet a guy at work today, and of all places he winds up at our show? If that ain't fate, hon, I don't know what is." She looked at her watch. "What it is, is way late and I've got to go. I'll see you tomorrow night at the Orange Lantern, right?"

"Sure." Bettie smiled and waved. "I've gotta go, too."

"Tomorrow night it is," Karalynn said.

As she walked into her little apartment in Hoboken, Bettie contemplated what Angelina had said, as well as Veronica's words. Fate. Did she even believe in fate? It was an awful coincidence that Jon wound up at the same place she and the band were playing. What were the chances of that happening?

. She undressed and went to the mirror, looking at herself, at her scars, wishing she could take them back and her skin would be unblemished. She ran her fingers over the pink slices and wondered what Jon would think of them. Would he understand or be scared off or say he didn't notice them? Would she let him in that close? If he was willing to come that close, would she keep him back?

He's married, Bettie. There's no way anything's going to happen between you. Even if you let him in as close as you've ever let anyone, he won't go that far. He can't.

Turning away from the mirror, she slipped into a pair of silk shorts and silk tank top. Then she shut the lights and climbed into bed.

"I kissed him," she said out loud, staring at the white ceiling. "Why did I kiss him?" But she knew the answer. She'd wanted to, and the adrenaline from performing made her do it. Had she kissed him on the lips, it would've felt good afterward and she would've been high for the rest of the show, but come tomorrow at work, it would've been damned awkward. As it was, things might still be a bit awkward. After all, she'd kissed him after knowing him for only eight hours. "I'm not really that desperate. Am I?" Rolling over, she closed her eyes and waited for sleep. "Not desperate. Just lonely." Then sleep took her away.

IN THE DARK: BERNIE

He came to in one of the air ducts and blinked, unsure if he was blind or not. But then he realized there would be no light in the ducts, so it was just complete darkness. Even when he held his hand up in front of his face, he couldn't see it.

"Shit." The duct was tight, but not tight enough he couldn't move. So he rolled on his stomach and crawled. He had no idea where he was going, but any place was better than where he was. He had crawled maybe twenty feet when he heard a sound he didn't understand. Metal scraped metal, and the sound moved toward him. Not a single sound but multiplied several times. The cables that had pulled him into the ceiling had blunt ends, but they were still metal cables. That's what he assumed the sound was. But because the duct echoed every sound, he couldn't tell if it came from in front, behind, or above him. Instead of waiting to see what happened, he continued on, hoping to come to a vent or something to give him some idea of where he was.

The first cable caught him around the ankle and dragged him back. The second one, with a knife-like edge, slit his shirt open and sliced his back from his waist to his shoulder.

He gritted his teeth. "Son of a bitch." He rolled over, feeling the cold metal on his back and tried grabbing the cable that had cut him, but it moved too quickly and he was going by feel alone. It coiled around his wrist and pinned his arm to his side. One thing was for certain: they didn't need any light to find him.

Three more cables brushed over his legs and torso. Then they centered on a point right below his sternum. The three cables sliced into his flesh and cut outward. He screamed from the intense pain. Hot blood pooled on his stomach and ran down his side. With his free hand he grabbed one of the cables and held it away from him. It wriggled like a fish, but he didn't let go.

The other two cables cut into his arm, not deep, but enough to make him flinch and let go. With one leg and one arm held fast, all he could do was lie there and let the cables slice his arms and legs. He tried his best to swat them away but they moved too fast—like snakes.

He felt consciousness leaving him from the pain, but just when he thought the cables would finish him off, they disappeared. One minute they were leaving little slices all over his skin and the next they were gone. The ones holding him slithered away into the darkness.

"Keep yourself together," he mumbled. "Don't pass out now." Though he knew he had to do something, he rested for the moment. He had little strength to do anything other than breathe. But soon he'd start crawling again and, God willing, he'd find a means of escape or at least a way to defend himself.

He wondered if this was what happened to Sharon, if she lay dead somewhere in the building, bled to death by cables that had to be controlled by someone. But who? Even Leo wasn't capable of something like this.

The first thing Bernie had to do was get out. After that he'd figure out some kind of plan. In the meantime, he hoped Leo had called the police and told them what happened. He was afraid that because of Leo's prior run-ins with the police, he'd flee the building and never call them. But there was no way the police could blame Leo for this. They probably wouldn't believe him. That was the bigger problem. And if they didn't believe him, they might not come and investigate.

He was exhausted, and his thoughts started going in circles. He'd rest and then start crawling again. Hopefully, he'd make it out alive and wouldn't end up as another dead body in the air duct. He prayed Sharon was still alive, but he had his doubts. If she had been pulled into the ceiling on Tuesday, she was probably dead by now. If only he had known, he could've tried finding her. Marcy had said something about cables attacking her and Paul, and he thought she was just stressed out by Paul's advances.

Stupid, Bernie. You should've believed her.

And then darkness descended fully, stripping him of consciousness.

FRIDAY

MARCY

The sound was like a fire alarm, urgent and insistent, but it didn't help Marcy get out of bed. Instead, she rolled over, hit the snooze button, said "leave me alone," and closed her eyes. But the sound continued, and Marcy realized it was the phone, not her alarm. "Who's calling so early?" She rolled over. Why wasn't the answering machine picking up? "Damn." She reached across the bed and picked up the receiver, almost dropping it. "Hello?"

The dull *ba-dum* of a generator filled her ear, then creaking, like someone speaking so slow it wasn't words but a sound. It chilled her and she hung up.

In the living room, the television came on.

Marcy gasped and listened for footsteps. Her first thought was that Paul had found her. She moved to the side of the bed and got the Smith & Wesson from the nightstand. Whoever it was, they were in for one rude awakening. Sitting on the edge of the bed, she held the pistol in both hands, her finger on the trigger, and waited.

There were no footsteps. No voices. No sound other than the TV with the volume too low for her to hear what was on. It was a low mumble of indistinguishable words.

She stayed on the edge of the bed, her grip on the pistol tightened against the sweat that made the handle slippery. But she wouldn't let it slip from her hand, not if there was a chance Paul had broken into her apartment and was waiting in the living room for her.

Five minutes had elapsed since the phone had rung and the television had come on. It was a waiting game. Who would outwait the other? She should call the police and not try to play the hero. If she threatened him with the gun and he came at her, would she be able to pull the trigger? Better to be safe and call the police. Just like five years ago when Jess had broken into the house and attacked her. The restraining order meant nothing to him. He was on coke and fearless, and the police had taken too long. But Paul wasn't an addict, just single-minded and stupid.

Out in the living room, the television volume jumped up. Now Marcy could hear what was on, and coldness seeped through her body, leaving gooseflesh on her arms. That insane creaking voice sounded, as if who or whatever made the sound was in the apartment. Someone pounded on the wall, yelling, "Turn that down! Do you know what time it is?"

Marcy dropped the gun, covered her ears, fell to her knees, and shouted "Stop it!" over and over.

Silence.

Wiping away tears she hadn't realized she'd shed, Marcy listened to the cold, empty silence. She checked her alarm clock to see how much time had gone by, but it was dark. Underneath the bed the plug was still in the wall, which meant the problem wasn't with the clock.

The gun lay next to her. She picked it up and stood on shaky legs. Her breath was ragged, and her heart beat like a hummingbird's wings. She wished she was dressed already and not in the pink nightshirt she'd slipped into after the bath. If someone was in her apartment, she wasn't wasting time to change. She'd just have to deal with him as she was, though she felt exposed and vulnerable, dressed as she was with only the gun to protect her.

She thought to call out to see if it was Paul, but she didn't want to let whoever was out there know where she was, so she stayed silent, praying that she saw him before he found her.

It's all right, Marcy. We can handle this. We handled Jess.

Taking painfully slow steps, she made her way down the hall toward the living room.

We killed Jess.

The sound of a mechanical heartbeat, like a huge generator, was barely audible; the creaking voice was silent.

He deserved it.

Five feet away from where the hallway wall ended, she paused. Her breathing was the only other sound besides the television.

We can handle anything.

Was there someone here? If the TV came on, there had better be; televisions didn't come on by themselves.

The Ladysmith was heavy in her hands and her fingers ached from holding the pistol so tightly, but she wouldn't let it go. She knew to aim low to take out his legs; she didn't want to kill anyone, Paul included.

She held her breath and covered the last five feet in several quick steps. The wall ended. The living room opened up. No one. But—

She dropped the gun and screamed.

On the television screen was a mockery of Sharon's face, the silhouette revealed, and when the thing opened its mouth, all that came out was the horrible creaking noise. The face had been Sharon's, but now it was ruined. One eye socket oozed a whitish fluid while the other eye was sunken in like her cheeks. The skin was pasty, bruised black and purple and covered with holes as if someone had used construction nails for acupuncture. Her lips looked as if they had been cut away as they tried forming words but failed.

"Stop it!" Marcy turned away and squeezed her eyes shut, but the flickering picture of her friend stayed like an afterimage.

Abruptly, the creaking sound vanished.

Marcy crumpled to the floor weeping, unable to get Sharon's once-beautiful face out of her mind. "I can't ..."

The phone rang three times before the answering machine clicked on. Marcy stared at the phone, waiting to hear who it was. When silence answered she wasn't surprised. When a woman's voice creaked over the phone and finally said a word, Marcy broke down and sobbed. The voice was Sharon's. The word: *help.*

JON

Jon woke up and realized he was alone in his bed for the first time in five years, and he wanted to feel bad, to feel lonely. But he didn't. Bettie's kiss lingered in his mind, and though he knew he should be concerned about his marriage and working things out with Alyssa, he looked forward to seeing Bettie again while he felt nothing but rage for Alyssa.

The marriage was over. Before last night he had wanted to try to fix what was broken, but now, any interest in making their marriage work was history.

He got out of bed; no matter how he felt, he had to go to work. He'd have lunch with Tony and Junior again, and there was Bettie to keep him distracted. Would she explain the kiss or not mention it? He contemplated saying something, but didn't want to make her feel uncomfortable.

After showering, Jon went to the kitchen, poured himself a glass of orange juice, realized he had no time for anything else, and decided to get something to eat on the way. He dressed and left the apartment.

In the lobby, he signed in. Glen wasn't there, but another, older guard sat behind the desk flipping through the latest *Entertainment Weekly*. Jon smiled, said "hello," and went to the elevator where another man waited. They got on at the same time and the man went to push the 5 button, but seeing Jon had already pressed it, stepped back.

"You don't work at Dasher Financials, do you?" The man was in his fifties, thin and fit, dressed in a gray suit. He had a natural smile.

The elevator doors slid shut.

"Osprey Publishing. I'm a temp. Started yesterday."

The elevator began its rickety ascent.

"You didn't look familiar. Name's Ted Bacon." He grinned and held his hand out.

"Jon Simon. Nice to meet you." He shook his hand, a firm handshake.

The elevator trembled as it rose.

"This is some old building," Bacon said.

"It feels old."

"I think it was originally built in the 1920s."

"Wow, that old."

"There've been so many renovations done to this place. I don't know why they don't tear it down and put up a more modern building. I know the neighborhood is fairly old, but still ... they could make it look as old as they want. This place needs to be torn down before it falls down." He laughed.

The elevator stopped. The doors opened.

"Boy, it's dark," Bacon said.

Jon looked up at the row of floor numbers. The 2 was illuminated. "This is the second floor."

"Why'd we stop here?" Bacon leaned over and pressed the door close button, but the doors stayed open.

"That's strange. The same thing happened to me yesterday, but the elevator stopped on the fourth floor. No one was there, but I had the feeling someone was watching me. The doors closed eventually and it went up."

Bacon pressed the Door Close button again. "I guess we'll give it a moment or two and then wa—"

Outside, somewhere in the dark reception area, something clattered like plastic on cement.

"What was that?" Bacon asked.

Jon had the same feeling of being watched, but from where he stood, he couldn't see anyone. "Maybe we should take the stairs."

"It's only three flights up." Bacon got out of the elevator and Jon followed.

As soon as Jon stepped into the reception area, the elevator doors closed.

"It figures," Bacon said.

Red emergency lights winked on, bathing the area in bloodred light.

"What's going on?"

"I don't know, but we should get to the stairs." Jon hurried to the stairwell door, turned the handle, and pushed, but the door didn't open. The feeling of being watched intensified as if the person had moved from behind a closed door. He glanced over his shoulder, but beyond Ted, there was nothing but red shadows.

"The door won't open." He threw his weight against it, but it didn't budge. "I think it's locked."

"There aren't any offices here; that would make sense. I guess it's back to the elevator."

"All right. Hopefully we won't be stuck here too—"

"Jesus."

"What?" Jon turned from the door and froze. Tony, deformed and crippled, shambled toward them. At least Jon thought it was Tony. The man's eyes were sunken and faintly glowing; it looked like every bone in his body was broken. "Tony? Is that you?"

The other man didn't speak, just stared at Ted as if he hadn't heard Jon.

"He's dead," Ted stated.

"What? No, he's not. He can't be." Jon shook his head. "Tony, what happened to you?" His friend couldn't be dead, though he looked ... shattered. Things like this didn't happen in real life, Jon thought. Maybe in bad horror movies, but not in the real world. "Tony!"

"Jon, I don't think he hears you."

Tony threw himself at Bacon, knocking him to the ground, and then fell on him, wrapping pale hands around the man's throat. Ted screamed as smoke rose from where Tony's hands strangled him, filling the reception area with the stench of burning flesh.

Two nights ago they had played pool together, Jon was there when Jenny was born, he had been Tony's best man and Tony had been his; they'd known each since high school and now ...

"Help me!" Ted shouted.

That snapped Jon out of his reverie. "Tony, what are you doing?" Jon winced, felt his stomach twist from the stink, but ignored it and rushed to pull Tony away from Ted. He reached for him, but an electric charge surrounding the two of them stopped him. "What the hell ..." The closer he came, the stronger the current got until the surge forced him back. "Tony, stop it! You're killing him!"

Tony looked around as if something had disturbed him, but he didn't see it. Jon was right next to him, yet Tony looked right through him as if he wasn't there. Then he turned his attention back to Ted, tightening his grip on the man's throat. The stench worsened as the smoke thickened. Ted screamed in agony, writhing under Tony's burning hands.

Jon's vision blurred. His friend was gone, replaced by this mockery bent on killing Bacon, and Jon didn't know what to do. He looked around for a weapon. The area was clear of debris except for a fire extinguisher on the far wall, which he yanked from its alcove. Tony alternately choked Ted, let him go, then choked him again. Jon hesitated; he didn't want to hurt his friend, or what was left of him, because surely some part of Tony was still in there. But this wasn't the Tony he knew. This was ... something dangerous that had no compunction about killing.

Heedless of the shock effect, Jon rushed at Tony, ready to swing the extinguisher at him. *It's not Tony,* he told himself. When he slammed into the electric energy surrounding the creature, he had no doubt it wasn't the friend he had known. He kept moving forward as the jolts of electricity wrapped around him and made him falter. He was so close but the pain was intensifying, enveloping him like angry bees. Though he had been stung only once in his life, he knew this was what it would feel like to be in the middle of a swarm of killer bees.

As much as he wanted a point-blank shot at Tony's head, he couldn't get any closer without suffering worse. He would have to take his chances from here and hope it was enough. "I'm sorry, Tony." Hefting the extinguisher, he threw it, aiming for Tony's head.

It struck the creature in the temple, and for a few seconds Jon thought Tony was going over, but the thing just stared at the extinguisher and then *through* Jon. For whatever reason, Tony couldn't see him. He saw it when Tony frowned, disappointed there was no one there. The thing opened its mouth as if wanting to speak, but all that came out was a strange creaking sound as if it couldn't form words properly. It reminded him of old door hinges and was the same noise he'd heard in the stairwell yesterday. He'd never heard anyone make such a sound. Was Tony—or whatever the thing was—in pain?

It picked up the fire extinguisher and in one fluid motion brought it down on Ted Bacon's face.

"No!" Jon took a step too late.

The weight and force of the extinguisher crushed Bacon's face with a sickening crunch. Jon backed away, refusing to look at the trembling body, unable to believe what had happened.

The thing that was Tony stared down at Ted, then looked around the room as if searching for anyone else. Satisfied it was alone, it staggered off into the darkness at the far end of the hall.

Jon watched Tony walk away. The extinguisher covered Ted's ruined face; Jon wouldn't go anywhere near Bacon. The body convulsed several more times before it was still.

The elevator doors opened.

Jon was torn between helping his former friend—it wasn't Tony anymore—and fleeing to the stairs. He went to the stairs and found the door opened with no trouble. In the stairwell, his world spun and he had to sit down. Tony was dead, but he wasn't. But he was ... what happened to him? The way he had staggered and lurched had made him look like his whole body was broken. Tears came to Jon's eyes. This wasn't happening. But even now, the stink of burning flesh reminded him that a man lay dead out in the reception area. He had to get upstairs and warn the others.

By the time he reached the fifth floor, Jon was out of breath and almost fell over when he shoved the stairwell door open. He went straight to Bernie's office to find the door locked.

"He's not here."

Jon looked at Sheila. "What? Where is he? I have to tell him what just happened."

"You look a wreck. Why don't you sit down in my office and tell me."

"Call the police. Ted Bacon's been murdered on the second floor."

"What?"

"Please, just ... let's go back to your office."

She turned but gave Jon a curious look over her shoulder. "This way."

In Sheila's office, Jon was only too glad to drop into one of the chairs. This was a cubicle, unlike the office Bernie had. But she had turned it into a home away from home with photos of cats, children, and a particularly attractive woman.

"Now. Start again. Tell me what happened."

Jon didn't want to start at the beginning. He wanted to tell her to call the police immediately because Ted Bacon from Dasher Financials was dead. But Sheila would just keep interrupting him to force him to start at the beginning. So he told her about meeting Ted in the elevator and how it stopped on the second floor. He repeated how when they got out, Tony was there, but he looked messed up, like he'd been in a bad fight or worse.

"You saw Tony?" Sheila interrupted. "Tony who works here?"

"Yes, but he was all beat up. His arm and his legs were twisted like they were broken and ..." Remembering his friend, ruined and shattered, Jon couldn't go on. It was bad enough he'd lost Alyssa, but now to lose Tony, as well, was too much for him.

"I don't understand. I saw Tony before I left yesterday and he was fine."

"Well, he's not fine anymore." Jon explained what he'd just been through and even as he told Sheila, the experience didn't seem real.

Sheila stared at him in disbelief.

"Okay. So that sounds nuts." This was only his second day at the job and the first real conversation he'd had with Sheila. What was she thinking of him? "How about this? I just saw Tony kill a man with a fire extinguisher."

"I ... I don't know what to say. Tony's worked here for years and I've never known him to be violent."

"I've known him longer and you're right, but that doesn't change what happened."

"I'll call Security and have them check the second floor." Sheila picked up the phone. "What is that noise?"

Even from this distance, Jon heard the eerie creaking voice

that sounded like Tony coming through the receiver. "That's the same sound Tony made. It sounded like he couldn't speak or was trying to say something and couldn't form words."

Sheila pressed the Hang-up button and released it. The sound was still there, so she hung up and took out her cell phone. "No signal? That's impossible. I always have a signal in here." She sighed. "Hey, Patti?"

"Yeah?"

"Check your phone. Do you have a dial tone?"

"Jesus. What is *that*? No. I have some sort of ... I don't know what it is."

"Thanks." She glanced at Jon. "The phone connections are in the basement."

"Of course they are."

"It's infected the electrical system as well as the phones." Sara stood outside Sheila's office.

"What are you talking about?" Sheila frowned. "What's infected the phones?"

"The living energy." She glanced at Jon. "It's what I told you about. The being has insinuated itself into the building's systems so it can control everything."

Sheila sighed. "Sara—"

"I know what you're thinking, Sheila, and that's fine. I'm crazy. But the being is here, and it's taken people into the ductwork. It's killed people to inhabit them, to understand what we are."

"Sara, please." She rubbed her forehead as if trying to massage away an oncoming headache. "I don't think you're crazy, but right now I need to think clearly and you're not helping."

Sara came into the office and slammed her fists on the desk. "Listen to me. Everyone here thinks I'm crazy, and I don't give a damn. But people are dying because a monster is experimenting on us to see how scared we can be and ..."

Sheila glared at Sara. "How do you know this? Do you talk to this monster? Does it talk to you? Does it tell you when it's going to kill people? Because if it has and you haven't said anything—"

"I *feel* it. I know it's here. I sense its intentions, but it doesn't talk to me and I can't tell you what it's going to do next."

"You've got to be kidding me." Sheila lifted the phone and heard the same creaking sound. "How can you sense its intentions but not know what it's going to do?"

"It feeds on our fear. It didn't used to, but something's wrong with it and now it's realized how nourishing our fear is."

"So what? It's scaring us to eat our fear? Sara, do you have any idea how that sounds?"

"Of course I do. I hear people whispering about me. I'm not deaf, and I'm not stupid. Everyone thinks I'm crazy because I'm sensitive to things other people can't begin to comprehend. But it doesn't matter. What matters is that this monster has to be stopped or else it's going to keep attacking us."

"How do we do that?" Sheila asked.

"I don't know."

"You don't—" Sheila stopped, exasperated. "If you know what this thing is, why don't you know how to kill it?"

"It's not like that." Sara sat down next to Jon. "I'm aware of this being's existence and I'm aware of its hunger and how it sees us as nothing more than food. But I don't know what it is."

"All right. This is getting us nowhere. Right now, the phones aren't working and the quickest way to fix that is to go to the basement and check the phone box."

Jon shook his head. "But—"

Sheila held her hand up. "No offense, Jon, but I don't know you at all. I'm not saying you're making up what you saw, but I can't believe Tony would kill someone."

"You're saying I'm lying?"

Sheila hesitated before replying. "No, Jon, I don't think you're lying." She looked from Jon to Sara. "I don't know what to think anymore. This is crazy. I'm not calling you crazy, Sara. But whatever it is that you both say is happening … I don't know what to make of it. Right now, I want to go find out what's wrong with the phones." She held her hand up to keep either Sara or Jon from saying anything else. "You're coming with me." Standing, she waved them to their feet. "Let's go."

Jon nodded and followed Sheila and Sara out of the office.

He wanted to ask Sheila where Bernie was but never got the chance. He hoped he was all right. The three of them headed to the stairwell. They had just passed the fourth floor landing when the lights went out.

BETTIE

Jon was too far ahead for her to catch up, even though she really wanted to talk about last night. When she woke up, a mild headache clouding her mind, she remembered very clearly kissing him on the cheek at some point in the night. The question was whether that was a bad thing or not. Obviously she wanted to kiss him or she wouldn't have. But why did she want to and, more importantly, how did he take it?

He was married. What more was there? No matter what she had said to Marcy yesterday, Bettie never played games with married men; it was a no-win situation. She had been put in situations by married men who were looking for extracurricular activities, and as soon as she found out they were married, she gracefully—and once or twice not so gracefully—backed out.

Bettie waved at the security guard and realized it wasn't Glen. "Good morning."

"Morning," the older man said.

She tapped the Up arrow and waited, wondering where Glen was. Having just missed Jon, she also missed the elevator that was taking him up to the fifth floor. She debated taking the stairs, but was too tired to make the effort, so she waited for the elevator to return.

While she leaned against the wall, trying to figure out how she'd make it through the day, she caught the guard staring at her legs. The skirt was a little longer than her usual; today she was self-conscious of her scars. But it was still short enough to catch even an old man's eyes.

After waiting for what seemed like ten minutes, she gave up and went to the stairwell, where she looked up at the five flights of stairs and groaned. It would be worse if the building had ten stories and Osprey was at the top. At least it was only five flights.

She considered taking her heels off. In bare feet it wouldn't hurt as much by the time she got to the fourth floor, but she didn't want to rip her stockings on the concrete steps. It was better to keep the shoes on and take it slow.

On the second floor landing, she paused to rest; her schedule had to change, though she refused to give up the rock-star lifestyle. If only she could find a job that started later than nine, it would be better. Then she could keep gigging with the band and still get a respectable amount of sleep. As she rubbed her tired feet, she thought of life without Laughing Jezebel. Not an option. Those women were her best friends, and if she lost the band, all she'd have left was Osprey, a dead-end temp job with no future. She'd keep the band and ...

Someone was in the stairwell coming up. She froze, and without knowing why, wanted to hide. But she forced herself to stay until the good-looking guy, someone she didn't know, reached the landing.

"Good morning," he said, his voice smooth and deep.

"Morning." She smiled at him and watched him walk past.

He had gone three steps up the next flight.

"Oh, shit!" His briefcase fell and landed at Bettie's feet.

When she looked at him, he held onto both banisters to keep his balance. Was he drunk or ... His feet were gone. He was ankle-deep on the stairs as if they had turned to quicksand, swallowed his feet, and then semi-hardened again.

"What—what the hell's going on?" He stared down where his feet had been.

Bettie stared in wonder and shock. *This doesn't happen. Stairs don't do this.*

He turned as much as he could and looked down at Bettie. "Help me."

"I don't know what to do." She came up to the first step and paused; she wouldn't take the chance of getting herself stuck.

"Then get help! Don't just stand there!"

It wasn't her imagination that he was sinking into the stairs. He had sunk up to midcalf.

"*Please.* For God's sake, get help!"

The only person she thought could help was Leo, but even if

he was in his office, that was three flights down. Would the guy still be there? The longer she stood staring, the less chance there was he would be there when she returned.

Taking her heels off, she hurried to the first floor lobby, ran across to the basement door, and pulled. It wouldn't open.

"Hey!" she called to the security guard. "Why's this door locked?"

"It's not locked. Just give it a good tug."

She tried, but it wouldn't budge. "It's locked."

"Sheezus." The man came around his security desk and shuffled in Bettie's direction.

"Have you seen Leo this morning?"

"Who?" The guard reached for the door and pulled. He grimaced and pulled harder. "Hm. That's strange. They told me this should be open."

"Leo, the maintenance guy."

"I'm sorry, miss. I don't know who he is. This is my first day. Glen didn't call in this morning and—"

"What do you mean, Glen didn't call in?" She let go of the door and stared at the new security guard.

"He didn't call in. That's all."

"Did anyone call him to make sure he was all right?"

The guard looked quizzically at Bettie. "I'm sure someone did." He pulled on the door again to no avail. "I don't get it. Let me call Maintenance. You said his name was Leo?"

"Yes." Bettie hurried back to the desk while the security guard took his time as if he had all day to make it back. "Look, I'm sorry, but there's an emergency on the second floor. A man—"

"Second floor? There're no companies on the second floor." The guard shook his head as he came around and picked up the phone.

Bettie restrained her desire to reach out and choke the life out of the old idiot. "I know that. The emergency is in the stairwell at the second floor."

"Someone fall?" He paused in mid-dial. "Because Maintenance ain't gonna help with that."

Hands clenched into fists, Bettie glared at the guard. "I know that."

"Then what'cha need Maintenance for?" The guard scowled at her.

Bettie was struck by the utter absurdity of the conversation. Someone was sinking into the steps as if they were quicksand, and she was arguing with an old man who refused to listen to her. "There's a man caught in the stairs on the second floor and—"

"Caught in the stairs? What do you mean?" Now it was his turn to stare in disbelief.

As impossible as it was, she had seen it with her own eyes. "A man—I don't know who he is—is stuck in the stairs and he's sinking."

"Ma'am, are you sure you didn't hit your head?"

"You think I'm making this up? Give me that." Snatching the phone from his hand, she leaned over and dialed Leo's extension.

"Hey! You can't do that!"

"Shut up!" Bettie waited for Leo to pick up. Several people passed the desk, stared at her, and either took the elevator or the stairs. Well, unless she was dreaming, someone else would come running down very soon.

Leo's answering machine came on. "Come on, Leo. Pick up the phone." But he didn't, nor did the answering machine beep. Instead, the creaking voice filled her ear. She gasped and dropped the phone at the same time someone screamed in the stairwell.

"What the hell?" The security guard came around his desk and went straight for the stairs. He paused, looked up, and went in. Bettie followed behind him, knowing what they'd see. Several people stood on the second floor landing. The man on the stairs begged the onlookers to help him, for God's sake, *help him*. He'd sunk to midthigh and was still sinking.

"Sheezus." The guard scratched his head. "I've never seen anything like that."

"Don't just stand there!" Bettie shouted, her voice echoing around the stairwell. "Call the fire department."

"What good are they going to do?" the guard asked. He came close to the sinking man, but not too close. "How'd this happen?"

"I came up the stairs and they turned to ... I don't know what." The man turned as best he could to look at the guard. "Please *help* me!"

More people had gathered in the stairwell, some she'd seen around the building, some she didn't know. They all gawked at the sinking man, but none of them made a move to help or try to pass.

The building wasn't just haunted, Bettie thought, it was ... possessed. That noise on the phone was the voice of the thing that possessed the building. This was something way beyond anything she could've imagined, and maybe the best thing for everyone was to just get out.

But she didn't want to start a riot. Somewhere above her a door opened and people started down the stairs. She was about to yell to them to get out of the stairwell when it was plunged into darkness.

LEO

The crowbar was cold and heavy in his hands, but if he had any hope of finding Bernie—one of the only people who gave a crap about him—he'd need something to defend himself with. He didn't own a gun, and the steak knives would be useless; only guns and axes were useful against zombies. Of course he hoped to be in and out before he ran into Tony, but just in case the worse came to worst, he was ready.

The problem that Leo slowly came to realize was that he had no idea how to find Bernie without getting himself snatched up. He certainly didn't want to crawl in the ductwork because he didn't know what else was up there. Wherever that electrical thing came from, it was probably still around. If it could travel throughout the building, then Bernie and Sharon, and whomever else the thing took, could be anywhere. He needed another plan, and he needed one fast, before the shit hit the fan and Tony found him.

What surprised him was that the police hadn't come back. Surely the other company managers had called the police when their employees didn't show up for work. He hoped after the police had harassed him the other day, they did the same with everyone else in the building so they'd have to know there were other people missing. What the hell were they doing about it?

He went to the phone in his office and picked it up to dial the police. As much as he hated bringing them into this—because, even if they found everyone and the killer electrical thing, he'd somehow get blamed for it—he couldn't do nothing. Better to leave this to the pros than to try to be some kind of hero and wind up dead. *Or worse ... a zombie.*

There was no dial tone, only that creepy-ass voice creaking away like it couldn't speak properly. Leo hung up; he didn't want the thing to know where he was. But it probably did know and was right now coming to get him. He should get out of the building. He wanted to save Bernie, but he couldn't do it dead. Plain and simple.

"Christ alive." He looked around his office as if something would help him. But help him do what? He had no clear idea of what he was up against except that he'd seen Tony floating up the elevator shaft and had seen him again later as some kind of zombie. And then something had snatched Bernie. He hadn't even seen it. But one minute Bernie was there and the next he wasn't.

How's Tony involved in all this? Is he really a zombie?

No, you dumbass, those are only in movies.

Well, he sure as shit looked like a zombie.

The memory of Tony floating up into the elevator shaft made Leo shudder. He'd heard the man scream and then the sound of his body hitting the floor. By the time he'd gotten there and opened the doors, Tony was already floating up. *Floating,* for Christ's sake. People just didn't float. Maybe whatever snatched Bernie also made Tony look like he floated in the shaft, but he was really being carried or pulled up.

Some ... thing had taken Tony and turned him into this staggering and shambling creature that looked an awful lot like a Grade-A, George A. freakin' Romero zombie. That kind of shit didn't happen in real life. If Tony had fallen down the shaft, then he'd be dead. So that meant he was a reanimated corpse. A freakin' zombie.

He searched around the office again; there had to be something he could defend himself with other than the crowbar in case he ran into Tony, the reanimated corpse, again or, worse, the thing that had reanimated him. The more he thought of Tony, the more he realized the crowbar was pointless.

Why in the name of God would something reanimate the dead?

To take over the planet.

So it snatches people up, kills them, then reanimates them?

It was that thing in my room. That … creature or whatever it was that's responsible for all of this, I bet.

Yeah? So now what?

Yeah. Now what?

The thing seemed to be made of energy or electricity. What about water? If he cut the power to the building, would that stop it or slow it down or have no effect at all? If it could move through the electrical system and he shut the breakers, then it would be trapped wherever it was. Unless it went into the phone lines. If only he knew more about what it was, then he'd have a better idea of how to stop it. After seeing Tony on Bernie's computer, he figured the thing could do anything it wanted, be in the phone lines, the computer cables. Anywhere. He suddenly felt as if he were being watched.

You're just freaking yourself out here. Knock it off. Go cut the power and get your ass out of here. If you kill the thing, then when the police come, they can find Bernie and everyone else trapped in here.

"And I'll be a freakin' hero." He thought about it. "No, I won't." As far as he knew, he was the only one to see the creature, which meant no one would know what he was doing or why and they would probably laugh at him, especially the women on the third floor. But that was fine. If they wouldn't listen to him, then he'd let them die. No great loss.

Somewhere overhead something slithered, metal on metal. What the hell was he thinking? Let them laugh. At least he'd be outside and alive.

Leo went out to the basement and looked around. The slithering noise was louder out here, reminding him of the buzzing sound in the elevator shaft. It was the same creature, the one who had appeared in his private room and burned the pictures. That made him move to the breaker box a little faster. He opened the door and stared at the switches. There wouldn't be much time once he cut the power; the thing would know what was happening and come after him. The sensible thing to do was to go to his private room where a trapdoor under the rug led, by an old wooden ladder, down to an unused sewage tunnel that ran to the outside. It might be the only way he had to escape, which meant he had to unlock all the doors between here and there first. When he went back to his office to retrieve the keys and a flashlight, he realized for the first time in his life that he was waist deep in the shit and didn't know how to fix it.

Twice he dropped the keys trying to unlock the first door. Finally, he had the key in the lock, turned it, and shoved the door open. It only took him two minutes to run down the hall, unlock his door, uncover and open the trapdoor, and hightail it back to the breaker switches. As he ran back, he realized there was some kind of vile stench coming from down the hole. Whatever it was, he'd have to deal with it in a matter of minutes.

"Here goes nothing." He held his breath and threw the main switch, throwing the basement into complete darkness. Even the emergency lights didn't come on. He switched the flashlight on and hurried across the basement to the hallway that led to salvation and freedom. His eyes registered a blur of movement near him, but he ignored it. If he stopped now …

The doorway to his room was to his left. He slowed and turned into his room, flashing the light over the women. "I love you all, but I've gotta—"

Another blur of motion and then the burning explosion of pain in his chest from the knife-edged end of a cable staggered him. He choked on blood as the cable yanked free and slithered up into the darkness.

"Not … like … this." But then he fell over, the last thing his eyes seeing, hundreds of women staring at him, watching him die.

MARCY

When she arrived at the office, Marcy had the Smith & Wesson Ladysmith in her purse, prepared to use if she found out who had taken Sharon, even if it meant shooting the cables. She knew shooting at thrashing cables would achieve nothing except waste ammunition, but if that's what it took to get whoever was behind everything to come out, then so be it. Most likely it was Leo. She wouldn't kill him, just threaten him until he helped her find Sharon. Thinking back to the television, she wondered how he had hacked in to send the signal of Sharon asking for help. No, begging for help.

She gritted her teeth and walked in, immediately surprised that Glen wasn't at his station. It was barely after nine, later than she wanted to arrive, but her desk, Bernie, Jon, and Bettie would have to wait until she found Sharon. Right now she had to get to the basement, the last place anyone had seen her.

A crowd of people stood by the stairwell door all talking at once, but Marcy ignored them. Whatever they were clamoring about was none of her concern. Only one thing possessed her, and if it took all day Bernie would have to understand. Opening the door to the basement, she hesitated. The last time she'd been down there was Tuesday with Bernie when Leo had stared lewdly at her. She had the gun this time. If Leo harassed her, she'd back him off quick.

Giving one last look at the crowd, she stepped onto the cool landing and realized the red emergency lights were the only lights working. What happened to the fluorescents? She couldn't remember if the lights were on in the lobby; daylight streamed in the front doors. The door closed with a soft click, and she started down the stairs.

The basement was too quiet. If Leo was down here, he wasn't making any noise. That frightened her; he could be anywhere. At the bottom of the stairs, thick silence filled the cavernous room and her heartbeat was the only sound. It beat even faster as she looked toward the elevator, then toward Leo's office. She drew the gun from her pocketbook and kept her finger on the trigger as she stayed near the wall and made her way to Leo's office.

The room was as she had seen it on Tuesday, but Leo wasn't there. Her nerves were on edge as she looked around the basement.

Where are you, Leo? Come out where I can see you.

From behind her and down the far hall, she heard that damnable creaking voice echoed through into the main basement. Marcy felt her blood chill, but though she wanted to run upstairs, she held her ground, ready to see who made the noise. No one knew she was down here, and if she screamed no one would hear her. She should've taken Bettie with her so if one of them got hurt, the other could get help.

She had the gun, but her courage was dissipating too fast and she was ready to run back to the lobby to be with the others. This had been a stupid and foolish mistake, and as she backed away from the creaking voice, she understood why she was here. Marcy had failed the family, worse, her own sister, and now she was trying to make it up by helping the friend she'd failed. But getting herself killed wouldn't help Danielle or Sharon. She needed to get upstairs and find help. Staying down here would accomplish nothing but—

Leo stepped out from the hallway and stared at Marcy. His work shirt was covered in blood from a hole in his chest.

He's dead. Someone stabbed him and killed him. So why isn't he lying on the ground? Why's he standing there staring at me with—

His eyes were gone, replaced by a bright white light that flowed from his sockets. The room stank of ozone. He was over ten feet away, but she felt electricity come from him that made her arm hairs stand on end.

"Leo?" But she knew it wasn't him. It was the thing that had taken Sharon.

It opened its mouth as if unfamiliar with its own body. The voice was thick and slow and creaked out like an old door that hadn't been opened in years, like what she imagined the door of a tomb would sound like after not having been opened for centuries.

It took a slow step toward her; it was still getting used to being in Leo's body. She could outrun it. Never turning her back, she made her way to the stairs, keeping a good distance between herself and what had been Leo. The air was charged with electricity that came off the thing in waves, surrounded her, and sent tendrils of mild shocks across her skin. She couldn't get any closer; the creature's electricity could kill her.

The gun was still in her hand, but she was hesitant to fire in case the electrical discharge caused an explosion. She wasn't ready to die, even if it meant killing the creature. Would the explosion even kill the thing? Thank God it wasn't used to Leo's body or—

"Mmmaaarrrccccyyy."

The gun slipped from her hand and clattered to the floor. Her blood turned to ice. She shuddered and felt her heart slam, about to burst out of her body.

The Leo-thing buzzed at her. It grinned and said her name again, its voice creaking, as it turned the two syllables into a flow of electrical static that crawled in her ears and penetrated her brain. Cold fear made her skin crawl even as she broke out in a fine sweat. She tried blinking the dizziness away, but the soft droning buzz lulled her further into a state of vertigo until she had to hold on to the boxes in front of her to keep from falling over.

"Stop it." The sensation intensified until she doubled over, nauseous, and dropped to one knee. "*Stop it!*"

"Wwwaaaannnt tooo seee Shhhaaarrronnn?" it buzzed and creaked.

"What are you?" Darkness crept in at the edges of her vision and she fought to maintain consciousness, but she felt so tired, so exhausted and drained, she only wanted to lie down and sleep. The nausea disappeared, replaced by bone weariness. But she couldn't give in to it, couldn't let it take her energy. She had to find Sharon. Pushing herself away from the boxes, she stumbled toward the stairs and the elevator.

"Donnn't llleeeavvve."

At the stairs she grabbed the railing and pulled herself up, but the stairs had turned into a concrete ramp straight up to the basement door. She slid down and staggered toward the elevator. "Stay away from me." If only she had the gun—but her hands were empty. Where did she leave it? Stumbling, she almost fell but leaned heavily against the wall to keep her balance.

"Mmmaaarrrcccyyy."

The elevator dinged. Who was here? She pushed herself away from the wall and collapsed into someone's arms.

"No!" She screamed and fought the man with what little energy she had left, but it was pointless. He held her and wouldn't let go. Struggling in his arms, she decided that if this was the end, so be it. She had no fight left in her and it was probably better this way. What she hadn't been able to do with the gun the other night some monster would do now. It would end her miserable life, and that would be it for Mousy Marcy.

She laughed and then cried. Her entire life had led to this moment. All her failures, her few successes, her brief loves, and years of loneliness would come to an insignificant end in the basement of her workplace. How goddamned pathetic. But life went that way sometimes. Bad things. Good people. You couldn't fight it. You just couldn't—

"Marcy!"

She glanced up into Bernie's face. It was cut up pretty bad, but when he smiled, she knew everything was going to be all right.

"It's Leo," she mumbled. "He's dead." She lifted her arm to point at him, but couldn't muster the strength. "I'm so tired." The last of her energy drained away, and she slumped in Bernie's arms. "Sleep."

He pulled her over and helped her sit with her back against the cold wall. "Rest here."

For a moment she opened her eyes and watched Bernie walk toward the Leo-thing, and then the blackness rose up in her vision and swallowed her whole.

JON

The lights went out and Jon froze in the pitch blackness. No emergency lights came on, and waiting for his eyes to adjust, he realized there was nothing for them to adjust to.

Sheila should be a couple of stairs below him with Sara behind. "Jon, are you still there?" he heard her say. "Sara?"

"Still here." Jon looked back where Sara should be.

"I'm here," she said.

Their voices echoed in the stairwell. Jumbled, frightened voices came from below them; something bad had happened and now, in the darkness, it was impossible to help.

Jon trembled when he thought of the Tony-creature coming through the door. Could it see in the dark?

"There should be emergency lights," Sheila said. "Why aren't they coming on?"

"Someone shut off the lights," Sara said. "This isn't the entity's doing."

"Who the hell shut the lights off?" Sheila asked.

Jon blinked several times, hoping his eyes would adjust to the dark, but even a cat needed some light to be able to see. "If we go back to Osprey, we could find a flashlight and then head down." The last thing Jon wanted was to run into the Tony-thing in complete darkness.

"That's a good—"

The voices downstairs quieted.

"Get off the stairs!" It was Bettie. "They're not stable. Someone down here's stuck. The stair turned to mud or something, and he sank into it. Get out of the stairwell!"

"Come on." Sheila backed up.

"Wait." He didn't want to abandon the others—specifically Bettie—to whatever was happening. But the only way to help was to go down three flights of stairs. Or take the elevator.

"We can't stay here." She was above him, making her way in the darkness. "We can take the elevator down."

After what happened to him earlier, that was the last thing he wanted to do, but he couldn't stay here. Keeping his hand on the banister, reluctant to walk away from helping the others, he made his way up to the fourth floor landing one step at a time, feeling each stair under his feet. Time had lost all meaning in the dark. Whether five minutes or ten minutes had passed, he couldn't tell. *Damn it, why don't the emergency lights come on so I can go down and—*

Someone grabbed his arm and he almost shrieked.

"Let's go." It was Sara pulling him up.

"I'm right behind you." Jon followed, making sure each step was under his foot before going for the next one. In the pitch darkness he didn't want to miss a step and fall. He also didn't want to spend too much time getting upstairs after what Bettie had said. Stairs turning to mud? What was next?

The door to the third floor landing opened with a crash as if whoever flung it open had tremendous strength.

"Jon?" Sheila called.

"Someone's coming," Jon said, trying to move faster without falling. He knew it was Tony, but he doubted the man would know him any longer. Deprived of his sight, he could hear Tony shuffling on the landing, moving up to the stairs. If he moved with the same speed he had on the second floor, they'd easily be able to get away from him. But if he could see in the dark, where they were disadvantaged, he could catch them.

Jon was almost to the fourth floor landing when he missed a step. His foot slipped and he slammed his knee against the edge of the next step. He gasped in pain as he slid down several steps.

"Jon?" Sara called. "Are you all right?"

Jon winced at the pain, but he knew he hadn't broken anything, and so he reached for the cold banister. "I slipped. I'm fine. I'll be right there."

Tony was climbing the stairs, albeit at a slow pace, but he was getting closer. If Jon didn't move, Tony would reach him soon.

"Do you need help?" Sheila asked.

"No." But he really could've used a hand to get up. He didn't want to put the other two in more danger. The pain wasn't that bad, so he forced himself to get up and crawl. The fourth floor landing was right above him. Tony had made it to the landing between floors. *Just a few minutes to rest and then I'll be fine,* he thought. *It'll take Tony that long to reach me.*

But he already felt the first tingles of electricity on his skin.

No more time. Pulling himself up, he got to the landing.

"I'm right here," Sara said.

"I told you to keep going," Jon said.

"I know."

"Let's go, you two." Sheila was only a couple of steps up.

"Tony's behind us," Jon said. "We have to go." He felt for Sara's hand, grabbed it, and the three of them continued in the darkness.

"I hear him," Sheila said.

So did Jon, shuffling up one stair at a time. "You believe me now?" He hadn't meant it to sound angry and sarcastic, but it came out that way.

"Yes," Sheila said.

Sara pulled away from him.

"What's wrong?" The stink of ozone filled the stairwell along with the soft crackle of electricity. Jon's skin crawled, and he was sure Sara and Sheila felt it as well.

"I don't know. All of a sudden I'm so tired. I have to rest."

"No time." He pulled her up, but she resisted.

Tony's shambling footsteps echoed below them. That damned creaking sound filled the stairwell, echoing so it sounded as if it was coming from all around them.

"Let me rest." Sara pulled her hand free. Jon heard her stumble backward.

"Sara." Jon reached for her, came back toward her, and felt around. "Sara."

Tony was on the fourth floor landing. He and Sara had only been four steps up.

"Sara!" Sheila shouted.

"Tired." She was one step away from Jon. He reached for where he thought she was and brushed her shoulder. "Why won't you let me rest?"

The force of the electrical current around Tony grew stronger, reaching out like sharp tendrils scraping Jon's skin.

"So tired," Sara mumbled, falling away from Jon.

He grabbed her around the waist. "Sheila, help me." He tried pulling Sara up, but she was deadweight, barely able to stand on her own.

"I'm right here," Sheila said next to him. "What's happening? I feel exhausted."

"Just help me get Sara up the stairs. Don't worry about it."

"Shhheeeiiilllaaa."

Jon's breath caught, and his heart skipped a beat.

"Hhhelllp mmmeee."

"Tony?" she said.

"It's not Tony," Jon said.

"Are you all right?" Sheila asked.

"He's not all right," Jon said, pulling Sara up. Sheila wasn't helping. "Sheila, focus. We have to get up the stairs. I need your help."

"But, Tony—"

"Tony doesn't need our help." How close was he to the landing between the fourth and fifth floors? He couldn't be that far. With one hand on the banister and the other around Sara's waist, he kept going. "Sheila, please, *help* me."

Sheila screamed.

Jon made it to the landing and let Sara slump against the wall. "Sheila?" He imagined Tony choking the life out of her as he had to Ted. "Sheila?" Starting back down the stairs, he hesitantly took steps so he wouldn't trip. The wall of electricity was stronger now, and though he had no idea if Tony had started up the next flight of stairs, he had to rescue Sheila.

He was so focused on each step, ignoring the intense shock of electricity on his skin, he almost collided with her. Without hesitation, he wrapped his arms around her and pulled her up.

"Shhheeeiiillla?"

The sensation of a thousand ants crawling on his skin, biting him, made him wince, and he almost let go of Sheila. But he fought against it and kept going.

The woman was crying. "My arm. He touched me."

"We'll take a look when we get upstairs. Are you all right otherwise?"

"I think so. I'm just wiped out."

"We have to get Sara back to the office."

"I'm all right," she said. "I feel so drained."

Without another word, the three of them ascended the last

set of stairs to the fifth floor.

Tony was on the stairs below them, the field of electricity reaching out to scratch Jon's skin, every hair on his body standing on end. He pulled the door open, and Jon, Sheila, and Sara went to Osprey's offices. In the office area, Jon locked the door behind him in case Tony came after them.

Through the frosted glass door, Jon saw Tony's shadow, and then Tony slammed against the door and fell to the reception area floor. Counting to ten, Jon cautiously opened the door to see what had happened to his friend and was assailed by the stench of burning flesh. Smoke rose from Tony's body, which lay curled on the floor. His skin was blackening as Jon watched, as if he were being roasted from the inside.

Sara had said the monster was living energy. Apparently, it couldn't survive in a human host for long without destroying it. Small consolation, but it was something. Jon closed the door and went to Sheila's office, where he found the two women slumped in their chairs.

"What was that?" Sheila asked.

"The monster." Sara sat up a little straighter when Jon came in.

"Tony's outside in the reception area." Jon reiterated what Sara had suggested about the creature burning up bodies

"I'm sorry I doubted the two of you," Sheila said. "We have to get everyone out." She looked from Sara to Jon. "Maybe we can starve it."

"We have to be careful," Sara said. "If it senses we're trying to escape, it will try to stop us."

"Stop us how?" Jon thought of Tony and already knew the answer.

"However it can," Sara said matter-of-factly.

"All right." Sheila sat back. "Jon, you get the A/P people, and, Sara, get the A/R people, and meet me in the conference room. Tell them it's important, but nothing else. I don't want people freaking out."

Jon left Sheila's office and headed over to collect the remaining A/P staff. Around him, eyes watched but couldn't see.

BETTIE

Jon, Sara, and Sheila were in the stairwell. Bettie barely heard them over the surrounding people, all talking at once.

"Can everyone please stop talking for a minute?"

Those nearest her stopped talking, and soon the rest had quieted.

Bettie looked up, wishing they were down here with her. "Get off the stairs! They're not stable. A guy down here got sucked into one of the stairs and he can't get out." Glancing at the man caught in the stairs, Bettie wished she knew what to do.

"*Help me!*" he shouted.

Someone rushed into the stairwell, shoved his way through the crowd, and came up to the second floor landing. "Roy? What happened?"

"Susan, thank God you're here. I'm trapped and these people are standing around doing nothing."

"What can I do?" Susan asked. "How'd this happen?"

"I don't know. I was coming up the stairs, and then suddenly I was sinking. I almost fell, and then they turned solid again," Roy said. "But I'm still sinking."

Susan stared at the stairs, then at Roy. "I don't know—"

Something that sounded like a gunshot came from upstairs, but Bettie realized it was probably one of the stairwell doors being thrown open. She hoped it was Jon and Sheila getting out.

A beam bounced into the stairwell. "I have a flashlight!" The guard shone the light around, then finally up the stairs toward Roy. He was turned, facing the collected group, visibly sinking into the stairs.

"Help me!" He reached out his hand, but no one moved. "*Susan!*"

Bettie saw the woman look at the stairs. "I—"

"Please!" Roy shouted.

The stair melted and within seconds, Roy was pulled down until only his forearm was left out, reaching to the heavens for help. Then the stair turned to concrete again.

"Everyone out of the stairwell!" Bettie shouted. "*Now!*"

The crowd rushed down the stairs, and for a moment Bettie thought people were going to get trampled. It was as if the devil himself pursued them. Even the guard had left, leading the exodus into the lobby.

Bettie glanced up. "Be safe, Jon."

In the lobby, people ran for the glass doors that led to freedom, heedless of the people in front of them, but if they weren't careful someone would wind up going through the glass doors.

"Please!" the guard shouted. "Don't run! Take it easy!"

No one listened. It was everyone for themselves. The coffee table with the magazines was shoved out of the way to make room for the twenty or so people rushing to the glass doors. The first people at the vestibule—two men Bettie didn't know— slammed against the doors and were momentarily crushed by the crowd behind them.

"Who locked the doors?" a woman shouted.

People looked at each other, searching faces for someone who had sealed them in, someone to blame.

"What's going on?" The guard pushed through the crowd to get to the front set of doors.

"The doors are locked," the woman said. "Why'd you lock them?"

The guard shrugged. "I didn't lock them."

"Then who did?" One of the men who had been first to the doors turned to face the crowd. Although physically unhurt, he was angry and embarrassed for crashing into the locked doors.

"The doors aren't locked," the woman said. "They're stuck."

The guard made it to the vestibule and examined the doors. "Not stuck. Fused."

"Fused?" someone asked. "How can they be fused? Fused by what?"

Bettie looked around the familiar lobby, seeing a place that had suddenly turned alien, and unless someone could figure out what this entity wanted, they might very well end up dead.

"Why don't we break the glass?" A guy went around to the Security desk and picked up the fire extinguisher. "This should solve our problem." He hefted it to the vestibule, said, "Stand back" and threw it at the doors.

"Wait!" Bettie shouted, but her words were drowned out by the shattering glass.

"There," the man said, ignoring her. He took a step into the vestibule to retrieve the extinguisher in case he needed it to shatter the outside door. He was careful of the jagged edges left around the metal door frame. Some of them were wickedly sharp, though most of the glass lay in the vestibule. "You just have to be careful where you—"

The glass around the door frame grew inward, seeking to repair itself. It crackled with a life of its own as it wove broken pieces together, elongating toward the center, stretching glass fibers heedless of anything in its way. The man was half-turned when the glass cut through his clothes, through his flesh, slicing its way to wholeness. Blood ran down the glass, thickened by gore.

Bettie turned away, unable to look, wishing she could be deaf to the ripping of flesh, the cracking of his bones, and his screams as he was cut in half.

BERNIE

After helping Marcy sit against the wall, Bernie turned to the thing that controlled the cables. He had passed out twice or maybe three times during the course of their attacks, only once did he scream, but he was never afraid of the cables; he had faced torture as a POW back in Vietnam and remembered how to ignore the pain.

Apparently, whatever controlled the cables didn't like his apathy, and just when he thought the cables would kill him, he had been unceremoniously dumped on the first floor in a locked office. His cuts were bad, would need medical attention, but he had to figure out a way to stop this thing. He was sure other people were in the ducts being stripped of their flesh, and they weren't as hardened as he was.

So where were they? He hadn't heard anyone. After he had been dumped in the abandoned office, he had roused himself and broken out. Then he'd taken the elevator to the basement, hoping Leo would be there to help him. They had both seen Tony on his computer screen and heard that bizarre creaking voice. Maybe Leo had found a way to stop whatever was happening.

He'd practically walked into Marcy.

Now Leo stared at him with blind, glowing eyes.

"Berrrnnniiieee." Leo's mouth curled into a smile. "Nnnooo fffeeeaaarrr."

"That's a problem for you, isn't it? I don't show fear and that bothers you." He had no idea what he was dealing with, only that it used cables to snatch people, and if his experience was like what others were facing, they were dragged through the air ducts and left in complete darkness for what might've been hours. Then the cables returned, randomly slicing their arms and legs, drawing blood, trying to scare the shit out of them. It wasn't about the blood, but the fear.

Marcy had said the cables attacked her and Paul, but not to kill them, just to scare them. If this thing fed on fear, then it had a ready supply of food. Who wouldn't be scared to death of being kept in utter darkness and then suddenly attacked, especially when you couldn't see where the attack was coming from? That was part of the thing's way of feeding, Bernie was sure of it.

The creature that had taken over Leo twisted its head up as if listening to something. Then it looked at Bernie and forced its lips into a sadistic grin. "Fffeeeaaarrr." Leo's eyes went dark and he crumpled to the ground, his skin darkening, peeling. Smoke rose from his charring flesh until his entire body was covered in burned skin.

"Shit." Bernie backed away from Leo, fascinated by the spontaneous charring of Leo's body as if a great heat had burned through him. He glanced back at Marcy; he'd have to get her upstairs and out of the building before the cables came for her.

Marcy opened her eyes. "What happened? Did I fall asleep?"

He came to her side. "Something like that."

"I have to get my gun and then ... Where's Leo? Is he dead?"

"Yes, he's dead." Then he realized what Marcy had said. "You have a gun here? Why?"

"I saw Sharon on my TV asking for help." Scowling, she

stood, leaning against the wall for support. "I knew she was still here and I was going to help her." She pushed herself forward. "I dropped it when that thing was … I don't know what it did. It sucked the life out of me. Here it is." She bent down and lifted a small pistol.

Bernie recognized it as a Smith & Wesson. "And what were you planning to do with that?"

"I don't know. I thought if Leo had her, I'd use it to make him let her go."

"Leo doesn't have her, but I think I know where she is."

"Where?" The look of desperation on Marcy's face made Bernie ache.

"I think she's somewhere in the ductwork."

Marcy gazed up at the ceiling. "Down here?"

"Somewhere in the building, probably on one of the lower floors, between the first and second floors most likely."

"Why?"

Bernie was concerned that they were alone, and if the thing chose to come back, he'd rather be with more people. "Let's go upstairs."

"But the stairs …" She looked at what had been a ramp.

"This thing has the power to reshape the building at its whim. That's why we have to get out of here as soon as we can. But I'm not going to leave any Osprey employee behind. We'll go upstairs, but I want you to go outside and call the police. I'm going to get everyone else out."

They were halfway up the stairs when they heard glass shatter. Bernie hurried with Marcy right behind him. He tried opening the door, but there were people leaning against it. When he was finally able to push it wide enough for the two of them to get out, he found himself in the midst of utter chaos.

At first, he couldn't tell why everyone was pushing and shoving until he saw into the vestibule and the pieces of someone lying on either side of the glass door. Bloody spiderweb cracks ran across its surface but those disappeared until the door was one complete piece again. Searching around for other Osprey employees, Bernie spotted Bettie and shouted her name, but there was too much noise from the crowd.

"What's going on?" Marcy hadn't seen the dead man. She pulled away from Bernie to make her way to the doors, but Bernie held her back.

"Don't go up there. Something bad's happened. Stay away from the doors." Marcy was still focused on the front of the building. "Marcy." He held her arm and shook her. "Marcy!"

"What?" She turned to him, a look of pain on her face. "You're hurting me."

"I need you to focus." He didn't like treating her this way, especially after everything she'd been through, but he needed her to stay with him. "I have to go upstairs and get the rest of the Osprey staff down here. I want you to get over to Bettie and the two of you keep each other safe. When I get back down, we'll figure a way out of this place."

"You can't go." Now she grabbed his arm. He winced from the pressure of her hand on his cuts. "Sorry." She let him go. "I need you." Her eyes were wide and wet with fear. "Please don't leave me."

"I have to, Marcy. Bettie's down here." He glanced around the crowd. "Bettie!" But he had lost track of the other woman. "Damn."

"What?"

Bettie was next to him. "Marcy, you're all right. What's with the gun?" She pointed at the Smith & Wesson.

"Nothing," Marcy said, avoiding Bettie's gaze.

"Bettie, I have to go upstairs and get the rest of the staff down here," Bernie said. "Stay with Marcy and the two of you stay out of trouble."

"We're trapped in here," Bettie said. "That guy tried getting out and the glass grew back while he was getting the extinguisher." She frowned. "It cut him in half."

Bernie was afraid Bettie was losing it. "Bettie, can you stay here with Marcy out of harm's way?"

"There was no warning. He was there and then the glass just ... Now he's dead."

"Bettie." Bernie gripped her shoulders. "Please, Bettie, I need you to stay with Marcy and stay away from the doors. Just ... just stay here. Don't go anywhere or do anything. All right?

No matter what anyone else says, don't do anything. Do you understand?"

She gazed at him, but he saw the unfocused gaze of someone in shock. There was nothing he could do. "Marcy. Stay with her. Okay?"

Marcy nodded but he could tell she was reluctant to let him go.

"I'll be right back."

She nodded again.

Before he could change his mind, he went into the stairwell.

"No!" Bettie screamed behind him, but he didn't stop. Even when he saw the arm of a man sticking out of the stairs, he kept going. There were people depending on him and he had to get to them before the entity did.

JON

Going through the A/P side of the office, he realized Junior and Sara were the only ones left. Sharon was missing, Marcy and Bettie were downstairs, Paul had been fired, and Tony was dead. At Junior's cubicle, he knocked on the door frame.

"Hey, Jon, what—"

"We're going to the conference room."

"What for?"

Jon didn't to have to explain what was happening when he knew Sheila would do a better job at it. "We're having an impromptu meeting. Sheila's calling it."

He got up from his desk and followed Jon. "What about the rest of the staff?"

"Sheila's getting everyone together so she can explain what's going on."

"Jon?" He put his hand on the other man's shoulder and turned him. "Do you know what happened to Tony? He didn't come in this morning."

"I know." Jon pulled away but didn't answer. He didn't want to tell him Tony was dead; he didn't want to believe it himself. "Come on."

Sheila, Nicole, and Yvette, all from Accounts Receivable, were already there. Nodding at Jon, Sheila said, "Sara's rounding up the rest of the staff."

"What's with her, anyway?" Nicole asked. "Freak."

"Enough." Sheila's voice was tight and angry. "Leave her be."

The two women stared at Sheila as if they thought she was as crazy as Sara.

The rest of the A/R people filed in, with Sara coming in last and going to stand next to Jon.

"I hope this works," Sara said. "These people think I'm insane."

No one sat; no one spoke. Anyone who had picked their phone up or tried calling on their cell phone knew something was wrong.

"What's happening?" Nicole asked.

Everyone stared at Sheila.

"What's the emergency?" Yvette asked. "Sara said there's some emergency?"

After glancing at each of them, Sheila straightened. "I don't pretend to understand what's happening here, but we need to leave the building."

Everyone spoke at once.

"Please." She held her hand up, and after a couple of moments they quieted. "We're going to take the stairs to the roof and go down the fire escape."

"What's wrong with the elevator?" Cathy asked.

"The elevator isn't working properly, and the lights are out in the stairwell."

"What's wrong with the phones?" Will asked.

"I can't get a signal on my cell phone, either," Nicole said.

"Maybe we can get one on the roof." George laughed.

"Sheila, what's the emergency?" Patti asked.

"I … I don't know how to explain it." She looked at Jon and Sara. "I don't."

Everyone turned to look at them. Jon thought some of the women frowned at Sara, but no one said anything. He wished he knew them better, had worked with them longer, so he wouldn't feel so estranged, like an outsider trying to convince everyone the best plan was to follow him. Sara wouldn't fare much better. "Where's the rest of the A/P department?" Yvette asked. "And Elaine?"

"They're most likely dead," Sara said. "At least we know Tony is. The rest of them are missing. And if we don't get out of here soon, we'll be dead, as well."

"What is she talking about?" Will asked.

"Nothing," Nicole said. "She's just crazy."

Jon wondered if anyone caught the wicked smile Sara offered Nicole. Before the others could speculate further, he figured it was time to lay it on the line and let them believe whatever they wanted to. "The truth is—"

"I'm not crazy," Sara said.

Nicole shook her head. "Okay, Sara, you're not crazy. None of us think you're crazy. A little insane maybe, but not—"

"I'm not crazy!"

Nicole wasn't close to Sara, but not far enough away that Sara couldn't rush over and attack her.

"Look," Sheila said. "We don't need any animosity now. Whatever your feelings are for each other, just stuff them. We need to work together and—"

Ceiling tiles broke, sending chunks of plasterboard down on the table next to Sheila. For a moment, no one moved. They all stared at the black, square hole. A braid of colorful wires came down from the ceiling and wrapped around Sheila's wrists, pulling her arms up over her head. More wires streamed down and slipped around her neck as she fought to get free.

"Help." She gasped.

When Jon realized no one was moving to help, he pushed through them with Sara behind him. He made it to Sheila and reached for the wires behind her head, around her neck, pulling on them, but they held firm, not giving an inch. "Someone get something to cut these with." He turned to those gathered. "Now!"

Several women went to the door and tried pulling on the handles, but nothing happened. "The door won't open," Alexa said. Then she looked closer. "Oh, my God. It's a solid piece of wood. There's no opening."

Jon knew panic would set in very soon.

"What's happening?" Nicole asked.

"Why can't we get out?" Alexa asked.

Jon climbed on the table to get a closer look at the cables and wires. They were slowly moving back up into the ceiling, taking Sheila with them. She struggled against them but to no avail. "Is there anything in here to cut them with?" He watched helplessly as more wires slithered down and crawled around her neck, while the ones holding her wrists undid themselves. If he didn't do something quickly, she would be hanged.

"Nothing," Will said.

His eyes came to rest on the fire extinguisher. Could he freeze the wires so they'd break? "Get me the fire extinguisher." He had to resolve this soon before the tension in the room multiplied and the creature fed off their fear. But it was already too late. The one person they'd trusted to get them out was Sheila and they all were watching her, eyes wide.

Someone screamed.

Jon turned in time to see thicker cables come out of the ceiling, weaving like snakes. He stumbled back on the table.

"Do something!" Alexa shouted.

The wires around Sheila's wrists loosened further while the ones around her neck tightened. She tried pulling at them to no avail. Her eyes pleaded with Jon, but he had no idea what to do.

"Here." George handed him the extinguisher. He hefted it and pulled the pin. "This is going to be real cold, but maybe if we can freeze the wires, they'll break."

"Please," she wheezed.

"Close your eyes." He held the nozzle up to the ceiling, trying to avoid Sheila's body, and squeezed the handle. A thick cloud of white spray exploded from the nozzle, and Jon held it for a count of five, hoping the wires would either freeze or let her go.

At three, Sheila's arms fell to her sides, and for a brief second Jon thought they'd won, but then her body shook violently.

At four, thick blood soaked Sheila's blouse. He stopped spraying and waited for the cloud to dissipate.

At five, he felt a spray of hot fluid across his face. He dropped the extinguisher and turned away, wiping at his face to get her blood off. His stomach tightened as the sensation of her blood splattering on his skin repeated until he rolled off the table to the floor and vomited.

People started screaming and rushing toward the solid piece of wood that had been a door.

When his stomach was empty, he took his dress shirt off and wiped his face. Against his better judgment, he turned back. The white cloud was gone, and he gasped in revulsion at what he saw. Sheila still hung with the wires wrapped tight around her neck and her blouse turning dark crimson. The thicker cables had sliced her throat open, killing her instantly. Those cables danced in the air like snakes, probing where the coldness had come from, most likely seeking the source. The wires around Sheila's throat shook her again, like a cat making sure the mouse in its mouth was dead. When there was no reaction, the braid and the cables loosened until she fell into a lifeless heap on the floor. The smaller wires retreated, replaced by thicker cables that streamed from the ceiling in the direction the cold attack had come from.

Sara was by his side, helping him away from the cables.

People pounded on the door, shouting.

The cables and wires retreated into the darkness.

He looked up at a creaking sound coming from the ceiling over the table. Others turned, as well, and watched the metal ductwork melt away so that a black maw opened in its center and something vomited onto the table. It splashed across the dark wood with a wet thump. Jon and Sara turned away from the splatter that had once been a person, but was now bloody chunks and scraps of innards spilling from the ceiling, dripping across the table.

Will and George pounded furiously on what had been the door, trying to break through with their bare hands. "Try a chair." George hefted one of the chairs and tried ramming it through the wood. The door chipped but little more.

"*Please!*" Cathy shouted. "I don't want to die!"

"Why are we trapped in here?" Yvette cried. "Who did this?" She banged on the door. "*Help!*"

"What happened to the door?" someone said on the other side.

"Someone's there!" Alexa said.

"It's Bernie," the man said. "What happened to the door?"

"Bernie's here!" Yvette shouted. "I don't know, but we can't get out."

"Sheila's dead!" Nicole shouted.

"I don't want to die." Cathy sat in the corner on the floor, weeping.

"All right," Bernie said. "I'll get something to open the door."

"Bernie. Wait. There's ..."

If he heard her, he didn't reply.

"Please! Hurry!" Yvette shouted.

Will went to the door and tapped on the solid piece of wood. "Who did this and why?"

"It's feeding."

Everyone looked at Sara.

"What are you talking about?" Will asked.

Sara hugged herself, and stared into the ceiling where pieces of flesh were still dripping down. "It's feeding on us. On our fear."

"What's feeding on us?" Will asked.

"I—I don't know what it is, only that it's been here in this building for a long time, and it nourishes itself on fear. That's why we have to get out of the building."

"Jesus Christ," Nicole said. "Don't listen to her. She's crazy."

Sara scowled at the other woman. "Fuck you."

A solid whack hit the wood, splintering it. Everyone moved back, keeping their distance from the muck-splattered table.

Jon felt a rush of relief that Bernie was still alive and was trying to get these people out.

The door cracked and fractured until it collapsed. On the other side, Bernie appeared, holding a fire extinguisher. He looked terrible. Jon waited for something to happen; everyone stood frozen, expecting an attack, but there was none.

"It's sated," Sara said quietly. "For now."

"You mean that thing?" Bernie asked.

"The entity," Sara said. "I think it's become attracted to crowds, but that doesn't make sense. It had always gone after people who were alone. Unless it doesn't care. Unless it's decided that mass fear is more satisfying."

"That would explain why I made it up here without incident." Bernie put down the fire extinguisher.

The others hurried out of the conference room and gathered around him.

"We have to get everyone to the roof," Jon said. "Then they can climb down the fire escape." He contemplated what Bernie had said. "If people go a few at a time and not all at once, maybe the ... entity won't notice."

"Do you think that's safe?" Bernie asked.

"It's better than staying in the building," Patti said.

"All right. I have to go to the other companies and get them out. Sara, you seem to know something about this thing, so I want you with me. Jon—"

"I'll get everyone out." Patti saw Bernie's frown. "I want to do this. Jon can go with you."

"You sure?" Bernie asked.

"Absolutely."

"Okay, then. We'll see you outside."

Jon went over to Patti. "Remember, go a few at a time. If this thing senses too many people are leaving at once, it may try to stop you."

"Thanks. Take care of yourself. And Bernie." She gave his arm a gentle squeeze and looked at Sara. "And Sara, too."

"Sure." Jon joined Bernie and Sara as they headed to the office doors. Behind him, Patti explained the plan, making sure everyone understood what was expected of them.

"So what is this thing?" Bernie asked.

"All I know is that it's been in the building almost as long as the building's been here," Sara said.

"I didn't see Sheila in the crowd," Bernie said. "What happened to her?"

"The thing attacked Sheila in the conference room and killed her," Jon said.

"Sheila's dead?" Bernie asked. "Damn it. It controls this building and everything in it, and if we don't find a way out soon ... What else?"

"It's hungry. It's learned fear is very satisfying. It's also learning what we're frightened of and is using that to scare us."

"But if you don't show it fear, it has no use for you," Bernie said. "I was up in the ceiling. It tortured me, but when I wouldn't show fear, it kicked me out. I believe Sara's right. If we don't show we're afraid, then it won't hurt us."

"But it feeds on energy," Sara said. "Even if you don't show fear, but you're still afraid, it will still feed."

"Easier said than done," Jon said, then to Sara, "you said it was sated. What did you mean?"

"It's not hungry anymore. It's had its fill of fear—for now."

Bernie nodded. "There's a group downstairs in the lobby and they're pretty terrified."

"That would explain why it's not hungry anymore," Jon said. "When I was on the second floor and ran into ... that thing, it couldn't see me. I hit it with a fire extinguisher and it looked right through me as if I wasn't there."

"So there's something special about you."

"Unless it was just that it was using Tony and—"

"What do you mean, 'using Tony'?"

Jon realized Bernie didn't know, so he explained his encounter with Tony and everything that had happened since.

Bernie sighed. "Let's just get this over with and get out of here."

They went through the office doors and into the reception area where Tony's charred body lay.

"Apparently, it can't sustain itself in a human host," Bernie said. "It burns the body out."

The elevator was in front of them, and the stairwell door stood ajar. The lights flickered, strobe-like, creating shadows, then just as quickly destroying them. To their left, the glass doors of Dasher Financials were closed.

"Come on." Bernie led them across the area toward the other office.

Jon expected something to happen with every step he took: The ceiling to break open and another body to come plummeting down. The floor to turn to mud. Cables to come streaming from the broken ceiling, slicing skin, puncturing flesh. By the time they stood outside Dasher Financials, Jon was nearly shaking. This was ridiculous. As much as he wanted to help, he wanted to flee the building. If only he'd convinced them he should go with Patti. But Bettie was downstairs, probably trapped, and he couldn't run out on her.

"It's awfully quiet," Bernie said, before pushing the doors open.

"Oh, my God," Sara whispered and turned away.

Jon stared into what used to be an office but was now a chamber of death.

"We're too late." Bernie let the door close. "I wonder if they had any idea of the danger they were in, if they had a chance to get out."

"The thing turned the conference room door to a single sheet of wood." Jon couldn't get the images of the bloody dead out of his mind. "It could've locked this door and there was no way out."

"We have to get to the companies on the third floor." Bernie headed to the stairs.

"I hope it's not too late," Sara said.

"I want to hear about this connection," Bernie said. "I want you to tell me everything you know about this creature." He pulled the stairwell door open and started down the stairs. "Maybe we can figure out a way to kill it."

Jon wondered what would happen if the entity suddenly got hungry while they were in the stairwell. Then he realized how unique the group was: the entity had already spit Bernie out, it couldn't see him, and Sara had some kind of connection to it. Patti and the others were probably in more danger than they were.

"Sara," Jon said. "Do you know if there's any way to stop it?"

"No, I don't."

"You said it was a living energy and it's feeding on our fear. If we got everyone out of the building, then it would starve."

"The same thing could happen if we calmed everyone down so they weren't afraid," Sara said.

At the next landing, Bernie stopped them and put a hand on Sara's arm. "I know something happened to you before you came here. I never asked because it was your own business. But now you're talking as if you know this ... entity, and I need to know how you know and what you know so we can figure out how to get out of here."

"Please." Though Jon expected her to start crying, she didn't; she began shaking.

"Sara, all these people, your co-workers, are depending on me to get them safely out of here and I plan to do just that. If you know something, anything that'll help us get out alive, then you have to tell me."

She leaned against the wall. "I felt it when I first started working here, like a dull buzz, not uncomfortable, but noticeable. I was able to ignore it for the most part until a few months ago. I guess it was around the time a couple of companies moved out. The sensation went from a dull buzz to a mild humming sound as if whatever it was had ... turned itself up."

"It's always been feeding on us, then?" Bernie asked. "Draining us? That would explain why we're always so damned tired. When the companies left, it had less people to feed on."

"But it had never physically attacked anyone before." Sara shook her head. "Only within the last couple of days did it start attacking people. Since Sharon disappeared."

"Trying to scare them."

Jon said, "If companies are moving out of the building, maybe it's desperate for food, so it decided to scare people to feed off of their fear."

"Fear is pretty potent," Bernie said.

"Then we have to get everyone out of the building," Jon said.

"It might die." Bernie glanced at Sara. "What do you think?"

"I think you're right. But there's more." She looked at the two of them as if waiting for their approval to go on. "What I've been feeling has changed over the last few years from a calm, steady sensation to, at times, something very erratic, almost chaotic. It's as if, for lack of a better word, the entity is going insane."

"Why didn't you say something?" Bernie asked. "All this time you've been here and you never mentioned it before."

"I've been through a lot of things no one believed. I saw a

lot of therapists to help convince me the demons that visited me, the ghosts I saw, and all the other terrible things that happened to me were just figments of my imagination. The best thing I learned was to keep my mouth shut."

"All right," Bernie conceded. "I see your point. We'll talk more about this later. Let's get down to the third floor and see if anyone's still alive. If so, we'll get them upstairs to the fire escape. I think it'll be too far to get to the lobby and there are already enough people down there."

BETTIE

Marcy faced the vestibule, the gun clasped tightly in her hand. *She's going to shoot someone*, Bettie thought. She glanced at the stairwell, too afraid to see if Bernie was caught in the stairs. That poor man—Roy was his name—*drowned* in the stairs. Nowhere was safe, and there was no way to get out of the building. They would die here for certain. She had the box cutter in her purse. If she could find somewhere to go, just for a little cut, she'd feel so much better and ease the pressure in her chest.

Marcy was saying something to her, but she couldn't hear over the loud din the others made talking over each other. Everyone had the plan. Everyone knew what it would take to get out.

Break a window and jump before it resealed itself.

Get into the vestibule and break the next set of doors.

Find a back exit.

Call the police and fire department. Except no phones would work.

A man—someone had called him Doug—came toward her. He was saying something, but she couldn't hear him. He looked angry as if they were all too stupid to see what the answer was, or too stupid to understand he knew how to save everyone. No, he wasn't coming at her, but at Marcy, pointing at the gun.

"Marcy," Bettie said.

But Marcy had turned to the stairwell door as if willing Bernie to come back.

"Marcy," Bettie said louder.

"Give me that fucking gun." Doug snatched the Smith & Wesson from Marcy, and turned to face those gathered. "All right. Listen to me. You're all going to do what I say and we'll get out of here fine."

"Who the hell are you?" Bettie asked.

The guy wheeled on her. "I'm the one you're gonna thank later when I save your ass." He glared at her and though she didn't want to, she shrank away from his gaze.

Stand up to him. Don't let him do this. She fought against herself to find the courage to stand up to Doug. She clenched her fists and held her breath, counting one, two, three, four, five. This wasn't like any of the other men she'd given control to, not her father demanding she do as he said or else. It was just ... some guy, some prick who thought he knew better, and would probably get everyone killed.

She glared back at him. "What are you going to do, shoot your way out?"

"I have no idea, but I sure don't hear you coming up with a better plan. Got one?"

"No." Bettie watched the pistol pointed at her. "But I don't think you can shoot your way out of here."

"Why not?"

"Because whatever this entity is, it's capable of manipulating—"

"The entity? What are you talking about?"

"What do you think made the glass grow back? Magic?"

"What are you saying? It's some kind of creature?"

Bettie shook her head. "All I know is that there's some sort of energy moving through this building, controlling it."

"Controlling the building? How?" Doug looked at the others, most likely to see if anyone believed her, or if anyone was trying to come close to him. "I know what you're doing, missy. You're trying to distract me so someone'll come and take the gun from me. Get over there." He waved the gun and then came around so he had his back to the wall. "Now, tell me again about this energy."

"I don't really know anything about it." Bettie didn't like having her back to the glass doors, but with Doug pointing the gun at her, she had little choice.

"You just told me that it controls the building we're in. How do you know that?"

Bettie laughed unintentionally. "Look around you. Stairs turning to mud and sucking people down. Glass doors that repair themselves. Does that happen in any other buildings you know about?"

"Of course not. But it doesn't mean there's some kind of force controlling this place."

"What would you call it?" Bettie was getting pissed. They were wasting time debating when they should be finding a way out. "Look, we have to work together to get out of here instead of arguing."

"You'd like that, wouldn't you?"

"What are you talking about?" Bettie realized Doug was probably scared shitless. If he was used to reality behaving in a predictable, rational way—as they all were—then he wouldn't know how to cope when things were unpredictable and irrational. How she was coping was something she didn't know, but at least she thought she was, as best she could.

"Why should I help you?"

"Doug, this is no time to be a jerk." One of the other women stepped forward. "You want to be a manipulative boss, that's one thing, but this is no time to keep up the act. This woman's right. We have to work together to get out of here."

Doug laughed. "I'm a manipulative boss? Well, Wendy, why haven't you spoken your mind before?" He waved the gun around. "Why wait until now?"

"Give me the gun." Bettie started at Doug, but stopped short when he aimed at her.

"I have a great idea." His grin was predatory. "You know so much about this energy force, then you're going to lead us out of here."

"I told you, I don't—"

"Shut up. Let me think."

Marcy walked up to Doug, and though he saw her he made no move to stop her or back her up.

"What do you want?"

"My gun." Marcy reached out to grab it, but Doug turned it on her.

"Why don't you get back with the others?" When she didn't move, he turned the gun toward the crowd and fired.

People screamed and fell, hands over their heads.

Bettie dropped to the floor and heard the sound of breaking glass by the front doors.

"See how easy this is?" He walked up to the vestibule, avoiding the remains of the dead man.

The whole door lay in broken pieces in and out of the vestibule.

"Now we'll see how fast your energy force fixes the glass." Doug stared at the empty door frame for several moments and when nothing happened, he smiled. "I don't know what you people are so afraid of." He went to step through.

"Don't!" Wendy cried out.

Bettie wondered why Wendy cared so much, giving her previously stated feelings about the man.

"Maybe I killed it." He stepped into the vestibule. "See? I'm fine."

The glass door repaired itself, stretching the jagged glass across the opening until it looked as if nothing had happened. Doug slid the gun into his belt and hefted the extinguisher that lay next to the other half of the dead man, making sure he had a good grasp on it. He moved to the front door. The glass on the floor began to slide across the vestibule as if stirred by an unseen hand.

Bettie and Marcy moved forward with the others to see what was going on. Bettie heard tinkling as pieces skidded over each other. Doug looked down at the glass that lifted off the floor in an ever-expanding circle.

His eyes wide with fear, he lifted the extinguisher and was about to launch it through the front glass door when the gold metal of the frame expanded in a crisscross pattern across the glass. When the extinguisher hit the door, the glass shattered and fell but the metal prevented him from getting out.

"Oh, my God," Wendy said. "Doug! Get out of there!"

Doug turned with the extinguisher, preparing to smash the

inner glass door. Everyone backed away.

The glass on the floor swirled to life as if a tornado wind swept it upward.

Doug's jaw dropped open and the fear in his eyes turned to pain as jagged shards of glass swept around him, slicing his pants to shreds and cutting into his skin.

"Oh, shit." Bettie pulled Marcy back. "Everyone get away from the doors!"

As the glass fragments swirled faster and higher, gathered speed and force, and swept all the broken glass into a tightening funnel around Doug, the extinguisher fell from his hands, and he screamed. Fat red drops spattered on the glass doors as his legs were sliced to ribbons.

It was like being in a blender, Bettie thought. Though she knew what would happen, she couldn't look away; she was fascinated by the glass whirlwind that swirled with ever-increasing force. There was no way anyone could survive it. The gentle tinkling of the glass had turned into a mad cacophony of broken chimes as it rang fiercely, dulled by the enclosed vestibule.

Bettie couldn't see Doug, only the sprays and drops of blood that splattered on the glass doors. When pieces of gore hit them, she had to turn away.

A man screamed. Then a woman joined in. *Why are they looking?* Bettie wanted to scream; she felt the fear squeezing her lungs, threatening to overwhelm her, but she had to think, had to stay clearheaded if she hoped to get out of this alive.

People around her were crying, and she realized she was as well.

All at once the swirling glass in the vestibule fell to the ground in one deafening crash. She refused to look because she knew her mind would shut down if she saw what was left of Doug. The silence that rushed in was painful, and as Bettie wiped the tears away, she waited, nerves fraying, for something else to happen. Other people were crying, the nearest one Marcy. Bettie pulled her closer and hugged her tight, keeping Marcy faced away from the glass doors.

Someone said, "Oh, God," repeatedly.

Bettie saw a door off to one side of the vestibule, and realized there was one on either side of the main doors. How many times had she passed those doors and never realized they were there? Where did they lead?

"Marcy, do you know where that door leads?" She nodded toward the door to their left.

Marcy sniffed and wiped tears from her face. "I think it's a small conference room. I don't know. I've never been in there."

"There's another door on the other side. What about that one?"

"I think it's another conference room."

"I have to see if the door's unlocked. We may be able to get out through the windows of the conference room."

Marcy gripped her tighter. "Don't leave me."

"Then come with me."

"No. We have to wait for Bernie. He's going to save us. I know it." She clutched Bettie tighter. "It's going to be all right."

"Marcy, please, we have to find a way out. Bernie will be back, but right now we have to figure out how to get these people out of the building before we're attacked again. Come on, honey. Let's do this." She tilted Marcy's face up to hers. "If this works we'll be heroes." She grinned, hoping she sounded sincere.

Marcy stared at her for several moments before a weak smile crept across her lips. "All right."

Around them, people tried their best to comfort each other, to deal with the impossibility of their situation. Bettie was sure they wondered what would happen next and if any of them would make it out alive.

Curiosity got the best of her, and she glanced at what was left of the body in the vestibule, covered in shards of glass and blood. All the skin had been sliced away, leaving pulped muscle and tissue. Even if those doors fell open right now, she wouldn't go that way. Turning from the bloody mess, Bettie pulled Marcy toward the far door, surprised when she found it unlocked. She cautiously pushed it open in case the energy force had something planned for them. But when the door was opened wide, nothing happened.

"So far, so good."

"Now what?" Marcy's voice was small and timid, like a frightened child's.

"I don't know yet." She wanted to see what was in the room, and if there was any way to get out that way. It was a small conference room, most of it taken up by a large wood table and seven chairs. A fire extinguisher hung by the entrance and blinds were closed over the old-style windows. Otherwise it was empty.

"We could put the extinguisher through the window," Bettie said. "But then we'd be no better off than we were out there."

"Unless we prop something in the window, like the table. But the glass would still grow back anyway." Marcy dropped into one of the chairs.

Taking the seat next to Marcy, Bettie faced her. "Unless we can stick something in the window like a big tube. The glass would still grow back, but at least we'd be able to crawl through the tube and get out."

Several people wandered into the conference room.

"What are you doing in here?" Wendy looked around the room. "Is there another way out of here?"

Bettie was exhausted, ready to put her head down and take a nap. The last thing she wanted to do was argue with someone. "Unless we can figure out how to jam something in the window to keep the glass from growing back, we're no better off."

"Except we don't have to worry about the glass slicing us to bits," a man said. His ID badge read Jeffrey Watkins, employee of Dimension Graphics.

"Agreed." Bettie stared at the blinds covering the windows. "Why don't we get everyone in here and—"

"And what?" Wendy asked. "Give the building an easy chance to kill us all at once?"

Bettie sighed, maybe a bit too loud. "The building's not trying to kill us. There's an energy force here, and it's what is controlling every part of this place, so when we tried to escape, it attacked."

"How do you know all this?" Jeffrey asked.

"Pure conjecture." Bettie turned and looked at him, tired of repeating herself. "I've felt the energy moving around. The rest is all hypothesis. Maybe there's something else that turns stairs to mud and sucks people down. Maybe it's just my imagination that made the glass doors slice someone in half. But I figure it like this: If there's something out of the ordinary, then that will most likely be the source of the disturbances in reality."

"Oh," Jeffrey said.

"If you don't want to get stuck in here, don't come in. Stay out in the lobby, and if you come up with an idea of how to get out of here, let me know." Bettie turned away and stared at the blinds again. "Let's get some light in here." She opened the blinds so that sunlight streamed into the room. "Much better." Returning to her seat, she reached for Marcy's hand. "How are you doing?"

"I'm all right. I just want to get out of here."

Bettie squeezed her hand. "We will." But she had her doubts. Even if Bernie, Jon, and the rest of the Osprey staff made it down, even if everyone in the building made it down to the lobby, how would they get out? If the energy force wanted them dead, it would kill them. But it hadn't killed them yet. Maybe it needed them alive. But why? "Marcy, didn't you say you've been feeling more tired than usual lately?"

"Yes. The last couple of weeks I've been leaving here almost exhausted."

"So've I," Wendy said.

The echo of agreement went out into the lobby, and then everyone was coming in, either sitting at the conference table or standing around it, but avoiding the windows.

Bettie looked at each of them. "Are any of you temps?"

One man and a woman raised their hands.

"How do you feel?"

"Fine," they said at once.

"No more tired than usual?"

They both shook their heads.

"Okay," Bettie said. "This is going to sound crazy, but hear me out. This energy force draws its sustenance from us. It's living off our energy. That's why it hasn't killed all of us. It needs us. But for some reason, temps aren't affected by it."

"That's crazy," one of the temps said.

"What about your computer and your phone?" Marcy asked.

"I've only been here a month. It's possible that it thinks I'm the same person who always sat at the desk."

"You're saying it hasn't killed us because it needs to feed on us? What about Doug?" Jeffrey asked. "It certainly killed him."

"And Roy," one of the women said.

Bettie thought about that. She glanced at Marcy, then at the others. "It's fear. The force is willing to sacrifice one of us to frighten the rest of us."

"It would be like a rush of adrenaline," Marcy said.

"Do you two have any idea how insane you sound?" The woman's ID badge said Rita Williams from A&R Collections. "You're suggesting there's some sort of creature in the building that's been feeding on us all this time, and now suddenly it's decided to scare us because fear is … what? More appetizing?"

"Pretty much," Bettie said.

"I think I can speak for most of us here," Rita said, "when I say the two of you are nuts. If there's a creature here, why haven't we seen it?"

"Because it's energy. It's not physical like we are. Look, the bottom line is simple. We're trapped in this building while the building changes at random around us, scaring the shit out of us. I don't know about anybody else, but I've learned that a number of people at Osprey Publishing have had weird experiences with their computer monitors and phones malfunctioning. All of them felt that, at one time or another, they were being watched, but no one was there. Some *thing* is in this building."

"And it's taking people," Marcy said.

"Taking people?" Rita asked.

"Yes," Marcy said. "Have you noticed anyone missing from your offices?" She glanced around at the others who all agreed they hadn't seen certain people in a day or two but hadn't thought anything of it.

"So the building's taken them?" a guy asked. "Why?"

"To torture them," Marcy said. "Bernie Thompson is my boss, and he was taken up into the ceiling and tortured. When he wouldn't show it any fear, it tossed him out."

"Do you hear yourself?" Rita asked.

Bettie saw no reason to keep arguing. She knew what she felt, and no one would change her mind. If they wanted to keep arguing, then let them. She was too tired to keep the game up. "You know what, Rita, if you want to believe we're crazy, then go ahead. I have no problem with that. Whether you believe us or not doesn't change the fact we're trapped in here."

The room fell silent.

Just as I figured, no one wants to argue with the crazy person.

"So what do we do now?" one of the temps asked. "Whether you're right or wrong about this energy force, we still need to figure a way out."

"Anyone check the basement?" Wendy asked. "Maybe there's another door down there that'll lead out."

"Don't you think the energy force will be aware of that and have the door blocked or fused or whatever?" The speaker was an older man in his fifties with "Ed Howe" listed on the Dasher Financials badge hanging from a lanyard around his neck. "I've never heard of anything so absurd. An energy creature that sucks the life out of us. Next you're going to say it's a vampire." He shook his head. "I will say this: as ridiculous as she sounds, she's the only one coming up with anything that remotely explains what's happening to us."

Bettie held her breath, waiting for the argument to continue. While they were arguing, the entity—she had no better word for it—was probably planning its next attack, and if they didn't act soon someone else would be killed. Maybe there was something in the basement that could help them keep a window open so everyone could get out. It was worth checking.

"So you think some *creature* is holding us here?" Rita asked. "Some monster that none of us can see but she can feel?"

"You saw what happened to Doug and Roy," Wendy said. "They're dead."

Bettie leaned toward Marcy. "I'm going to the basement—"

"No! You can't leave me alone." Marcy grabbed Bettie's arm. "I'll come with you."

"No, you can't. Listen to me. I believe that for whatever reason, this entity can't see me or any of the other temps. I don't understand why it can't, but I'm satisfied to believe it can't. I have to go downstairs to see if I can find anything to keep one of these windows open. I want you to stay here and try to keep these people from doing something stupid like Doug did."

"But …"

Bettie hated the puppy-dog look Marcy gave her, and she almost gave in, but she couldn't afford to have someone with her whom the entity could see. She could get a lot more accomplished being invisible. "You'll be fine."

"I wish I had my gun."

Bettie was grateful she didn't. The last thing she wanted was for anyone to get shot because someone got frightened.

She stood up and listened to the arguments continue. "I want the two temps to come with me."

"Why?" the female temp asked.

"I'm going downstairs to look for anything we can use to keep one of these windows open, and I want you to come with me. Three people looking around will get it done much faster than one."

"But what about the creature?" she asked.

"I don't think it can see temps. I don't know why it can't, but I haven't been affected by it and neither have any of the other temps."

"It has to be the ID badges," Ed said. "The temps have to sign in; they don't have badges like the rest of us. We scan ours in when we come in. Maybe this thing can interface with the building's security system and know who's who."

The others in the room sat still as if waiting for the entity to make an appearance or in some way prove the man right or wrong, but nothing happened.

"But the badges are set to a code," Jeffrey said. "It's not the specific person, but the code on the badge. If you give your badge to one of these women—he indicated Wendy and Rita— then they'll have that coded badge. If whatever it is can get into the electrical system that the security scanner works on, then it might be able to track that coded badge around the building."

"What if I leave my badge here and leave the room?" Wendy asked. "Will it still see me?"

"The only way it could is if it processes energy signatures."

Everyone looked at the guy—he couldn't have been more than twenty-four—sitting quietly in the corner. "My name's Freddie. I just started at Dimension Graphics." He held up his ID badge as if proving he really did work there. "If it processes energy signatures with the badge codes, then it could track individuals around the building."

"What?" Wendy asked.

"We all have unique energy signatures," Freddie said.

"Auras," one of the other women said.

"Okay." Freddie nodded. "We'll call them auras. Everyone has an aura that's unique to them. Everyone here also has a coded ID badge, except the temps."

"The temps still have auras, though," the woman said.

"Right," Freddie agreed. "But they don't have ID badges, so it's like they're free floating energy forms with no identification tags. The rest of us have these badges, so this thing can identify a particular ID code with an aura. Even if you leave your badge in here and walk around the building, it would still know who you are."

Rita snorted. "You've got to be kidding me. Do you hear what you're saying? Auras? Energy signatures?"

"How else do you explain it?" Ed asked.

Rita's smile slipped.

"We can discuss this all later," Bettie said. "Right now I'm going to the basement, and I want the two temps coming with me. The sooner we find something to prop these windows open with, the sooner we can get out of here." Bettie turned to go, not waiting for the temps. She refused to look at Marcy again because the woman looked like she was about to cry.

The other two temps caught up with Bettie halfway across the lobby.

"I'm Chris," the guy introduced himself.

"Doreen," the woman said.

"Bettie, and thank you for coming along." She stopped and turned to them. "It doesn't matter what you believe. Do you understand?" When they nodded, she continued. "Buildings don't change like what we've experienced. Are we in agreement about that?" Again, they nodded. "Good. So whether you think it's some kind of energy creature or a kind of magic or just an 'off day at the office,' we all agree we need to get out of here before something else happens." They nodded. She went to the basement door and pulled it open. "All right. If I'm correct, which I hope I am, the entity can't see us, which means we can move around the building without being bothered." Holding the door open for Chris and Doreen, she started down the stairs. "We need to find something that, once we break a window, we can use to keep the glass from growing back so we can get everyone out."

"Should we try to find a door down here?" Doreen asked. "If one of us can get out, we can call for help."

She had a valid point. If one of them could call for help, then at least the rest of them could wait for the police and fire departments to arrive. "Absolutely. Do you want to look for a way out while Chris and I search for something to prop in the window?"

Doreen nodded.

At the bottom of the stairs it was cold and dark and Bettie shivered. She'd never cared for the basement, as it always seemed dank and depressing. The only lights were the emergency ones shedding bloodred illumination across the cavernous room. The door to Leo's office was wide open.

Bettie wondered where Leo was. She hadn't seen him in a couple of days. The most likely answer was that the building—

Doreen screamed.

Chris and Bettie rushed over to where she stared down at Leo. He was dead, stabbed in the chest. That answered Bettie's question.

"That's the maintenance guy, isn't it?" Doreen asked. "God, what a jerk."

"Someone killed him." Bettie looked around the basement. If someone was down here and killed Leo, she wanted to be able to see, and for that she had to find the breaker box and get some light.

"Someone?" Chris asked. "Don't you mean the entity?"

The breaker box door was open. Bettie squinted at the labels and when she found the three basement switches, she flipped them to the On position. "Maybe, but I don't think it kills just to kill, and this looks like someone stabbed him." Bettie wasn't going to get any closer to him to check the stab wound. "Let's keep looking around."

Doreen started walking toward the back hallway.

"What do you think'll work to keep the window open?" Chris asked.

"I don't know. It has to be something strong enough to keep the window from growing back and also big enough so people can crawl through."

"Maybe like a piece of the ductwork?"

Bettie imagined shoving the metal square through the broken window and people climbing through it. "That would be the exact thing I'm looking for. Now where would you keep pieces of ductwork?"

"Do you really think this is some kind of monster?" Chris asked.

Bettie paused. "Does it matter?"

"No, I guess not. Just curious."

Bettie had no desire to start a discussion or an argument. Maybe later, when they were all safe, over a few drinks, she'd be more than happy to start a debate on what had really happened. But it was still happening and she wanted nothing else but to get out.

Following in the direction Doreen went, she hoped she'd find a storage room with a few pieces of ductwork lying around. "Why don't we check down here?"

"Good idea." Chris glanced around. "I don't—"

"Bettie!" Doreen's voice was weak.

"Oh, no. What now?" Bettie rushed down the hallway, made the right, and went to the last room on the left. "What—" Even before she stepped into the room, she saw the walls, the open trapdoor, smelled the foul stench, and knew things were about to get much worse.

JON

The first office they came to, A&R Collections, looked like a war zone. Desks were overturned, papers scattered everywhere. Several dead bodies lay on the floor while others were still in their chairs, their necks sliced open.

"Jesus Christ," Bernie whispered.

"We're too late," Sara said.

"Maybe there's someone left alive." Jon went into the office, knowing full well everyone—whoever hadn't been taken—was dead. But if there was the chance anyone was still alive, he could try to save them.

"Let's not take too long. We still have Dimension Graphics to check out," Bernie said.

"I'll check over there," Sara said. "I'll meet you back here."

"Be careful, Sara," Bernie said. "Anything, Jon?"

"No. Not yet." He wanted to find someone alive, he realized, so he wouldn't feel hopeless. If at least one person was still breathing, he'd feel there was a hope of getting out. If not, what hope did Patti and the others have once the entity discovered they were leaving?

But there was no hope. Chairs were broken, computers smashed, desks deeply scarred, bodies carved up.

"Come on, Jon," Bernie said. "There's nothing here we can do. There are people downstairs who need us."

He left the office and the two of them walked to the graphics company.

"I'm sorry, Jon. I hoped we'd find someone alive, but when that thing decides to kill, there's nothing to stop it."

Sara came out of the Dimension Graphics office. "There's no one there. Either they got out or the entity took them."

Bernie looked up at the ceiling. "Damn it. Let's go down to the lobby." Bernie led them to the stairs and down. "With luck everyone's all right down there and nobody did anything stupid."

"Why do you think the creature isn't attacking us?" Sara asked.

"We're three people," Bernie said. "and if what Jon said is true, then we appear as only two to the entity and it's already decided I wasn't any fun."

Sara glanced at Jon. "I wonder why it can't see you?"

Jon shrugged. He had no idea, but he was more than grateful to be invisible.

"Be careful when you go down the last flight of stairs," Bernie said. "When I came up, there was an arm sticking out a few steps above the second-floor landing."

"An arm?" Sara asked.

"The stairs turned to mud," Jon said. "And someone sank into them until he was almost gone and then they resolidified."

"Fear," Sara said. "There were probably people standing around and it was scaring them to feed on them."

Sure enough, when they reached the final landing, Jon saw the man's hand and arm almost down to his elbow sticking out of the stairs, reaching for help that would never come.

The lobby was empty except for something Jon couldn't identify. "What the hell is that?" As he came closer, he realized it was the remains of a person. "Jesus Christ." He spun on his heels and went to the wall to steady himself. His stomach twisted and tightened. He was grateful he had nothing left to vomit or he would've.

"Where the hell is everyone?" Bernie asked. "I told them to stay put and not to do anything."

"Maybe ..." Sara said but didn't finish her sentence.

"No, that thing didn't get all of them." Bernie and Sara walked to the vestibule doors.

"What in the name of God is that?" Bernie asked.

Jon turned to look in the vestibule at what first appeared to be a pile of broken glass. But then it moved, and Jon froze, staring in disbelief at ... what was it?

Sara was backing away, one hand on her stomach, the other over her mouth.

Jon heard the tinkling of glass. He'd seen enough of the man—or what was left of him—to know he had to be dead. If he was moving, it had to be a trick of the eye. But he heard the sound of movement and knew it wasn't a trick. The thing in the vestibule climbed to its knees, and stared at Bernie with glass-pierced eyes.

Bernie moved away from the doors.

Fascinated, Jon watched as the thing put its bleeding, skinless hands on the door but then fell back in a crash of broken glass. There was no more movement; the thing was still, as if it had only one last gasp of energy to frighten them and that was it. Good riddance.

"There's an open door over here." Bernie pointed to a door to the left of the vestibule. "I hear people." He walked over with Sara following.

Jon pressed himself against the wall, keeping an eye on the vestibule in case the thing had one last burst of energy, but it was for naught; it was completely still. *As dead people should be,* Jon thought.

He turned into the conference room and looked at the handful of people milling about. He didn't see Bettie or Marcy.

"Where's Bettie and Marcy?" Bernie asked.

"Bettie went downstairs with a couple of temps," one of the women said. "And the other woman … she was here a minute ago. I don't know where she went."

MARCY

As she sat waiting for Bettie to return, the woman in her head started talking.

Why don't you go retrieve the gun and make yourself useful? Why are you sitting here while Bettie looks for a way to save the day? Wouldn't you rather get the glory for saving these people than let her get the spotlight one more time?

Leave me alone.

You hate the truth, don't you? Bettie is down there looking for a way to save these people. Go get the gun, go downstairs, and maybe you'll see the creature, the gun will go off "accidentally," and all your problems with Bettie's smug attitude will be over.

She's not like that. She's not trying to be in the spotlight.

Oh, no? Every woman dresses like she does. Don't you think she's trying to be noticed because her ego demands it? And every man would fawn over her more than give you a second glance. But with her gone, there's nothing stopping you from going after Jon, and you know you want to.

I can't do that.

The woman laughed. *Go get the gun and I'll help you make things right. You can be the hero and get all the glory for saving these people. Bettie will be gone and you can have Jon all to yourself. You've always been jealous of Bettie, haven't you?*

No. I ...

But she got up. No one saw her leave the conference room. *Because no one cares about me.* Out in the lobby she saw the gun in the vestibule lying on top of the pile of glass that had once been Doug. *What a stupid man,* she thought. *But how am I going to retrieve the gun, unless ...*

She pushed the vestibule door and it easily opened. Reaching in, careful not to get cut by the glass, she held her breath, expecting Doug to come to life any second and grab her arm. But he didn't and she retrieved the gun with no problem. She contemplated trying to get out, but didn't want to come to the same fate as Doug.

Now, the woman in her head said smiling, *the basement.*

Marcy held the gun and went down the basement stairs. The building was silent except for her footfalls on the cement steps. "This is a mistake." She paused on the stairs and stared at the Ladysmith in her hand. "I can't do this."

If you can't go down the stairs, find Bettie and kill her, then just take the gun, suck the barrel down, and pull the fucking trigger, you good-for-nothing piece of shit.

"No!" The gun started slipping from her hand, but her fingers curled around the handle before it fell.

It's either you or Bettie. One of you isn't coming back up the stairs. It's your choice.

Marcy stood frozen, unable to move. Why couldn't she just shut the woman in her head up? Why couldn't she be normal like everyone else?

The day you failed your family, you made me real.
That was the truth. And the only way to get rid of her, to silence her for good, was to ... She held the gun up to the side of her head, right behind her ear. Could she somehow miss and wind up paralyzed for life? She opened her mouth and placed the cold metal barrel on her tongue. One, two, three, pull the trigger and there would be no more Marcy and no more judgment. Easy. Simple. Maybe count down from five. Four. Three. Two. One. She squeezed her eyes shut and gently pulled back on the trigger.

Four. Three. Two ...

BETTIE

She found the light switch and turned it on, then wished she hadn't. All four walls were covered from floor to ceiling with photographs of women and girls. Some of the ones to her immediate left were curled and blackened as if a controlled fire had burned them.

"Oh, my God," Doreen mumbled.

"What the hell is this?" Chris asked.

"Leo's sick little world." Bettie went over and kicked the trapdoor shut.

"Okay," Doreen said. "We're done in here." She ran out with her hand over her nose and mouth, followed by Chris, who was shaking his head.

Bettie was about to shut off the lights when she noticed photos on the wall of her and Marcy, as well as other women who worked at Osprey, in the bathroom. She shuddered, glad Leo was dead, and closed the door, wondering where that trapdoor led to.

The gunshot echoed throughout the basement.

Bettie remembered Marcy had a gun and ran back to the main basement. No one was there. She checked the stairs to see if anyone had fallen. Marcy's gun lay on one step and a shoe lay on its side several steps down. "Oh, God, Marcy, what were you thinking?" She glanced up into the darkness of the ceiling, hoping to catch a glimpse of her friend, but there was nothing to see.

"What happened?" Chris asked.

"I don't know." Bettie picked up Marcy's gun and her shoe. "Damn it."

"Should we keep checking down here?" Doreen asked.

Bettie thought about the back room with the walls of photos and its stench, and she didn't want to go back. She preferred to run upstairs and be with everyone else where it was safe, though she knew nowhere in the building was safe. Glancing into the dark ceiling, she wondered if there was any way to save Marcy without going into the ductwork and crawling around. Why had Marcy been coming down here with a gun?

"Bettie?" Chris said quietly.

Without looking at the two temps, she said, "Check Leo's office for keys or something to unlock those other doors. Maybe there's something in there we can use."

How many more people were dead that she didn't know about? *Keep it together, Bettie, these people need you. God knows if Bernie and Jon made it; you may be their only hope. You don't want this on your shoulders. You can't do this alone.* A weight in her chest grew, then constricted. *I'm … I'm not helpless. I'm not helpless.* She repeated the three words over and over, hoping to overcome the pressure building in her chest, the tightness that always came when she felt overwhelmed. Marcy's shoe fell from her hand. It was a panic attack and it paralyzed her, made her question her ability to function, brought her to the edge of self-worth, and threatened to shove her over. If only she had her cutter. Just a small cut would soothe her, would remind her of the power she had over herself, the power of the blade. Seeing her blood always dragged her away from the edge into a sensation of calmness. People said that when she cut herself she was looking for attention, but she knew better. It overwhelmed the agony in her soul so that some degree of clarity could come to her.

The familiar sensation of coming unhinged started first in her chest, and then sank deeper. She was too small and weak to do this. She needed Bernie, like Marcy had, and she was a fool to think she could do anything to save these people.

Not now.

She started counting. There would be a number, maybe twenty, maybe fifty, when the creeping cold in her body, the icy fingers of fear clutching her heart, would cease and she'd be in control again. She sat down on a box of paper and closed her eyes. Ten. When she tried taking a deep breath, it shuddered through her. Twenty. Someone was talking to her. Thirty. Someone, a woman, was calling her name. She opened her eyes and for a moment, the two people in front of her were strangers.

"Are you all right?" The man's name was Chris.

"Bettie?" The woman's name was Doreen.

"We found keys," Chris said. "Do you want to wait here and we'll check those other rooms?"

She held her breath. Forty. She desperately wanted to stay right there and cry through the pain, but if anything happened to Chris or Doreen, it would be her fault. "No." Her voice sounded like a child's. Fifty. She cleared her throat and shook her head. "Let's go. I'm fine." Using the boxes around her, she steadied herself as she rose to her feet and tucked the gun in her belt.

"Are you sure?" Doreen asked. "You can wait here, and if we find anything, we'll let you know."

Oh, how she wanted to say, "Thank you, please, I'll be right here, scream if you need me," but she couldn't. Underneath the helpless child was a woman who was a survivor, and it was that woman from whom she summoned the strength to finish this. "No. Come on."

The first and second rooms were empty. The third room had exactly what they were looking for: five pieces of metal ductwork that were too heavy for them to lift.

"Now what?" Doreen asked.

"We get help." Bettie turned and almost collided with Jon.

"Need a hand?" Bernie asked.

MARCY

The cables came down and embraced her. The gun went off, but the bullet shot off into the darkness. She cried, so close to ending the pain and misery no one but her understood. While she decided she wouldn't struggle against the cables, they took her up into the ceiling, into the blackness of the heart of the Howard Phillips Building. They didn't crush her, nor did they attack her, but bore her upward, pausing only to break through ceiling tile and set her down in a dark room. She was on one of the abandoned floors in one of the empty offices. Why had it brought her here? If it wanted to kill her, it could've done so in the basement. If it planned to torture her, it could've left her in the ventilation system.

Wiping tears from her eyes, she walked around the room. It had been one large office area, but if there had been fabric walls, they were gone now. She went to the windows and turned the blinds open, flooding the room with gray daylight. It hadn't seemed long enough to have gone up five floors, but when she glanced out the window she saw she was definitely on the fifth floor. The view was just like that from Osprey's, facing the parking lot.

There were voices outside the office door, and for a second she thought she was dreaming. People were still here? She walked into the reception area and came face to face with Sharon—or what was left of her. She staggered toward Marcy, and Marcy felt a wall of electricity around Sharon, reaching out to her.

"No." She gasped, tried to scream, to warn the others, but no sound came out. Even the woman in her head was silent. Tears filled her eyes. "Why?" Her heart raced and her knees began to buckle. She could barely stand. Her hands started shaking. This was too much. She backed up against the nearest wall. Tears ran down her face and she quickly wiped them away so she could see.

It lurched at her and the wave of electricity swarmed around her, enveloped her like an electrical blanket, smothered her until she could barely breathe, barely see. The darkness of unconsciousness rose up to overwhelm her, but she fought it. There were people outside who could save her. Tiny lights exploded in her vision, white sparks like fireworks, like she was watching the synapses in her brain firing off—and then she giggled.

Dull, buzzing warmth pressed down on her, until she fell to one knee and thought she was going to pass out. The pain coursed through her head and down her back, then wound around and back up her spine with an icy coldness that knocked her over. She fell, trembling, out of control, her body not her own. All she wanted was to scream the pain out as it burned her nervous system, but she couldn't make a sound. In a tiny part of her mind, she expected the woman in her head to chime in and she thought she heard the familiar chant.

Mouuuuuussssssssss ...

Static filled her ears, washing the voice away in a tidal wave of sound that crashed over her, leaving her breathless, lying on the floor shaking as if she were having a seizure.

Finally, the buzzing subsided, the static faded, and her body was still. She opened her eyes and looked around. Everything seemed a uniform, dull gray.

What's happening to me? (happening to me?)

I ... (I ...)

What? (What?)

Oh, my God. (my God)

She touched her face, ran her hands along her arms, making sure she was still Marcy Browne (*Marcy Browne*) and—

Her skin glowed with a faint redness, and with each breath she felt something in her chest like a gentle rumble, like a ... purring sound.

"What's happening to me?" (*happening to me?*)

"Oh, God. It's inside me." (*inside me*)

She stood up on wobbly legs but felt a rush of energy like she hadn't felt in years. She felt alive! All traces of exhaustion were gone.

"Whatever it is, I think I like it!" (*like it*)

She glanced down where her friend lay dead. All she could see was a fading red tint around Sharon that quickly flared up but then died out. She quickly moved to the front of the office, to the glass doors. There were people, well, a person, going into the stairwell. Then, a few seconds later, another person came through and into the stairwell. The window was frosted so she couldn't tell who the people were, but they were either from Dasher Financials or Osprey Publishing, and if they were from Osprey and knew a way out …

She unlocked the door and stepped out into the hallway.

"Marcy?"

"Patti?" (*Patti*) Her co-worker glowed red with lighter tinges around her body and a brighter red in her chest right where her heart was. "Oh, my God." (*my God*) *Shh*, she told herself or whomever it was that repeated everything she thought or said.

"Are you all right? You don't look so well."

"I … I'm not sure." She giggled. "Something happened in there and I can't explain it but I see … Everything's weird." Marcy glanced around. The walls radiated grayness, but Patti and the person coming up behind her were vivid reds, yellows, and oranges. Will stopped in front of her and again she gasped. Two spots, both very dark, almost violet, lay in the center of his chest. His lungs. He smoked too much. She should tell him he was going to die soon but didn't.

"Are you all right?" he asked.

"I don't know." She turned back to Patti. Though she could see the woman as she always had, this new vision was amazing. She should be worried, but she couldn't feel fear, only a calmness that warmed every fiber of her body.

"We're going up to the roof and down the fire escape," Patti said. "It's the only way to get out of here. There's some sort of … creature that's been draining us and keeping us here, scaring us so we'd be frightened and it could feed on our fear."

Marcy giggled. "That sounds silly."

Patti stared at her. "You're not all right. Poor dear. Come with us and I'll make sure to get you help."

"Okay." Marcy almost skipped to the stairwell, but controlled herself. It was obvious Patti and Will were scared; she could feel their fear and it was delightful. She stopped with her hand on the stairwell door.

"Marcy?" Patti said.

She shouldn't be able to feel fear. But it was as if all her senses were amplified. Backing away from the door, she leaned against the wall. "Why don't you go first? I'll be right behind you."

"Are you sure?" Patti asked.

Marcy nodded.

Will held the door open and the two of them went up.

Just another minute. (another minute)

Yes. One minute more. (minute more)

Marcy realized two things at once. The entity that she had been so afraid of was inside her, and in reality there was no reason to be afraid of it at all. The entity was harmless! With that, she opened the stairwell door and, laughing, followed the others up to the roof.

Patti was there with Will and a couple of others. Most had already gone over the side to the fire escape.

All my friends are going away. (going away)

The purr in her chest grew louder, as if the recognition of her co-workers made the entity happy or angry that they would leave it. A sudden jolt in her stomach brought her to her knees. These were the worst hunger pains she'd ever felt. It wasn't merely as if she hadn't eaten in a day, but more like a week. She needed food fast. Her head grew dizzy from the buzzing sound that rose from her chest.

Must stop them. (stop them) Catch them. (them) Feed. (feed)

The easiest way to slow them down was to turn the roof to molasses. Energy streamed out from her hands, and she watched those still on the roof sinking into what had been concrete a moment before. Her revulsion at her own actions was slowly replaced by their fear, which soothed the ache in her belly. Yes, their horror calmed hers, feeding her until she felt sated, pleased at what these beings offered her. She'd keep them around for a while. She let them sink until only their heads were above ground and after she turned the roof back to cement, she sat and surveyed her work. Four of the beings were caught. They screamed and waved frantically, their fear coming off them in delicious waves.

She got to her feet and walked in the direction they were going. The woman (Patti) had said something about escape. The food stuck in the roof called for help, repeated a name over and over, but she no longer understood their language and it troubled her. She should know what they said, but all she heard were loud, frightened sounds. What was this "Marcy" they spoke of? She vaguely remembered the label that had been attached to herself, but now that the transformation was in full bloom, she had no need for names or labels or even language.

As she passed each piece of food, they screamed louder, and a smell filled her olfactory sense. The entity searched the host's memory to identify the odor and found roasted meat. Yes, it agreed, it smelled like roasted meat.

At the edge of the roof, she peered over and down. There was more food escaping. Kneeling, she reached out and touched the cold metal, allowing her energy to cascade downward. In moments there were more shrieks and screams. The metal had melted just enough to bond to the food, keeping it there for later when she was hungry.

Satisfied and sated, she turned back to the food trapped on the roof. They weren't moving or making any noise, but smoke rose from their darkened husks. Within the entity, a piece of the host felt a deep emotion that the entity found labeled as sorrow. Perhaps it would allow her to surface more so it could experience these sensations fully. Though it was sated from the fear, it found these other emotions amusing.

JON

It had taken Jon, Chris, and Bernie working together to get the three-foot piece of ductwork up the stairs and into the conference room. Doreen had suggested the elevator, but the other three agreed it was a bad idea.

"So now what?" Doreen asked once they were back in the conference room.

"We open the window," Bernie said, "and slide this through so all of you can climb through it and out." Bernie patted the piece of ductwork. "This was good thinking, Bettie."

She blushed. "Thanks, boss."

Sirens echoed in the distance, growing louder.

"Somebody's made it out and called the police," Jon said.

"Excellent," Bernie said. "We'll be out of this soon." He went to the window. "Ready?"

Chris and Freddie hefted the metal and waited.

"Wait!" Sara shouted. "It's gone."

"What do you mean, it's gone?" Bettie asked.

"What's gone?" Chris asked.

"The entity," Sara said. "It's not here anymore."

"How do you know that?" Ed asked.

"Where did it go?" Bernie asked.

"I ... I don't know." Sara stared at him. "It's just gone. I've been able to sense it, feel its presence." She saw the look people gave her. "I know. I'm crazy. Can we just get out of here?"

"All right. Wait here. No one move." Bernie went out into the lobby. "The doors are still fused." He came back in to the conference room. "Jon, open the window, but be ready to get that ductwork in so it doesn't close or whatever it's going to do."

Chris and Freddie stood by. Jon opened the window and stepped back as the two men moved in and—thankfully—fit the piece of duct into the window frame. It was a touch snug, but that just meant it wouldn't fall out.

"All right," Jon said. "Get one of those chairs over here. The easiest way out is to climb on the chair and slide out."

The first person, a woman from Dasher Financials, stepped up and tried to go through headfirst.

"Don't go headfirst or you'll have no way to land on your feet."

"Should we wait for the police to get here?" she asked.

"No." Bernie shook his head. "We should get out as quickly as possible." He looked around the room. "It might be gone, but it could come back at any moment."

The woman nodded before sliding herself through and out. "I'm out!"

The others went through until only Jon, Bernie, Sara, Chris, and Bettie were left.

"Ladies first," Chris said.

"No," Sara said. "I'll go out with these guys."

"All right." Chris climbed onto the chair and shoved himself out.

"Sara, go ahead," Bernie said. "We'll be right behind you."

Sara was climbing on the chair when the creaking noise came from the lobby.

They all turned as Marcy stepped into the doorway. She moved stiffly as if she were just learning how to use her body. Her arms hung at her side, while she shuffled her feet, each step a difficult gesture. Her head wobbled like one of those bobblehead dolls and her eyes glowed pale electric green.

"Oh, my God." Sara came down off the chair and stood with the others. "It's in her. The entity's merged with her."

"What?" Bernie, Jon, and Bettie said at once.

Marcy opened her mouth, tilted her head, and made that god-awful creaking noise that Jon had heard Tony make.

"Oh, shit," Bettie said.

"Is that possible?" Bernie asked.

"I didn't think so." Sara joined the others.

Bernie turned to face the transformed woman. "Marcy?"

The only sound the woman made was the creaking noise, as if trying to understand the language and speak it, but without the ability to do so. She placed her hands against the wall and the ductwork buckled from the force of the wooden window frame expanding.

"What the hell's going on in there?" A police officer stood outside the building looking in through the ductwork. "What's with the metal?"

Bernie ignored him. "Sara, get out of here."

"No, not yet." She pulled Jon back. "If we can get Marcy outside and isolate her, I've got something in my car that we might be able to use to capture the entity."

"What are you talking about?" Bettie asked.

"I can explain later. We need to get her outside and away from everyone."

Bernie shook his head. "I want everyone out now."

Marcy grimaced, her hands still flat against the wall.

The police officer came closer. "Could someone tell me what the emergency is?"

"Help the people outside," Bernie said, then glanced over at Marcy. "Someone get her away from the wall!"

The wooden window frame forced itself inward, creasing

the middle of the metal until the metal folded in on itself like paper.

"Holy shit," the officer said before backing away from the building.

Bernie turned back to Marcy. "Stop it!"

She took a step toward him, and he had to step back.

"There's some kind of energy field around her," Bernie said.

"It's like what happened with Tony," Jon said. "I think it's electrical."

"I don't know if it's electrical." Bettie took a hesitant step toward Marcy. "I feel it as more pure energy."

"Be careful, Bettie," Bernie said.

"Marcy? Can you hear me?" Bettie asked.

"She can't hear you," Sara said. "She can't see you or Jon, remember?"

The other woman cocked her head like a dog and stared at Bettie, with no recognition in her gaze, but then she opened her mouth and under the creaking voice was the word, "Bettieee."

"That shouldn't happen," Sara said. "She shouldn't be able to hear or see you."

"Aalllwaaaysss betterrr thaaannn mmmeee."

"No." Bettie backed up against the table, furiously shaking her head. "I wanted to help you. I never thought I was better than you."

"Alllwaaaysss." Marcy took a step toward her, forcing the four of them back away from her, but they kept the conference table between them and Marcy. The waves of current grew stronger, striking Jon's skin with a million tiny jolts.

"How can she hear me? I'm a temp." Bettie looked at the others. "We agreed the entity couldn't see us."

Sara said, "All I can think of is because it's using a human host, it has her memories and her senses so it can see and hear. Bettie, she remembers you, and the entity understands what it sees through her memories."

"Is she still alive?" Bernie asked.

"Tony couldn't see me even though we were friends," Jon said. "I don't think he heard me, either." He glanced at Sara.

"I think Marcy may still be alive." Sara shook her head.

"There are some thing I don't understand like the bond between the entity and its host and how the relationship between the host and others affects it. The entity might know those emotions through Marcy's experiences and see Bettie. If she's got strong emotions toward anyone, then the entity is probably aware of their existence."

"Marcy?" Jon moved around the table, keeping the conference table between them. She was near the windows, across the table, oblivious to him. "Marcy." She showed no sign of hearing him, which meant he was invisible to her, or so he hoped. Making his way toward the doorway, he had no idea what he was going to do, but he had to at least try to get her outside. The quickest way was to push her through the window, but even though she was possessed by the entity, he didn't want to hurt her.

There was the other conference room he could drag her to, but that was too far away.

"Berrrnnnieee. Liiike a faaatherrr tooo mmmeee. Buut nnnooo fffeeeaaarrr. Sssaaad yooouuu wiiilll nnneeeeverrr knnnowww thiiissss fffeeelinnng." She turned her gaze to Sara and Bettie. "Yooouuu willll dieee."

"Please, Marcy," Bettie said. "You don't have to do this."

"I know you're better than the thing inside you," Bernie said. "Let us go and we'll help you."

"Diiieee."

Marcy was slipping away; the entity grew stronger. The floor between her and the other three rippled and melted. Pulling the fire extinguisher from its rack on the wall, Jon came toward Marcy. Bernie, Sara, and Bettie separated, but it did no good; the floor turned to a viscous liquid.

"Marcy, stop!" Bettie tried to move away from the windows, but fell, her hands sinking into the thick ooze.

Bernie managed to keep from falling by leaning back against the wall.

Sara stumbled and fell face-first into the floor. She pulled herself up, molasses-like fluid dripping from her skin.

Marcy cocked her head at her.

The window closest to Sara exploded inward. Slivers like

daggers sliced Sara's face and arms while larger shards sunk into her neck and side.

Jon was torn; he didn't want to hurt Marcy, but the entity was trying to kill them. He couldn't worry about Marcy. She'd go to the hospital if she lived through this. The others might not be so lucky. He stepped into the field of electricity that surrounded her; it wasn't as strong as Tony's so he could get closer before the pain crawled across his skin like ants. All he needed were a few seconds to knock her out. He could stand the intense scratching of electricity on his skin for just that short length of time.

Raising the extinguisher, he swung at her head. She was oblivious to him until the moment of impact when she was thrown against the windows.

"We need help over here!" someone shouted outside.

Jon looked at the police officers staring, their guns out, pointed at him.

"Drop it!"

Jon dropped the extinguisher. He looked back at the others. The floor was still liquid. Bernie sloshed through it to Sara, turned her over, and shook her head. "Damn it. She's dead."

"Bettie?" Jon said.

"Sticky, but alive."

"Put your hands where we can see them," the officer outside shouted, his gun trained on Jon.

Jon put his hands on his head.

Marcy stirred. If he didn't act quickly, she'd finish them off. He turned to Bernie. "Clear the broken window. Get the glass out."

Bernie took up the extinguisher and used it to do as Jon asked.

"Help me get her outside." Jon knelt to pick Marcy up.

"Sir," the officer said, "get away from her."

Bernie came to his side. "What are you planning?"

"Sara said we had to get her isolated from any buildings and people. I don't know what she had in her car, but maybe if we keep her isolated, the thing inside her will starve and die."

"What will happen to Marcy then?"

Jon looked at him and shrugged.

"Great."

They lifted Marcy and brought her to the window. Several officers came over and waited to receive her.

"Get back," Bernie said.

"Pass her out."

Jon moved to the window to do as the officer said. "As soon as she's out, put her down and back away."

"Sir, she's injured. We're taking her to an ambulance to get medical attention."

"No," Jon said. "Put her down and back away from her."

Instead, the officer took Marcy, and with help from another officer, carried her away from the building and set her down on the grass.

"Back away from her!" Jon shouted, but they weren't listening to him. "Shit." He climbed through the window, followed by Bernie and Bettie.

Marcy reached a hand up and grabbed the arm of the nearest officer. He screamed as smoke rose from where her hand held his arm.

"Let him go!" The other officer fell back and drew his gun. "Let him go!"

Jon watched helplessly as she tossed the first officer back and stalked toward the other one. She closed her eyes and a sudden shimmering flashed out, encompassing the second officer, turning him into a human torch. His skin turned black in seconds, and before his last scream died, he fell to the grass, a smoking husk.

The nearest officers drew their guns.

"Stop!" Jon had no idea what the bullets' effect would be on the energy field around Marcy, but he didn't want to find out, especially if it were to cause a large scale explosion. "Don't shoot!"

As Jon predicted, they ignored him and opened fire.

If the bullets had any effect, Jon couldn't tell. Marcy stood, stared at the police, and moved away from them as if they weren't of any concern to her.

"Stop!" one of the officers shouted.

But Marcy kept walking and then ran, and Jon realized she

headed toward a small wooded area and beyond that, a couple of office buildings.

"We have to stop her," Bernie said.

"How?" Bettie asked.

The police had stopped shooting and now chased after her.

"Come on." Jon led them after the police. "All this time, the entity has been in the building feeding on people's emotions. Now it's isolated in Marcy. If we can keep it from merging into another building, maybe it won't be able to survive for much longer."

"It has to be killing Marcy," Bettie said.

Jon remembered finding Tony's charred body. "It's too much for a human body to sustain. Whether it's energy or electricity, the human body isn't built to be a host for it."

"Then we need to keep it from reaching another building," Bernie said. "It'll kill Marcy. But will it be trapped in her body?"

Ahead of them Marcy passed through the trees and headed across the parking lot.

"Where else will it go?" Bettie asked.

"Jon, you're going to have to do this. Bettie and I can't go near her. She doesn't see you, so you can get close enough to hold her back."

"Maybe we can knock her unconscious," Bettie said. "That way Jon doesn't have to get near her."

"Jon tried that." Bernie shook his head. "The entity did something to get her moving again. No, we need to physically stop her."

They ran behind the police. What the officers would do when they caught her was an unknown Jon didn't want to think about. He was sure Marcy and the entity could kill all of them, but would that exhaust the creature?

Between the two office buildings was an alleyway with utility entrances to both buildings. Marcy headed for it. If she made it, the entity could go into either one. Or could it split itself so that it could inhabit both buildings? Jon didn't want to consider the possibility. One murderous entity was enough.

"Freeze!" The policemen ahead of him had their guns

drawn and now pointed them at Marcy. She had just reached the alleyway and stopped. "Turn around with your hands above your head!"

She turned around and looked at the half-dozen officers closing in on her.

Jon wanted to tell them to back off, but they wouldn't; they were only doing their duty and didn't know any better. He stopped no more than twenty feet behind them with Bettie and Bernie at his side.

"She's going to kill them," Bettie said.

"Slowly and painfully," Bernie said. "She's recharging."

"It's recharging. That might be Marcy, but she's not the one killing people."

"Come forward," the lead officer said. "Keep your hands on your head."

She did as he asked.

"Do you think Marcy's in control?" Bettie asked. "Maybe the entity doesn't have the strength to maintain control."

Jon wanted to do something. Standing there watching the police attempt to handcuff her made him feel useless, and unless Marcy herself was somehow in control, the officers were in grave danger.

When the screaming started, Jon made his decision. Bettie and Bernie couldn't help; Marcy would kill them without a second thought. The police would never listen to him, and now they were suffering themselves. He was the only one who could get close enough to stop Marcy, however he could.

The officers were falling back, pulling their smoking comrades away from the entity's electrical field, calling for back up and EMTs. Marcy stood still for a moment before turning to the alleyway. Jon ran after her, hoping to keep her far enough away from the building until the entity ran out of energy or electricity or whatever sustained it.

When he passed the downed officers, he paused. Had the entity seen them? It attacked them as if it had. But that made no sense because it hadn't seen him. Or it hadn't heard him. He hadn't tried getting close enough to find out if the entity could see him; only if it could hear him. If he tried attacking it from the front, would he wind up a casualty, as well? Did he have any choice?

"I need one of your nightsticks," he said.

"What?" The nearest officer—his badge read Gregory—gave him a look like he was nuts.

"I need your nightstick. I'm going to knock her out."

"No, you're not. You can't get close enough to her to do anything. Besides, I won't let you put yourself in danger."

"What are you going to do? Restrain me?"

"I don't want to have to, but I will if you don't back away."

"Sorry." Jon turned to go.

"Wait," the officer said and pointed to one of his fellow cops. "Rawlins said there's an electromagnetic field around her. He doesn't know how it's possible, but there is. That building belongs to a communications company, and their equipment puts out—what did you call it?"

"Electromagnetic interference," Rawlins said. "It screws up EMFs."

"If you can get her close enough to the building, it might short out the EMF around her, and we can get a clean shot at her."

"Thanks." Jon didn't like that idea at all. Quite the contrary, he hoped to keep her away so the entity couldn't merge with the building. Hopefully, she'd be close enough that the interference would mess with her EMF. He ran after Marcy and stopped within ten feet of where she stood at the mouth of the alleyway.

She cocked her head to the side like a puppy. If she just stayed exactly as she was, he could … what? Tackle her? Knock her down?

He moved around her, careful not to get too close, so he blocked her way. Now he'd find out if she saw him or not. Showing no sign that she did, she took a step, but faltered. She winced and looked around as if something had affected her; the interference from the communication company's equipment was messing up her electromagnetic field. Or so he hoped.

"Marcy?" he said, but she didn't notice him.

They were too far from the building for her to make contact, and as long as he kept her away, the entity would be unable to get out. How long did it have before it ...

Her skin started smoking. At first he thought he was seeing things, but small trails of smoke rose from her arms and her face.

"Jonnn?"

She saw him.

"Jonnn? Paaiinnn."

How could she see him?

"Dyyyiiinnng. I ... nnnot ssstronnng eeennnouuugh." Her skin darkened where the smoke rose. She stumbled forward.

Jon went to catch her, but the surrounding field, though tight to her, was stronger than before, pushing him back. "Fight it," Jon said. "I know you can."

Several police officers had their guns drawn and were coming up behind Marcy. She shook her head. "Nnno ssstrennngthhh lllefffft." She staggered forward, and the field crackled outward as if the entity knew Jon was there and was forcing him back.

They were half the distance now. Another few steps and she'd be at the building, reaching out her hand so that the entity could leave her and merge with its new home. Jon searched for anything he could use to keep her back, but there was nothing.

"Marcy, please, stay back. I don't want to hurt you, but I can't let you get any closer."

"Sssommmethiiinnng huuurrrtinnng mmmeee heeerrre. I caaannn't thiiinnnk." Her eyes were sunken and her skin was pale; she looked close to death. "Huuurrrts." She nearly fell toward him, and this time, without thinking, he caught her.

The sensation was a dull buzzing across his skin, and he realized the entity didn't have the energy left to cause much of an energy field. The field was nominal. If she could hold on a few more minutes, maybe she could outlast this thing.

"You can do it, Marcy. I know you can."

"I'mmm ssorrryyy. I ... I cou ..." She winced and sobbed. "Love." She pushed Jon away, and as he stepped back, he realized the surrounding field had completely collapsed.

She had won. The entity had run out of energy. He turned to Bettie and Bernie. "The field's gone. She won. The entity's—"

"Now!"

Jon threw himself to the ground as the officer closest to him opened fire, followed by two others.

Jon's screams to stop were drowned by the deafening gunfire.

Marcy's body shook and her skin blackened as the bullets slammed into her. The force of the impact threw her forward against the closer building. Smoke rose from her body as she burned from the inside out.

Jon gagged on the stench of her smoking flesh and tears stung his eyes, but he watched her crawl toward the office.

They must've emptied their entire clips into her, coming toward her, following her into the alleyway until she fell to the ground, smoking and still.

Officer Gregory approached Jon. "I'm sorry. Once the interference took out the field around her, we had no choice."

"But ..." Jon couldn't make the words come out because he knew the officer wouldn't understand any of what he meant to say.

"What the hell happened to her?" one of the officers asked. "She's burning up."

Bettie and Bernie came to Jon's side.

"They didn't stop," Jon said, real tears running down his face. "They just kept firing." Through the blur of tears, he saw Marcy's body tremble violently.

"What the hell?" The officers backed away.

Her body continued to convulse as if she were being electrocuted.

"Get back!" Bernie pulled Jon and Bettie away from the alleyway.

Jon continued to watch. There was a faint crack and then a splash of blood erupted from her arm as it was torn from her body from the force of the convulsions.

"Oh, God." Bettie turned away.

"Jesus." One of the officers lost his lunch.

"Look at that," another officer said, taking tentative steps toward the alleyway. "Damned strangest thing I've ever seen."

Jon looked at where the officer pointed. The arm that had been wrenched from Marcy's body lay in a pool of blood, the hand pressed firmly to the office building. Jon's blood froze as he realized the implications of what the officer pointed at. He glanced up at the ten story building.

How many companies were there, with how many employees? How long would it take before the entity started torturing and killing people? Would anyone connect the two events, or would what happened at the Howard Phillips Building be forgotten by the time people started disappearing here?

"Her hand is stuck to the building," the officers said. "I don't get it."

Jon stared at Marcy as the EMTs arrived to help the wounded police officers. "It's going to start all over again, isn't it?" He turned to Bettie and Bernie. "Isn't it?"

Bettie came over to Jon's side. "You did the best you could." She drew him to her and kissed him.

When they broke, Jon searched her eyes. "What … ?"

"Oh. It was … you saved us … we made it. Right? I mean … You did your best and saved us."

"Oh." He'd hoped it was more. He doubted it was only that he'd saved them. The kiss lingered too long.

"Sir?" one of the officers said. "Come on, we're taking all of you to the hospital."

"Yeah, I did the best I could. But it wasn't enough."

The police led them to a waiting ambulance. As he was helped into the back, he had the distinct sensation of being watched..

ABOUT THE AUTHOR

Gary is the self-employed author of *Forever Will You Suffer*, a supernatural, time-shifting tale of unrequited love gone horribly wrong and Institutional Memory, a story of cosmic terror in the corporate workplace. He, with Mary Sangiovanni, co-edited Dark Territories, the anthology from the Garden State Horror Writers. Several of his short works has been published, including "Stay Here", "The Fine Art of Madness", and "He Loves Me, He Loves Me Not".

A member of the Horror Writers Association since 2005, Gary has also been a member of the Garden State Horror Writers since 2003, where he spent two years as president.

When he's not spilling his imagination on the page, he plays house-husband, and sometimes plays guitar. He's currently at work on his next novel or three, but that's another story.

Novels:
Forever Will You Suffer
Institutional Memory

Short Stories:
The Fine Art of Madness (*Now I Lay Me Down to Sleep* (Necon eBooks))

He Loves Me, He Loves Me Not (*Space & Time Magazine* (forthcoming))

Stay Here (GSHW anthology: *Dark Notes From New Jersey* – 2005)

You Just Can't Win (*Horrorworld* – 2005)

Other Bits:
On Writing Horror (WD Press): Roundtable discussion on new horror authors

Curious about other Crossroad Press books?
Stop by our site:
http://store.crossroadpress.com
We offer quality writing
in digital, audio, and print formats.

Enter the code FIRSTBOOK
to get 20% off your first order from our store!
Stop by today!

Made in the USA
Middletown, DE
24 June 2018